Lord Edward's
MYSTERIOUS
TREASURE

OTHER BOOKS BY LILLIAN MAREK

The Victorian Adventures series

Lady Elinor's Wicked Adventures
The Etruscan Adventure

Lady Emily's Exotic Journey
The Assyrian Adventure

A Scandalous Journey
The Ruritanian Adventure

LORD EDWARD'S
MYSTERIOUS
TREASURE

LILLIAN
MAREK

To Danny

The Beginning

Lord Edward Tremaine
Penworth Castle
Penworth, Dorset

Chateau de Morvan
September 26, 1871

My dear Ned,

I hope this finds you well and a trifle bored with your dusty tomes, because I plan to tempt you to travel.

You may be surprised to find me writing to you from a chateau in Brittany, when the last time I saw you I was headed for steel mills in Belgium. Well, my esteemed and reclusive great-grandfather, the vicomte de Morvan, has summoned me and my cousins to his bedside—a command performance, as we all have hopes of an inheritance—and I invite you to join us.

The bait I hold out to you is that the old man is in his nineties, old enough to have been alive at the time of that Breton rebellion that so fascinates you. Yes, my friend, the Chouans—those peasants who rose up against the Revolution. Ancient history to me (and to most people), but he remembers it. He not only remembers it, but he obsesses over it and over his relatives who died with them.

I can almost see your eyes, bright with eagerness. And yes, we can also offer you a moldering pile of a castle filled with bundles of ancient letters and suchlike, as well as the meanderings of the old *man. You know me. I would just as soon toss all those papers on the fire as so much antiquated trash, but I will restrain myself if you promise to come and relieve my own boredom.*

Ever yours,
Tony

PS I don't know if this qualifies as an additional lure or not, but the old man seems to think there is a lost treasure hidden someplace in the chateau. This is probably just the fantasy of a very old man, but who knows?

To M. Antoine Morvan
Chateau de Morvan
Finistère, Brittany

Penworth Castle
September 29, 1871

Dear Tony,
  I'll be there within the week.

Yours,
Ned

Chapter One

SIX DAYS LATER, NED CURSED HIMSELF FOR A ROMANTIC IDIOT. He could have traveled comfortably in the coach along with his valet and luggage, but no, he had to go on horseback to better explore the countryside of Finistère—that region called the end of the earth, the wild, westernmost part of France. And what had this adventure brought him thus far? Cold, wet misery.

The countryside was invisible, blanketed in a thick fog. He could barely see enough to keep his horse on the road, if one could call this muddy track a road.

But still… he could not shake the feeling that the fog also hid secrets, now just as it had done in the past. A dozen men—a hundred, a thousand—could be hidden in those woods, and no invading army would be able to see them until and unless they chose to be seen. And after they attacked, they could vanish into the mist again.

Eighty years ago the stubborn Chouans had done just that, resisting the armies of the Revolution. He could almost see the gray figures slipping between the trees. He could almost hear the owl's call that had been their signal.

The fog wrapped him in silence, as if the rest of the world had simply vanished, dissolved in the gray mists around him. It also seeped through his coat and condensed on his collar, sending drips of water down his neck. His horse, a decent enough mount, tossed its head in understandable irritation.

With a silent apology to the creature, he allowed it to move on, plodding doggedly ahead.

They finally crested a hill and everything changed.

Only wisps of fog lingered here, the rest left behind in the wooded valley. The road divided, one track leading down to the right where off in the distance a village of gray stone cottages with slate roofs circled a harbor, not very different from the fishermen's villages in his native Dorset. But straight ahead of him—here was magic. Ancient stone walls rose out of the waves, a castle almost completely surrounded by the sea. He pulled up so abruptly that the horse objected, but he had to allow himself a chance to simply look. He stared, drinking in the eerie romance of the scene.

Could anything be more perfect?

The Chateau de Morvan looked like an enchanted palace, set as it was upon a rocky promontory—an island almost, connected to the mainland only by a narrow causeway that dipped so low it must be covered by the waves at times.

At the moment, those waves were gently lapping against the rocks with a shushing sound barely louder than the horse's breathing, but he could imagine what it would be like in a storm. The chateau would be cut off, isolated.

The cliff merged into the stone of the ancient walls almost imperceptibly. It was difficult to tell where one began and the other ended, as if the castle had grown out of the rock. Behind the walls, he could see towers rising, a pair of crenellated medieval ones and several more fanciful turrets with conical roofs.

Ned gave a sigh of pure pleasure.

Then he laughed at himself. True, there were bits of fog clinging in tendrils to the castle, but to be truly romantic the scene needed a raging storm, with huge waves crashing high enough to reach the castle walls, cracks of thunder and flashes of lightning, winds howling like the cries of the damned, and torrents of rain lashing at the poor traveler seeking shelter. Now *that* would be dramatic.

The drama he was willing to save for another day. As it was, he felt quite cold and damp enough. The horse needed only permission to continue and set off with renewed energy down the road to the causeway, doubtless longing for a warm, dry stable and a bucket of oats. Ned could sympathize. He was looking forward to the warmth of a roaring fire himself.

However, warmth was not immediately forthcoming for either of them.

The heavy gate in the wall stood open, allowing passage through the thick fortification, but no one appeared to greet him when he arrived before the chateau itself. He faced a bizarre building: half a medieval castle, made of sturdy granite blocks with narrow slits of windows, and half a fanciful Baroque palace, no more than a few hundred years old. Yet it was the newer section that seemed to be crumbling into decay.

The chateau itself was set well back from the gate. A broad gravel road lined with beech trees—almost denuded of leaves at this season—led to a door as massive as the outer gate. It looked as if it had not been opened in centuries. The whole place seemed deserted. A bit of searching led Ned to the stables, which were in surprisingly good repair and housed what looked like a plow horse and a few decent-looking mounts, the only evidence that the chateau was indeed inhabited. In the absence of any grooms, he had to unsaddle and rub down his horse himself. At least he managed to find some oats, so he could leave the horse contentedly munching.

It then required several minutes of hammering on the nearest door to get the attention of someone within. Neither the high roof nor the stone pillars of the porte cochère offered any shelter from the damp. Irritation had replaced enchantment long before the door finally swung open, pulled by a desiccated old servitor in black who looked to be of an age with the castle.

"Lord Edward Tremaine," snapped Ned, striding into the dark hall without waiting for an invitation. "I am expected." He took off his hat to shake the water from it and gave himself an angry shake as well. The stone flags of the floor wouldn't be bothered by the shower, but they offered no warmth either. An oil lamp in one corner offered the only illumination, and a pitiful pinpoint of light it was. The walls bore a pair of enormous paintings, brown with age, of what might once have been colorful crowds of people. Nothing provided any note of cheer.

It was hardly the welcome he had been expecting.

"Oh!" A soft, high sound floated down from above.

Ned looked up, and the scene was suddenly transformed. He beheld a vision atop the stone staircase that rose beside him. The princess imprisoned by the dragon in the enchanted tower. The lady awaiting rescue by a knight in shining armor. A vision of sweetness and light with golden ringlets, huge eyes, and a rosebud mouth shaping a circle of surprise. Her face was all he could see before she vanished into the greater darkness above.

She must have been an angel. No one had ever heard of a ghost with blonde ringlets.

He was still staring up, stupefied, when the aged servitor coughed slightly to get his attention. Bringing his attention back to the hall, Ned realized that the man wasn't actually all that old or desiccated—just a bit cadaverous. There was another servant right behind him—a bit younger, but still with a lean and hungry look. The first one was dressed in black, like a butler, and the second was in some kind of livery. Both were watching him with extreme patience.

"If you would care to leave your things with Louis? M. Antoine is expecting you. I will take you to him." The butler spoke in English, but with a French accent strong enough to sound almost comic. Or it might have seemed comic had his face borne even the trace of a smile, and had his words not sounded like a reproof. He took the hat from Ned's hand and shook it again, before handing it to the footman and reaching up to remove Ned's coat.

Ned was tempted to say he wanted to keep his coat. He wasn't accustomed to being treated like a recalcitrant child, and the stone-flagged hall was both cavernous and chilly. But that would be foolish—especially since a wet coat would not keep him warm.

While the footman carried off his damp garments, Ned followed the butler first through a long, dusty hall to another set of stairs—he half expected dingy suits of armor festooned with cobwebs in the corners. Did anyone actually live in this place?

The elderly servant moved with surprising speed, and Ned had to hurry to keep up with him through a labyrinth of corridors in what was obviously the older, medieval castle. Eventually, tall doors were flung open, and the butler announced, "Lord Edward Tremaine," and Ned stepped into blissful warmth.

"Ned!" A long, thin gentleman unfolded himself from a plush armchair angled to catch the heat from a roaring fire, and reached out his hands in smiling welcome. He was wearing a brown sack suit of heavy wool and sported a carefully twirled mustache over a small pointed beard.

They exchanged the hearty slaps on the shoulder and laughing greetings of old school chums. In no time at all, Ned was ensconced in a chair of his own by the fire with a glass of whiskey in his hand.

"Good Lord, Tony, where did you get those whiskers? You've turned into a Frenchman." Ned laughed as he shook his head.

"But I am a Frenchman, at least a quarter of one, and the camouflage is useful these days. When I meet with potential investors, they think me a foolish *flâneur*, an idle man about town, and assume that any agreement we make is in their favor."

"You're still determined on that steel factory, then."

"Yes. And at the moment, it's a damned nuisance, having to spend my time dancing attendance on the old man here. He has the money to invest, all we would need, but I can't seem to talk any sense to him. Nothing modern means anything. He keeps meandering off into some nonsense about the Morvan treasure."

"Treasure?" Ned halted with the glass halfway to his lips and put it aside. "You mentioned a treasure in that intriguing postscript of yours. What sort of treasure is it?"

"Damned if I know. The old man mutters that it 'must be found,' but refuses to say what the hell it is. Or where."

"That must make it a bit difficult to find."

"Impossible is more like it." Tony's face twisted into a grimace of disgust. "The blasted chateau is enormous, a rabbit warren of rooms and passages, and I have no idea where to begin looking. Hell, I don't know if I should be looking for something the size of a pea or something the size of an elephant."

Ned's lips quirked up in a half-smile. "Is this treasure hunt the real reason for your invitation to me?"

"Well…" Tony had the grace to look a trifle embarrassed. "Maybe a bit. It seems to be important, and I do need help. There's a tower full of documents that might be connected, I suppose, but they're all in writing I can't read and half of them are in Latin to boot. You're the only one I know who might be able to decipher them—see if there's anything about a treasure that might give us a clue about what we're looking for."

Disappointment settled on Ned. "So the lure of the Chouans was just a trick to get me to come help you?"

"Not exactly. From what I've been able to understand of the old man's maunderings, that's when the treasure disappeared— when the Republicans were marching in, putting down the local resistance." Tony winced and rubbed his stomach.

Ned frowned. He'd been a little annoyed that Tony hadn't been exactly forthright, but perhaps there were problems. Now that he looked at him, his old school friend seemed even thinner than usual. "Is something wrong, or are you just forgetting to eat, as usual?"

Tony glanced down at the hand that was massaging his belly and gave a light laugh. "No, it's just that my stomach can't seem to get accustomed to the rich food the chef here insists on providing. I spent too many years feeding it English stodge. And what about you? You're so wet that you're steaming as you sit there. What did you do, travel in an open carriage?"

Ned grinned. "No, I was ferried over to Brest in Father's yacht and decided to ride. My valet's coming in the carriage with my baggage."

Tony snorted. "Decided to ride! And no doubt you were watching out for fairy creatures or noble knights or brave peasants all along the way, my romantic idiot friend. And what did you see? Gloomy gray villages and their mistrustful inhabitants, I expect."

"Not even that." Ned gave a rueful shake of his head. "Mostly what I saw was fog. It was hard enough to find the road much of the time."

"Well, come along." Tony stood and held out his hand to his friend. "I'll show you to your room, and you'll have a chance to dry off and regain your strength before dinner, when you'll meet the others."

"Your great-grandfather?"

"I'm afraid I can't take you to see him yet. He's pretty much bedridden and he's only up to visitors in the morning. That's when my cousins and I are granted our daily audience."

"Your cousins, yes. I always thought you didn't have any relatives, at least not on the French side." Ned looked a question.

"They were a surprise to me as well. It seems the Morvans are not a very close-knit family."

"What are they like then?"

Tony paused and then smiled, a slow teasing smile. "I'll let you form your own judgment."

Ned opened his mouth to ask about the vision he had beheld when he arrived, but decided to wait. After all, she might have been one of the servants, or her beauty might have been a mere trick of the light. He had endured enough teasing about his supposedly romantic streak ever since their school days at Rugby. He had no intention of giving Tony any more ammunition.

Chapter Two

BY THE TIME HE HAD ENJOYED A HOT BATH IN A SURPRISINGLY up-to-date bathing chamber and changed into dry clothes, which had arrived in good time, Ned's usual good humor had returned. He could appreciate the incongruities of the Morvan chateau now that he had experienced its luxuries.

The medieval castle, with its impressive gloom and maze-like corridors, would be dim even on a sunny day. The two windows of his room were mere slits in stone walls a good two feet thick. The stone flags of the floor were old enough to have been worn into a hollow by centuries of footsteps passing through the doorway. Though small, the room was dominated by a fireplace with a massive stone mantle at least five centuries old—and a roaring fire adequate to warm the room.

He was not a medievalist himself, but Ned knew enough to be able to recognize the authenticity of the architecture, and to be amused by the oddity of the modern furnishings. These were medieval only in the way that Pugin or the Pre-Raphaelites were medieval. The bed sported a heavy oak canopy supported on pillars that were in turn separated by pointed arches filled with carved traceries. Several chairs were placed around the room, chairs on which not a square inch of wood had escaped the carver's chisel.

He had seen similar pieces in the catalog his mother had been examining when she was considering redoing some of the rooms at Penworth. Now that he had tried sitting in one of the chairs, he was glad she had decided against the medieval look.

The stone walls of his room were hung, appropriately enough, with tapestries, but these had been woven not more than twenty years ago. On one, a knight with a soulful expression rode a horse as pale and wan as he. On another, an etiolated damsel leaned mournfully from her tower.

Tony might consider him a romantic, and Ned knew himself well enough to acknowledge that he might on occasion get lost in daydreams about the past, but he also knew the difference between the reality and the prettified version that decorated too many drawing rooms.

Whatever the shortcomings of the furnishings might be, the view from the windows could not be faulted. This part of the castle was built into the western wall. When Ned looked out, there was nothing to be seen but the wild Atlantic. Not so wild today, with fog off in the distance so there was no sea, no sky, no horizon, only a darkening mist. A timeless, eternal prospect offering nothing but infinite possibility.

A sudden gust of wind rattled the window, sending a chill to recall him to the present and prompt him to laugh at himself. The roaring fire under that stone mantle meant that the room was warm and the mattress on that grotesque bed would be soft. There was nothing like a day spent riding through a chilly fog to make a man appreciate creature comforts, and he was not such a fool as to prefer medieval reality to modern comforts. He was looking forward to that bed, but first came dinner and an introduction to the mysterious cousins.

Clivers, his man, gave a final whisk to his evening dress coat and nodded approval of his appearance. Ned stepped out into the corridor and realized he had no idea where to go. Fortunately, his confusion had been anticipated and Louis, the gaunt footman, detached himself from the wall and silently positioned himself to guide Ned through the gloomy corridors.

His destination turned out to be a room that had probably

once been the Great Hall of the medieval castle. A massive stone fireplace, at least double the size of the one in his room, stood at one end, with a blaze that almost warmed the room. Almost, because no contained fire could warm a room this size, any more than a dozen lamps could illuminate it. The corners of the room were hidden in darkness, and high above, the ceiling vanished in the gloom above the blackened beams that ran the full width of the ceiling.

Here was a medieval room, but furnished as a fashionable drawing room. Here the stone walls were hung with paintings of heroic scenes from history interspersed with gilt-framed mirrors. The half-dozen tables around the room were covered with draperies and topped with oil lamps and a clutter of knick-knacks. Various chairs were scattered about, all looking finicky and uncomfortable.

Tony looked up at Ned's entrance with a smile of relief. He seemed to have been trapped against a potted palm by an older man with grizzled whiskers and a lugubrious mustache.

"Milk, not brandy. And remember to take the tonic," the older man said, shaking a finger at Tony.

Tony nodded dutifully and called out, "Ned, come and meet Dr. Fernac, who is caring for the old man."

The doctor scowled. "A bit of respect for the vicomte on your part would not come amiss."

"You know that is beyond me, Fernac. But please allow me to introduce my friend, Lord Edward Tremaine, who will be delighted to listen to the old man's tales."

The introduction did not win a smile from the doctor, but his scowl lessened slightly as he inclined his head at Ned, who murmured polite greetings. Then the doctor looked past Ned and did smile.

Ned turned and stared. It was quite possible that his mouth was hanging open. He could not be certain, but he did not care.

It was the angel from the staircase. She was every bit as beautiful as he had thought. No, she was more beautiful. She was absolute perfection.

Those ringlets of pale gold framed a delicate face with a rosebud of a mouth over an exquisite little chin. Large eyes of soft blue looked up at him through thick lashes under a high, smooth forehead. The faintest blush of pink touched her rounded cheeks. Her figure was all soft and round, a full bosom above a tiny little waist. He could span that waist with his hands, he was sure.

She was all softness and roundness, looking as sweet and gentle as an…as an…well, as an angel. The very sight of such a delicate, fragile creature roused all his protective chivalrous instincts. Were he a knight, he would kneel at her feet, dedicating himself to her service. What greater joy could there be in life than to serve such a creature?

He could feel himself smiling, and that faint blush of pink on her cheeks deepened slightly.

"And here are my cousins." There was a hint of laughter in Tony's voice.

Cousins? Ned was confused for a moment until he realized that the angel was not alone. Beside her stood a tall dark woman, dressed in black. She was young, he realized, probably in her early twenties, so only a little older than the angel, but she looked stern and forbidding. Dark eyes under slashes of brows, a wide mouth pinched in a tight line… She was an intimidating creature, harsh and angry.

Still another woman stood behind them. This one was much older, though dressed in black like the tall young woman. Also like her, this one was stern and unsmiling. The pair of them were almost frightening, hovering over the angel like a pair of wicked spirits in a fairy tale.

Trailing them was a hulking young man, probably a servant since he remained in the corridor when they entered the room. Though he was not dressed in livery, as the servants in the castle seemed to be.

"Ladies, may I present my old school friend, Lord Edward

Tremaine, who has come for a visit. He will, I trust, help to entertain you while he is here. Ned, these are my cousins, Mlle. Delphine de Roncaille and Mlle. Marguerite Benda, and their companion, Mme. d'Hivers."

The ladies all curtsied—the angel with a graceful flutter, the other two with brief, chilly courtesy. Ned bowed and did his best to force his face into a courteous mask. He feared he had been looking like a moonstruck calf, and Tony had been finding too much amusement in the sight.

"Lord Edward Tremaine, we are enchanted to have you here."

The angel—Mlle. de Roncaille—had a soft, sweet voice with an enchanting accent. Just what he would have expected. Although they all spoke in English, she pronounced his name in the French way—*Edouard*—making almost three syllables of it. He managed to form a response. "How could I fail to be enchanted here, when I discover myself in such delightful company?"

Mlle. de Roncaille clasped her hands together at her breast. "Ah, but how delightful it will be, how much more amusing now that we have such an elegant cavalier among us. We shall have such gaiety!" She beamed her smile at him, looking up through those long golden lashes.

Ned swallowed. No one had ever considered him an elegant cavalier before. Certainly not his sisters, but perhaps all sisters viewed their brothers as something of a joke. That was certainly the case in his family. He hoped they were wrong and Mlle. de Roncaille had the right of it. Before he could frame an elegant response, the elderly companion spoke.

"Gaiety, Delphine? You forget how ill the vicomte is, and you forget that we are still in mourning." Mme. d'Hivers sounded as cold as her name.

Immediately contrite tears threatened to spill from Mlle. de Roncaille's blue eyes as she turned to her cousin. "Forgive me, Marguerite. I know how much you must miss your poor papa. I am desolated that I forgot for even one moment the pain you suffer, the pain I share."

Mlle. Benda turned a quelling look on her. "There is no need to be quite so dramatic, Delphine. It is simply that we should be grateful that the vicomte has offered us shelter here, even though he is old and ill himself."

"You are so cold, Marguerite." The younger girl pouted—quite prettily, but it was still a pout. "Gratitude is such a cold emotion. After all, he is our relative as well as Antoine's, and this is our ancestral home too, is it not? Why should we not reside here as well?"

"No reason at all," said Tony, intervening before Mlle. Benda could make the cutting retort that seemed to be on her lips. "Shall we go in to dinner?"

Mlle. Benda took Tony's arm with a sigh of resignation. Ned could not be entirely displeased, since this allowed him to lead in Mlle. de Roncaille. Still, there were currents he did not understand. The temperature of the room could not explain the shiver that ran down his spine.

Chapter Three

IF HE EXPECTED THE MOVE TO IMPROVE MATTERS, HE WAS mistaken. The dining room was another stone-walled room, as chilly as the hall. It seemed oppressed rather than lightened by the weight of gleaming silver on the table. An enormous epergne in the center of the table bore, for some unknown reason, a display of beaded fruit. It also blocked Ned's view of Mlle. de Roncaille so that he had to tilt his head at an awkward angle in order to see her, and his neck was beginning to hurt.

The discomfort lasted throughout dinner. It was not the food—which was very good in the French fashion, though not very warm—and the impeccable service made him realize that the chateau was indeed well staffed. In the fog, he must have chosen to enter through the wrong door. That would explain why it had taken so long for anyone to open to him. He would have to ask Tony later.

However, none of that had anything to do with the air of tension in the dining room. All of them, save Mlle. de Roncaille, seemed watchful, on their guard against something.

Tony's discontent seemed focused on his stomach, and looking at his dinner, Ned was hardly surprised. While the rest of them feasted on scallops cooked with mushrooms, shallots, wine and cream, Tony's plate bore a piece of plain boiled fish accompanied by a boiled potato. Even Tony's mustache seemed to uncurl and droop at the pitiful sight.

"Trust me," said the doctor. He signaled to a footman who poured a glass of mineral water for Tony.

Tony looked at it with despair.

"Trust me," the doctor repeated. "You must treat your liver gently."

Tony glared at him.

"Poor Cousin Antoine." Mlle. de Roncaille clasped her hands to her heart and tilted her head. "I do pray that it is not The Curse!" Her eyes grew round and she spoke as though the words required capital letters. An excited smile pulled at the corners of her mouth.

"What curse…?" Ned began.

"The Curse of the Morvans, of course. Do you not know of it?" Her eyes glittered and rosy spots of color appeared in her cheeks.

"Such foolishness," exclaimed Mme. d'Hivers.

"Delphine! Stop that nonsense at once," said Mlle. Benda. "You know there is no such thing as a curse."

"But there is. Why do you try to pretend it isn't true? Is that not why we are all here?" The girl lifted her chin defiantly.

The two older women exchanged glances.

"Delphine…" Mlle. Benda spoke softly. It was as if she were trying to soothe a frightened kitten.

Mme. d'Hivers was far less gentle, and her look was cold and stern. "You are upsetting yourself, Delphine. Do you wish to dine in your room?"

Mlle. de Roncaille froze and then drew back in her seat. "No, I am not upset." Her voice shrank to a whisper. "Do not send me away. Please."

"Oh, leave her alone," said the doctor, waving his fork in his hand. "Children like to frighten themselves with such tales. We all know that it is nonsense."

The young girl glared at him and opened her mouth as if to protest, but then looked at the older women, who were frowning at her, and subsided into a sulky silence. Mlle. Benda stared at her for a long minute and then returned to her meal.

Ned wanted to comfort the girl, but hesitated to say anything that might allow the other women to vent their displeasure on his angel. How ridiculous to get so upset over the mere mention of something as ludicrous as a curse. As if young girls did not always delight in frightening themselves with ghost stories. He searched his mind frantically for a neutral topic of conversation, but he had no idea where the explosive ones might be lurking. It wasn't that he had any objection to offending Mlle. Benda, who seemed accustomed to having things her own way. He just wanted to protect Mlle. de Roncaille, who was obviously too timid to stand up for herself.

This was preposterous. He was never at a loss socially. His family had seen to that, having inflicted thundering bores and irascible old ladies on him as dinner partners ever since he had been out of the nursery. Surely he could smooth the ruffled feathers here. He picked up his glass and drank off half the wine in an effort to calm down.

He turned to Mlle. Benda. "Your English pronunciation is excellent, but every now and then, your phrasing sounds French. Am I mistaken in thinking that English is not your native tongue?"

She smiled slightly—he was startled to see how even this tiny change softened her face. "My native tongue? I am not sure I have one. My mother grew up in England, so she spoke English to me to ensure that I learned it. My father was from Bohemia, so he spoke to me in German and Czech, and we lived mostly in Paris, so perforce we all spoke French."

"Don't be silly, Marguerite," Mlle. de Roncaille said. "Of course your native language is French. We are all French, after all, though we are delighted to speak English now that Lord Edward is here." She sent a beaming smile in his direction, which compensated in part for the frozen look that reappeared on Mlle. Benda's face.

All right. Languages were a bone of contention. What else could he try?

The weather. Surely they could talk about the weather without distressing anyone. No one got heated about fog.

But it was Tony who spoke up first. "I heard from Georges today. He's my partner in the steel venture"—he turned to Ned with that explanation—"and he thinks he's found the perfect site in Franche-Comté for a steel mill. Close to iron mines, close to transport for coal, and with access to workers."

"That sounds promising." Ned looked up with a smile. At last—an unobjectionable topic of conversation.

Alas, he was wrong. The doctor also looked up from his meal. "Franche-Comté? Too close to Germany. They've already taken Alsace and Lorraine. If they invade us again…" He shook his head.

"If France modernizes, we will be too strong for them to invade." Tony's color rose along with his voice. "That is precisely why we need steel mills and railroads."

"So you would dangle a rich prize in front of their noses?" Fernac's color matched Tony's. "They will be salivating at the prospect of the next invasion."

Mme. d'Hivers slammed down her wine glass, sending the golden liquid splashing across the cloth. "They will attack us or we will attack them, and what does it all mean? A few generals will have more medals, and a few bankers will have more gold. And for the rest of us? Death and misery once more." Mme. d'Hivers' sudden outburst of anger and anguish was such that Ned almost jumped in his seat. He would not have been surprised to see her hair turn into writhing snakes.

Mlle. Benda put her arm around the older woman and held her close, murmuring softly, "Be easy, Tante Héloise. Do not distress yourself." Her voice was surprisingly gentle, and even her features seemed to soften as she spoke to the older woman.

Mme. d'Hivers took a deep breath and seemed to pull herself in. "Please forgive my outburst," she said stiffly without actually looking at anyone in the room.

She stood and turned to leave, and everyone else rose as

well. The two younger women followed her, Mlle. Benda with an apologetic glance and Mlle. de Roncaille with a roll of her eyes. The doctor hesitated for a moment and then excused himself to follow.

The hulking fellow must have been waiting just outside, because he detached himself from the wall to follow the women. Ned frowned. Something about him, about the way he followed them, seemed odd. Was it the way he stood? Hovering, but not really protectively.

As soon as the ladies had withdrawn, Tony went over to the sideboard, opened the lower cabinet and, with a sigh of pleasure, brought forth a decanter of port and two glasses.

Ned took one look and began to laugh. "What? Port instead of cognac? And you call yourself a Frenchman."

"I call myself nothing of the sort," said Tony, carefully placing the decanter on the table. "My mother was English, my father's mother was English, so that makes me three-quarters English even if everyone here insists on calling me Antoine. I greatly prefer port to cognac at the end of a meal, and do not see why I should let an unknown ancestor decide what I may drink."

"As you like it. I enjoy both. But should you not be drinking mineral water?"

Tony gave that remark all the attention it deserved, poured himself a glass and slid the decanter to Ned before pulling out his cigarette case. He paused and said, "Do you prefer cigars? I am afraid I have none to offer."

"Quite all right. I'm not wedded to that habit either. But I would appreciate some explanations. Your letter mentioned cousins, but I thought your family was 'only son of an only son' all the way back. Where did these cousins come from? Are they some mysterious long-lost sisters?" Ned leaned back and prepared to listen.

"As you may have surmised, Delphine and Marguerite are not particularly close cousins—at least, not close to me. My mother had to explain the family tree to me when the old man invited me here.

"Their great-grandmother was the sister of my great-grand-father—the old gentleman upstairs. The old man and his sister were the only members of the family to survive the Revolution.

"After they fled to England, the sister, like a good little girl, married one of the other émigré nobles. They had one daughter, another good little girl, and she married another French noble-man—this one wasn't completely impoverished and managed to regain some property here. All very French and very expected. And then they had *two* daughters."

Tony grinned and winked. "That was when things changed. One of them—Marguerite's mother—was not such a good little girl. She ran off with a musician. Her family, especially her father, took great exception to this, my mother tells me, and made such a racket that even my branch of the family heard about it. It seems her papa took enormous pride in his noble heritage and had, besides, plans to make a profitable marriage for her. At any rate, she was disowned with great drama.

"The other sister—Delphine's mother—was more dutiful and married another French nobleman of her parents' choos-ing. These two girls are close to each other, though, despite the dramatics surrounding their mothers. And they are both far more French than I."

"So then Marguerite, Mlle. Benda, is a companion to Mlle. de Roncaille?" Ned frowned. "Somehow, that was not the im-pression I had of their relationship."

"And you should not. The parents were as foolish in their choices as parents often are. It seems that the musician was actually quite successful, a violinist. You know about that sort of thing. Maybe you've heard of him?"

"Benda? Do you mean *Matthias* Benda?"

"Yes, that's the name."

"But he's known all over Europe. They talk of him as the heir to Paganini. Complaining about him as a son-in-law would be like complaining about having Michelangelo or Raphael in the family. Were her parents fools?" Ned was thunderstruck. "I heard him play a few years ago when I was in Paris. It was an extraordinary experience. There was a woman accompanying him on the piano?"

Tony nodded. "Yes, that would have been Marguerite's mother. And the last year or two, ever since her mother died, Marguerite accompanied him herself."

Ned shook his head in silent amazement. It was difficult to imagine that cold, stern creature producing music.

"De Roncaille, on the other hand, was a dissolute spendthrift who ran through both his own fortune and his wife's dowry," Tony continued. "Then he died and left her and their daughter penniless. They had to take refuge with the Bendas."

Ned's head snapped up. "Good Lord! That poor child. When did this happen?"

Tony shrugged. "Some years ago, I think. I only know what I heard from my mother. And it seems that not long after that, both sisters died."

"Worse and worse." Ned shook his head. "And Mme. d'Hivers? I heard Mlle. Benda call her Tante Héloise. She is their aunt?"

Another shrug from Tony. "I don't think she's actually a relative—more of a courtesy aunt. I believe she came to live with the Bendas after her husband died. From what they've said, I gather that she's been with the family since Marguerite was a child. Benda seems to have had a tendency to pick up strays. Have you noticed Horace?"

"Horace?"

"That big fellow who follows them around."

"Oh, yes." Ned nodded. "I wondered who he was. Or what he was. A servant?"

"Not precisely." Tony wriggled in his seat, picked up his port and took a sip, rolling it meditatively around in his mouth. "I don't know what to say he is, to tell you the truth. Have you had a good look at him?"

"No, I've only seen him from a distance."

"Well, he's a bit simple. At least I think that's what he is. Apparently Benda picked him up off the street years ago when he was quite young. Some older boys were tormenting him or teasing him or some such. I don't know precisely. Anyway, Benda discovered that the boy was an orphan so he took him in. He's been with them ever since."

"A kindly action." Ned wondered if he should have made that a question.

An uncomfortable grimace crossed Tony's face, but he continued, "I'm sure it was but…I can't help it. He makes me uncomfortable. I know they tell me he's always been protective of Marguerite, and he certainly follows Delphine around with an absolutely dogged devotion. Still…" He threw up his hands. "There's something odd. I can't explain it."

Having barely glimpsed the fellow, Ned was not inclined to try to explain it either. Instead he shook his head and asked, "Why not send him back to stay with Benda?"

"You didn't know?" Tony was taken aback. "I hadn't realized… but then, why would you? There were so many deaths. Benda was killed during the fighting in Paris in May when the army moved in. That is why Marguerite is in mourning." He shrugged regretfully.

Ned looked at Tony in shock. "They were in Paris when it was besieged? And during the Commune? That young girl? " He was appalled by the danger Mlle. de Roncaille had faced. As reported in the English papers, the violence had been horrifying and indiscriminate, and the siege had meant near-starvation for the residents of the city.

Tony shot a sarcastic glance at Ned. "I gather they managed to shield Delphine pretty well. At least it doesn't seem to have distressed her greatly. Marguerite and Madame are the ones who have nightmares. Hence Madame's outburst at dinner."

Ned was not appeased. "Why didn't someone get them out?"

"Don't start looking at me accusingly," Tony snapped. "At that time I didn't even know they existed, and I'm not sure the old man did either. Who knows what he thinks about anything? After things had calmed down, he summoned them here to the chateau. Now he has us all under his roof, and I'm not really sure why.

"The only sense I can make of his maunderings is that there is some treasure hidden away and for some reason or other, it is important to him that we all be here—presumably to hunt for it. I'm hoping that treasure is something that will finance a steel plant—or persuade him to do so—and that you will help me find it."

Chapter Four

"An English lord. Lord Edward Tremaine." Delphine smiled happily as she twirled around in the small sitting room she shared with her cousin. "He is handsome, is he not? He has blue eyes, like mine. A bit darker, perhaps, but that is good."

"He has the eyes of an innocent," Marguerite said. "The eyes of one who has been sheltered all his life and has never had to look on the reality of the world."

"You should not talk so." Delphine paused before a mirror to take an admiring look at her smile. "It makes you sound bitter."

Marguerite held her tongue. What, after all, could she say? Denial would be pointless.

"But he is handsome," Delphine continued. "His hair is dark and thick, and he is tall enough. Not elegant as a Frenchman would be, though he could doubtless be taught. Of course, it will be only an English title I have when I marry him. Lady Tremaine." She shrugged. "It does not sound too bad."

Leaning back in her chair, Marguerite closed her eyes and rubbed her temples. She had promised *Maman*, and she would keep her promise. But it was not easy. She was so tired of having to rein in Delphine, of trying to keep the girl calm. So tired of trying to make her behave sensibly. So tired. "You are not going to marry him, Delphine," she said gently.

"Why not? I could if I chose to." She smiled smugly. "He is almost in love with me already. He could not take his eyes from me. Even you must have seen that."

Of course Marguerite had seen. Delphine was enchantingly pretty, and men always fell under her spell at first.

"You know…" Marguerite sighed. No, Delphine did not know. She did not understand. She would never understand. Another tack was necessary. "He is not really an English lord."

"But of course he is. Antoine introduced us. He is Lord Edward Tremaine."

"That is just a courtesy title. He is a younger son. His father is a marquess, but he has an older brother who will inherit the title."

"He is a younger son?" Delphine could not keep the disappointment from her voice. "How do you know this?"

"Tante Héloise spoke with his valet."

Delphine sniffed. "Servants' gossip."

"Not gossip. Information."

A distressed frown crossed Delphine's face, but she quickly recovered. "No matter. An older brother might die."

Marguerite inhaled sharply. Delphine must not be allowed to think that way. She tried to speak, but could not immediately find the right words.

Delphine waved aside the unspoken protest. "But it is true. One never knows what the future may hold."

That was only too true, but Marguerite strove to keep her tone calm. "No, Delphine, no. You must not think that way. There may be a dozen older brothers, and they may all have sons of their own. You do not want to think of him. After all, he is an Englishman, and you are French."

Delphine tilted her head and looked thoughtful. "Yes, that is true. I am of the true nobility, *la noblesse ancienne.* I would not want to contract a *mésalliance.* My situation is not like yours."

Marguerite steeled herself for what was coming.

"I do not understand why you rejected the comte de Louvois." Delphine smiled slyly. "I know he is no longer young, but his lineage is impeccable."

Marguerite's head was throbbing. Rubbing her temples was

useless. She wanted only to lie down in a dark room and wrap herself in silence, but she could not. Not yet. "You know he was not offering marriage." Just remembering the comte, his full lips and cold eyes, evaluating her, as if balancing the price he was willing to pay and the price she might accept, made the bile rise in her throat.

"Of course not. Given your parents, you could hardly expect that." Delphine moved a lamp to the table in front of the mirror, She had picked up a shawl and viewed herself in different poses, draping it in slightly varied folds. "Still, an alliance with a comte, even without marriage, would move you into higher circles, though not the highest."

Had the girl absolutely no concept of what she was talking about? Marguerite wanted to scream, but forced the words through clenched jaws instead. "He thought I would have no choice after Papa died. No matter that I disliked him, that I had told him so—I think my dislike pleased him in some way." She would never be able to make Delphine understand how the very sight of him revolted her. The thought of those fat fingers touching her made her skin crawl.

Delphine sniffed. "At least you would no longer have embarrassed me by performing in public."

Marguerite turned away. There was no way to explain, no way that Delphine would comprehend. If the invitation from the vicomte, the invitation to come here, had not appeared, what would she have done? What *could* she have done? She had been desperate. Delphine, Tante Héloïse, Horace—they were all her responsibility now.

This unexpected invitation had offered a respite, but that was all it was—a respite. It solved none of her problems. Dread settled in the pit of her stomach as it did whenever she thought about the future.

What was she going to do?

Chapter Five

MLLE. DE RONCAILLE FLUTTERED INTO THE BREAKFAST ROOM, followed once again by her dark shadows, Mlle. Benda and Mme. d'Hivers. Her smiles and pink ruffles were all the more delightful against the black robes and stern faces of her companions. Ned rose to his feet to seat her while a footman took care of the other two.

She rewarded him with an even more brilliant smile over her shoulder as she settled herself. "I am so glad that you are here, Lord Edward."

Ned returned to the other side of the table, the better to look at her. "And I am delighted to be here in such enchanting company, Mlle. de Roncaille." His smile caught briefly when he heard a quiet snort from Mme. d'Hivers but he did not look away.

"Mlle. de Roncaille, no, you must not call me that. It is much too formal when we are all living here at the chateau. You must call me Delphine, and I will call you Edward."

Her smile was irresistible. "I would be honored," he said.

"And Marguerite too, of course," she continued, waving a hand at her cousin.

"Of course," replied Mlle. Benda dryly. She looked at Ned and shrugged. "Attempting to maintain formality would be futile once Delphine has decided against it."

Ned suspected that the bow of agreement he gave to Mlle. Benda—Marguerite—might be too formal, but really, the woman did not invite informality despite her words. She had, he supposed, a sort of beauty, but it was a stern, almost fierce beauty with her strong features and proud carriage.

They were such unlikely cousins. Where Delphine's blonde curls danced around her face, Marguerite's dark—almost black—locks were pulled back harshly into a severe bun. Delphine's eyes were of a guileless blue; Marguerite's were fathomless dark pools. There could be a hundred—a thousand—secrets hidden behind those eyes.

But perhaps it was not their looks that made them seem so different. Delphine was all softness and sweetness, the sort of delicate creature a man instinctively sought to protect. Marguerite—he would try to think of her by that name—seemed surrounded by a hedge of prickles, fierce and independent. If she had red hair, she would make a good Boadicea.

His mother and sisters would probably like her. At least they might like her if she ever smiled again.

Ned felt that shiver run down his spine.

He turned back to Delphine. "Tony told me that you were in Paris during the siege. That must have been dreadful for you."

"Oh, it was. It was simply horrible. At the start, it was exciting, though. I went out to the ramparts with friends, and we could see the Prussian army in the distance. I had seen officers before that, of course, but it was different to see a real army."

"Especially when they began to shoot," said Marguerite.

"Surely not." Ned was shocked. "They would not shoot at women."

Marguerite shot a contemptuous glance at him. "They were besieging the city, bombarding the walls. Do you think they were particularly worried if their shells hit sightseeing fools?"

Ned felt like an idiot. Of course she was talking about the bombardment, but somehow he had imagined soldiers shooting rifles at the people on the walls. Surely no sniper would ever harm a delightful creature like Delphine.

"And it was so difficult to get food," Delphine continued as if there had been no interruption. "Some of the poor even ate horsemeat."

Mme. d'Hivers and Marguerite rolled their eyes.

"Even worse," said Delphine, "They killed some of the animals from the zoo at the Jardin des Plantes, and butchers were selling the meat. Truly. The English butcher on the Boulevard Haussmann was selling parts of Pollux. He was the elephant that used to give people rides. It was so sad." Tears of tender sympathy threatened to fill those blue eyes, and the rosebud mouth quivered.

"Delphine." There was a warning note in Mme. d'Hivers' voice.

Delphine ignored her, but the threat of tears receded. "Things got so expensive, and it was so difficult to buy food, that Marguerite sold my pearls. She insisted on taking them no matter what I said. I couldn't stop her." The girl's voice started to rise, and her eyes flashed. "Even when I said that she could sell her brooch instead, but she wouldn't."

"Delphine!" The warning note had sharpened. "You know perfectly well that Marguerite had already sold all the rest of her jewels and her mother's jewels."

"But I miss my pearls. It was cruel to take them from me." Delphine's voice softened, and her mouth pursed in a pretty pout. "We didn't even need all the money, because a week later it was all over."

"Yes, it was all over," Marguerite said, her voice barely audible. She rose and hurried from the room. Mme. d'Hivers went to follow but not before she snapped at Delphine, "Pearls can be replaced."

Delphine looked startled at the reprimand, so Ned commented gently, "You forget that Marguerite lost her father in that last week."

"Yes, I know that, but he was old, and it was all so silly."

"Silly?" That was not a word he could imagine associating with a death.

"The whole thing was silly. What did it matter to any of

us? I just wanted to be able to go shopping again, and see the handsome soldiers in their uniforms." The pout had returned. "My uncle wasn't involved in the fighting, but he made us all stay inside for days and days while it was going on. We weren't even allowed to go near the windows to see what was happening. And after all that, when it was almost over, a shot came through the window and hit him."

She spoke with the callousness of a child. Ned reminded himself that she was very young, but he still had to reprimand her gently. "It must have been terrible for Marguerite to lose her father that way."

Delphine frowned slightly. "I don't think she can have been terribly upset. She hardly cried at all. She just sat there for ages, holding him in her lap. And afterward, she would sit staring at nothing for days and days." She took a bite of her croissant.

She was obviously too young to understand grief. That must be it, Ned thought. He swallowed some coffee and found it hot enough to burn his mouth.

The gasp he made after he had swallowed it attracted her attention again, and she smiled. "It makes me feel safe, though, knowing that you will be able to protect us."

"Protect you?" Ned was still trying to breathe in cool air. "Protect you from what?"

"Why, from the curse, of course." She took another bite.

Ned closed his mouth, then opened it, then closed it again before he finally spoke. "Delphine, it may be amusing to joke about it, but you know that there is no such thing as a curse."

"Of course there is. How else do you explain it?"

"Explain what?"

She looked at him as if he were the simple-minded one. "Ever since the family fled the chateau during the Revolution, there has been nothing but tragedy. The vicomte's two brothers died in the fighting. Then on their way to England, his father died. When the vicomte married, his wife died giving birth to their son. That son died even before his own son was born. And that son died when Antoine was an infant. Brothers and sons all died before they were thirty. And his sister? She had only a daughter. And that daughter has only daughters who have only daughters. What can it be but a curse?"

She returned to her croissant with a shrug, and nothing Ned could say made any impression.

Mme. d'Hivers caught up with Marguerite in the hallway, and put her arm around the girl's shoulders and held her until her shudders eased.

Taking a deep breath, Marguerite lifted her head and huffed a sigh. "I am such a fool—I should know better than to let her disturb me. I know I promised my mother that I would take care of her, but sometimes… It's just that every now and then I suddenly cannot bear it."

"Pftt. Since when can we control our feelings to such an extent? One would have to be a saint to keep from being distressed by that one from time to time."

"Thank you for that." Marguerite lifted one side of her mouth in a crooked smile. "I just don't know what to do. We cannot stay here forever."

"I know it worries you, but for the time being we are safe enough here. We can stay until we know more. Have you sent the manuscript to Oscar Villoteau?"

"No, not yet."

Mme. d'Hivers shook her head impatiently. "If you do not write to him, we do not know, and so we cannot make any decision. Give it to me. I will take it down to the village to post. No one will see."

The girl nodded in acquiescence. "But what should I do about Delphine?"

"Do? Nothing. She is busy with the English aristo. So long as she is practicing her wiles on him, she will not be too difficult."

She shook her head. "True, but it seems unfair to him. He seems too kind, too gentle. Nothing like those arrogant Parisian aristocrats. Nothing like Louvois."

"Marguerite," the older woman said in exasperation, "kindness costs him nothing. If he does not seem like Louvois, it is because he has no need to be so at the moment. Just remember that he is an aristo, accustomed to having whatever he wants and expecting everyone to fawn on him. Delphine will do so, he will be charmed by her, and they will both be happy. He does not deserve your concern."

"You are doubtless correct." Marguerite did not look as if she believed her words. "But he seems…I do not know." She gave herself a shake. "It is of no importance, as you say, and in all probability she can do him no harm. Come. I will write to Oscar and send him the manuscript. And I must ask for his advice as well. Paris is not the only city in the world where music is played. Perhaps he will have some ideas about where we might go. Someplace far from Louvois."

Chapter Six

THE TAPESTRIES FLAPPED AGAINST THE WALLS AS THEY PASSED by, making it look as if the warriors brandished their swords and spears at the people moving through the corridor. Ned wasn't sure if this movement was because Tony was causing a breeze by the pace he set or because the chateau was drafty, but he had no time to investigate. He was too busy keeping up with Tony.

The women—with Horace keeping a silent guard over them— were waiting beside one of the doors that appeared between the tapestries in the corridor. Each of the doors along this corridor was flanked by stone pilasters and surmounted by a pediment carved with leaves and rosettes surrounding a shield with a coat of arms. An impressive—even oppressive—sight. This section of the castle must have been the residence of the lord and his family. Not diffident about proclaiming their importance, thought Ned, but then, what aristocratic family ever was?

Delphine greeted them with a bashful smile—she really had a delightfully sunny disposition, especially in contrast to the grim faces of the other two women. Ned felt a spurt of irritation. Yes, they were about to visit a dying man, but did they have to look as if they were already in mourning? Then he remembered that they actually were in mourning. Now he felt irritated at having to feel guilty. He would have liked to swear to relieve his feelings, but that seemed childish.

How was it that even on such short acquaintance Marguerite

always managed to make him feel as if he had put his foot wrong? Even when he hadn't opened his mouth. It wasn't anything she said—she barely spoke to him. Now, she wasn't even looking at him. She was standing there as still and impassive as a carved pillar, her eyes motionless as if her thoughts were far away. She certainly wasn't thinking about him. Delphine might be a bit silly, but at least she didn't make him feel like an idiot.

"We're not late then." Tony looked relieved. He was massaging his stomach again. Another attack of dyspepsia was the reason he had been delayed.

"No," said Mme. d'Hivers. "The doctor has not yet deigned to open the door for us."

"Tante Héloise…" Marguerite softened the reproof with another of her rare little smiles.

The older woman shrugged her indifference. "For all your life, the old man never acknowledged your existence, if he even knew of it. Why should we distress ourselves over him?"

"But think how sad it is," said Delphine. "He has lived here all alone all these years, without a family to love him, and now when we finally meet him…" Her voice drifted off into a sigh and tears glinted in her eyes.

Marguerite sighed as well, but it sounded more like exasperation than sympathy.

Tony pulled out his watch and glared at it. "It's one thing if the old man is truly not feeling well, but if Fernac is just playing with us…"

"The vicomte must be very old," Ned said gently. "A little patience must be necessary."

Tony glared at him. "Let's see how patient you feel when you ask him a perfectly simple question and instead of giving you a straight answer, he starts telling you fairy tales."

"Alas, the poor old man. To have his mind wandering so." Delphine tilted her head and clasped her hands at her breast. It was a very attractive pose, but Ned had the oddest feeling that he had seen it before. In a magazine illustration, perhaps.

The door had opened without their noticing, and the doctor stood there, frowning impatiently. "His mind is not wandering. He just lacks the strength to explain himself." He waved them brusquely in.

If the other rooms had been furnished in the latest fashion, this one was in the splendor of a long-vanished age. It was a room fit for a king, but not the sort of king who reigned from Versailles. This was the room of a warrior king.

Over the fireplace hung a sword and shield—the equipment of a medieval knight. Ned was not sure, but he thought they might very well be authentic. On the wall facing the bed was a large iron crucifix—also, Ned thought, genuinely medieval.

The hangings on the stone walls here were of crimson velvet, and the bed had a canopy and curtains of the same fabric, held up by richly carved posts of some dark wood.

It was an enormous bed. Half a dozen men could have slept in it. The sole occupant, however, was a wizened old man, whose hand, resting on the bed covers, had shriveled into a claw. His dark eyes were sharp, darting over his visitors with something that was not kindness, coming to rest on Ned.

"So you are the young man who fancies himself an historian." The voice was thin and high, but not weak, and not kind. "Live long enough and you will find yourself turned into history, like me."

"As will we all," said Ned, "but not all of us will have lived through such tumultuous times."

"Tumultuous," the vicomte repeated, savoring the word. "They were that." He fell silent, his eyes drifting away, as if looking into the past, until he returned to look at Ned once more. "They were brave, you know. All of them. At least that's what they tell me. My brave brothers, my brave father. Even the priest was brave. And they all died." He chuckled. It was not a pleasant sound. "They all died, and I survived."

Ned cleared his throat. "If you remember…"

"Of course I remember. I cannot forget," he snapped. The

clawlike hand picked at the cover, the eyes unfocused again. "I cannot forget. I hear them crying out. The obligation must be fulfilled."

The old man fell silent, and the others waited with various degrees of patience. Delphine seemed eager for the vicomte to speak again, while Marguerite watched her cousin with a mixture of worry and anger. That, Ned thought, seemed to be Marguerite's most common expression, though he could not see any reason for it. Mme. d'Hivers stood back watching them all contemptuously—her most common expression as well.

Ned felt uncomfortably like an intruder.

Tony, never a patient sort, spoke up with an attempt at joviality. "Well, great-grandfather, might you be willing to share those memories with us?"

The dark eyes snapped. "Are you a fool, like all the rest of them? The treasure—the treasure must be found."

"It might help if you told us a bit more about it." Tony was not in the least intimidated, only annoyed.

The old man did not seem to hear him. His face went slack, and his eyes lost their focus. "The priest hid it. Just before they came. He hid it, and then they dragged him off and killed him." He closed his eyes and his voice slowly faded. "I saw them. I saw them and I could not stop them. I did not even try. I ran away."

Silence filled the room as they all stood around, uncertain. An odd little rumble began. The old man had fallen asleep again and was snoring.

The doctor shooed them into the corridor and shut the door on them.

"Is it jewels, do you think? Perhaps the family jewels, diamonds last worn by a vicomtesse at Versailles." Delphine's eyes shone as she waved her hands to drape herself in imaginary necklaces and tiaras. "Or is it gold, saved from the hands of the revolutionary pigs, the *canaille*?"

"If there ever was such a treasure, it is doubtless long gone," said Marguerite. "Think, Delphine. This chateau stood empty for forty years. Anything the revolutionary troops missed would have been found by the enterprising thieves who followed them."

Delphine's face fell into a mutinous pout. "But he says there is a treasure."

"He says, he says! What does it matter what he says? He has lived here now for years. If there ever was a treasure worth retrieving, would he not have found it himself? He just uses this talk of a treasure to tease us, to make us wait here in attendance on him—and we are all foolish enough to do so!" Marguerite marched off in a swirl of anger.

"She is probably right, Delphine." Tony gave the girl a consoling pat on the shoulder.

Delphine shook him off. "No, she is not right. There is a treasure, and it is rightfully mine. She just doesn't want me to have it." She flounced off in the opposite direction from Marguerite.

Horace started to follow her, but halted to look questioningly at Mme. d'Hivers. She sighed and nodded permission before turning the other way to follow Marguerite.

Lifting a hand to rub the back of his neck, Tony sighed. "I have absolutely no idea what those women are on about. Everything with them is always a drama. I wish they would just come out and say what it is that is bothering them instead of expecting me to guess."

Ned nodded sympathetically, but his main emotion was frustration as his thoughts turned to the old vicomte. It was maddening. The old man had been here at the time of the Revolution. If only he could converse lucidly, and not just whisper gnomic hints, he could reveal so much about not just the events but the thoughts of people at the time. All that history, forever out of reach.

Or was it forever?

It might never be possible to unlock the vicomte's memories, but the chateau might contain other revelations. "Tony, you said there were papers."

"Lord, yes. Piles and piles of them. Not the legal stuff—deeds and what have you. The lawyers have all that. Just old letters, diaries, that sort of thing. Interested?"

"You know I am!"

Tony laughed. "Your kind of treasure. Buried not underground but up in the old north tower. And maybe you can find something in there that will tell us what this damned 'treasure' is."

Chapter Seven

NED MANAGED TO SHAKE THE DUST OFF HIMSELF, DRESS IN evening clothes, and slip into his seat at the dining table just as the soup was being served. Mme. d'Hivers frowned at him, leaving him feeling rather like a naughty schoolboy. He felt a bit better when he glimpsed a fleeting expression of sympathy on Marguerite's face before she retreated again behind her cool, imperturbable mask. But nothing could entirely dampen his enthusiasm about his afternoon in the tower.

Yet when he began to talk of his afternoon's discoveries, Marguerite shot him a glare and Tony spoke over him to talk of a book he'd been reading. To say he was taken aback by their attitude was putting it mildly. What was going on? Tony had invited him here to look at those papers, hadn't he?

Well, if they didn't want to hear about his discoveries, so be it. He retreated into offended silence while they talked about currently popular books.

Something by Jules Verne had caught their fancy—*Vingt mille lieues sous les mers. Twenty thousand leagues under the seas?* Ned didn't know the book, and he rather thought Verne was the author of children's books, but Tony and Marguerite seemed to be taking him quite seriously.

Tony was intrigued by the notion of an underwater ship, which sounded like a fairy tale to Ned, but Tony seemed to think the idea was actually possible. Marguerite contributed some gossip about the author's problems with his publisher.

While Tony and Marguerite talked—she seemed to actually relax a bit over the gossip—Delphine said to Ned, "That is the kind of people they knew, Marguerite and her father—artists, writers, musicians." She gave a dismissive sniff. "Never any people of fashion, people of importance. It was so very boring."

All thought of his own grievances vanished. Really, the girl's selfishness might be simply childishness, but still it should not be allowed to pass without reprimand. "Have I misunderstood?" he asked, looking at her sternly. "I thought that you and your mother were taken in by Marguerite's family after your father's death."

She shrugged. "Yes, yes. And I must be grateful, no doubt. I was no longer forced to be at that dreadful school. But that did not make it any less boring, to listen to them and their friends talk."

"Many would find the conversation of artists the most inter-esting talk to be found, and would be grateful to be admitted to their circle." He winced at hearing himself sound so pompous.

It didn't matter. Delphine was impervious. She did not notice the censure in his tone. Instead she looked at him with pity for his foolishness. "Musicians are, really, nothing more than servants. They simply play to entertain the important people, the aristocrats, the fashionable ladies and gentlemen. It makes one embarrassed to have to associate with them. And then one is faced with the reputation of the women!"

She seemed to think that he did not understand what she was talking about. "Consider," she said, impatiently. "What kind of woman would get up and perform on a stage, expose herself in front of strangers? Not a lady, not if she were possessed of any sensibility. She makes herself no different from an actress, and it was foolish of Marguerite to pretend to be insulted when the comte offered to make her his mistress. She should have felt honored."

This was so outrageous that Ned did not know what to say.

He was still sitting there with his mouth hanging open when dinner came to an end, and with it the conversation about Verne's book. When Ned looked away from Delphine he saw that Mme. d'Hivers was regarding him with something that looked almost like sympathy. Still, he was not in a comfortable frame of mind when they all gathered at one end of the great hall for their after dinner coffee.

"All right, Ned," said Tony, settling himself back in one of the well-padded chairs. "Now you can tell us what you found out today."

That set Ned's back up. "There's no need to humor me. I know you are not interested in my research."

"What makes you think we're not interested?" Tony looked honestly surprised.

Marguerite handed Ned his coffee. "Surely you can see that it would not be sensible to talk about a possible treasure in front of the servants. The news that you are searching for it would be all over the village in no time, and the chateau would be overrun with treasure hunters."

"I am not searching for it. Besides, I thought you said it had probably been found long ago." Ned tried to sound dismissive but feared that he sounded sulky.

"And that is probably true. But until it is known to have been found, or known to be imaginary, people will keep looking—as we are." One corner of her mouth lifted in a cynical half-smile. "Many find it difficult to remain sensible when people talk of a treasure."

She was really the most maddening creature. Did she really think he was such an idiot as to chatter away about some probably imaginary treasure in front of all and sundry? To say nothing of the fact that unless French servants were an entirely different species from English servants, those in the chateau doubtless knew all about it already. She should have realized that herself. "You need not have worried," he said. "I found nothing that shed any light on the treasure, though a good bit that bears on my own studies, as I began to tell you at dinner."

She gave him a considering look, not smiling. "I fear I may have insulted you. If so, I apologize. My only excuse is that in recent years there have been so many plots and counterplots, so many conspiracies, so much suspicion…" She shrugged. "I have perhaps grown overcautious."

He nodded a chilly acceptance of her apology and excuse, such as it was. "You need not fear. I have no interest in your treasure, whatever it may be."

"It is not *my* treasure. If it belongs to anyone, it is the old man's, and perhaps Antoine's. I want nothing to do with it. My only interest…" She broke off and shook her head. "No, let us forget the treasure, please. You were going to tell us about your discoveries."

A part of him wanted to remain offended, but she was making an effort. The least he could do was make an effort of his own. Turning to her, he noticed how the light from the lamp struck upon her cheekbones, giving a golden glow to the ivory of her complexion. It was really quite lovely… He realized that he was staring at her. So he cleared his throat and took a sip of his coffee.

"Yes, well, there are letters, diaries—it's an incredible treasure trove." He grinned at them all as his enthusiasm spilled out, offense all but forgotten. "There is a diary written by a girl who was at Versailles during the reign of Louis XVI. Letters from Lafayette before he even went to America. So many letters."

She sounded actually interested. "And these are helpful for your own researches?"

"I have barely begun to sort them chronologically, but your relatives seem to have known everyone—even Jean Cottereau. Just glancing through the letters, I saw references to Boishardy, Puisaye, Cadoudal."

"And that's important?" Tony was trying to look interested, but only looked confused. Delphine did not even try to hide her boredom.

"Of course it's important. These were all leaders of the resistance here in the west." Ned couldn't hide his irritation. He knew that people rarely shared his enthusiasms, but it was always a disappointment.

The conversation came to an abrupt end when the doctor made an appearance at the door.

"You will excuse me," the doctor said to the group at large, before he turned to Marguerite. "Mlle. Benda, I fear you are needed. If you would be so kind?"

"Of course." She immediately put down her coffee and followed him out.

None of the others seemed to think this at all remarkable or even unusual, and the conversation drifted into conventional inanities. But when Ned and Tony went up to bed, there was music, faint harpsichord music coming from the direction of the vicomte's rooms. It sounded like a gentle, peaceful memory of the past. Ned looked at his friend and raised his brows in inquiry.

"Oh, that's Marguerite. Sometimes when the old man is fretting and can't sleep, it soothes him to have her play for him."

Ned felt surprised. He wasn't quite sure why. Marguerite might seem cold but there was no reason to think she would refuse to help the old man. But the music… It was something familiar. Bach, he thought. One of the English suites. "She plays very well," he said.

"Didn't you know? I'm no judge myself, but I'm told she's considered quite an accomplished musician. She and her father were very much in demand before the war with Prussia knocked everything sideways."

"No," said Ned slowly, "I didn't realize." There was a purity to her playing, a sweetness that he would not have expected from Marguerite. She always looked so cold and stern.

Tony shrugged. "I don't know what she'll do now that her father's dead. I gather it was lucky for them that the old man invited them here." He flashed a grin. "Like me, they're waiting to see what happens next."

Penworth Castle

The sun was pouring through the diamond panes in the window of the breakfast room when Lady Penworth came down. She had never liked having breakfast in her room. Eating in the breakfast room not only meant that the eggs were still hot but—if she was quick enough—gave her the first look at the mail.

She was rewarded that day with the first letter from her son. Reading it brought a smile to her face, and when her husband joined her, she passed the pages to him as she finished them.

"Well, Ned certainly seems to be enjoying himself," said Lord Penworth.

"A bizarre chateau on the Breton coast, an ancient and apparently demented host, a mysterious treasure—how could he not be enjoying himself?" she laughed. "It sounds as if he has tumbled into one of Wilkie Collins' sensation novels. There is even a beautiful young girl and her stern, forbidding relatives. What more could he ask?"

Lord Penworth sighed. "Is he going to decide she is a damsel in distress and fall in love with this one too?"

"I don't think we need to worry," his wife said with a smile. "He only falls half in love with his distressed damsels. As soon as they turn out to be silly or vain or stupid, he ceases to feel romantic."

"But he doesn't stop feeling obliged to help them." Lord Penworth shook his head ruefully. "I hope this one isn't going to be too much trouble."

She smiled fondly at her husband. "He's still just a boy, and never gets too deeply involved. As for trouble, there has never been any that we couldn't extricate him from easily."

"Yes, but one of these days…" A worried frown passed over his face.

Chapter Eight

MORNING WAS NO MORE CHEERFUL THAN THE EVENING HAD been. Another gloomy day of clouds and fog meant there was no sunshine to brighten the gray dining room. Even the silver of the serving dishes seemed dull, and the steam from the coffee might as well have been more fog. Tony was pale and withdrawn, Mme. d'Hivers sat stiffly in black, and the only spot of color came from Delphine, smiling cheerfully in yellow ruffles.

No. Ned realized that he was wrong. Marguerite, though she was also in black, did show some color. There were two red spots on her cheeks. "I regret that I left so abruptly last evening," she said stiffly. "It must have seemed rude. And I do not want you to think I am not interested in your researches."

"Not at all," Ned assured her. "I gather your departure was something in the nature of an errand of mercy." The spots of color on her cheeks were obviously embarrassment. He doubted she apologized very often, and he looked at her assessingly, trying to see if this new information about her made a difference in the way he saw her.

No. In the cold light of morning—and it was a cold light— she was still a stern portrait in black and gray. Those spots of color faded from her cheeks. The dull black dress drained all remaining color from her face, framed by the dark hair pulled into a bun at her neck, and her brows were still fierce slashes above dark eyes that gave nothing away. Was there no womanly softness in her at all? She seemed to hold the whole world at defiance.

As he might have expected, she shrugged, as if to dismiss the notion that she might be considered anything so gentle as an angel of mercy. "But I must apologize. When you first mentioned your researches, I assumed you were just another dilettante looking for glorious stories about the heroic noblemen defying the rabble of the Revolution. But from what you said last night, I see that you are actually a serious historian."

"I hope I am." He offered his own self-deprecating shrug. "What interests me about the resistance here in the west—in the Vendée farther south and the Chouans here in Brittany—is the alliance between the noblemen and the peasants. That did not happen elsewhere. It occurs to me that there might be an analogy with the Highland clans, with lairds and crofters alike rising up to support the Stuarts. Since both the Bretons and the Scots are Celts, I wondered if there might be something in the Celtic heritage to explain it."

Her response was an incredulous laugh. "So you are romantic after all? Do you think the Celts have an inborn tendency to throw their lives away in a hopeless cause?"

That was offensive. "Hardly," he said stiffly. "Neither cause seemed hopeless at the beginning. But there was a collaboration between lord and peasant here, a loyalty that did not seem to exist in other parts of France."

Tony snorted. "I don't know that it was loyalty so much as proximity. The peasants here weren't as badly off as those in some places, and most of the nobles weren't all that wealthy. They mostly stayed here at home because they were too poor to try to make a show at Versailles. Besides, the Bretons have always considered themselves independent of France. The fact that the Revolution came from Paris was reason enough to resist."

"But brave! They were truly brave," broke in Delphine excitedly. "My mother told me stories about the vicomte's brothers. They were so heroic, dying with their men. They were like the

Marquis de Larochejaquelein. Do you know of him? Do you know what he said as he led his men to battle?" She stood up and gestured dramatically as she spoke. "If I advance, follow me. If I flee, kill me. If I die, avenge me!" She sat down again with a sigh. "Is that not splendid?"

"Splendid!" Mme. d'Hivers threw the word down in contempt. "Larochejaquelein was a twenty-year-old boy with dreams of glory and no idea what he was doing. They made him a general because he was an aristo, and his men were slaughtered because he had no idea how to lead them. As if being a marquis meant he had been born with any knowledge of strategy and tactics." She threw down her napkin and strode from the room.

Delphine rolled her eyes. "She is impossible!"

"I gather Mme. d'Hivers is not very fond of aristocrats," said Ned.

"Why should she be?" asked Marguerite, sounding defensive. "It is the aristocrats, the powerful ones, who start the wars and who benefit from them. They care nothing for those beneath them. What do they care if the poor suffer and die, as long as they are safe and comfortable."

"That is hardly a fair assessment." He was growing irate. "The vicomte's own brothers gave their lives."

"Pftt!" She snapped her fingers. "A few foolish boys who led hundreds of others to death. And the other aristos? They fled abroad until it was safe to come back to their chateaus and their hôtels and their wealth. Nothing has changed. They still trample on those they consider beneath them. They still think themselves entitled to everything and obliged to do nothing. Useless parasites!"

"That is ridiculous. It is no more just than saying that all peasants are brutes."

"But that is indeed what the aristos do say, is it not? Peasants are all brutes or ignorant fools who must be driven like animals." Marguerite had jumped to her feet and was facing him defiantly.

"No, it most certainly is not!" Ned stood as well, and flung down his own napkin. It seemed the appropriate gesture. With one part of his mind he noticed that Marguerite's phrasing became more French when she was upset, and that his own gestures became more florid in response. "It's absolute nonsense, and you know that perfectly well. You're an aristocrat yourself, after all. You and Tony and Delphine are all cousins, aren't you?"

"Are we? When one's mother has been disowned, it is hard to say." She spun around and marched out, head high.

Ned opened his mouth and then closed it. He could hardly shout after her, and he didn't know what to shout anyway. What had that been about, anyway? He rubbed the back of his neck and turned to Tony.

"Don't look at me." Tony held up his hands to ward off any questions. "I haven't the faintest idea. And I have no interest in your old battles." He got up with a grimace. "What I need is to study the figures Georges sent and see if I can think of any way to raise the rest of the money we need, so if you'll excuse me."

He added his napkins to those on the table and left.

Delphine had been sitting calmly through the eruption, dripping honey on a brioche. "She carries on that way at times. One must simply ignore it."

Ned looked at her in surprise. That did not sound like Delphine.

She shrugged. "That is what they say about me all the time. I thought it was time for me to return the compliment."

Ned frowned. Perhaps Delphine was not quite as childish and unknowing as he had thought. He filed that thought away, to be considered at some later time. Right now his confusion centered on Marguerite. "Do you have any idea why she is so, so angry? Why both of them are so angry?"

That warranted another shrug. "It is mostly because of Mme. d'Hivers, I think. She was assaulted by some aristocrats—I think she must have been pretty when she was young—and when her husband tried to protect her, they killed him. That is what she claimed, anyway, my mother said."

Ned was shocked, both by the story and by Delphine's indifference. "That is a dreadful story, and not at all the sort of thing someone would make up."

Delphine dismissed his comments with a wave of the hand. "It was years ago, but also just before the war with Prussia, my uncle was angry when a comte commissioned a series of concerts and then refused to pay the musicians. It is very bourgeois to think so much of money, is it not?"

"It is hardly noble to cheat people and to fail to pay your bills," Ned frowned severely. That was something his parents had drummed into him. "Taking advantage of people, abusing them, is contemptible."

Delphine waved a graceful little hand. "They should have felt honored by the opportunity to play for a comte. No. I think the problem is that Marguerite and Mme. d'Hivers are jealous."

"Jealous? Jealous of whom?" Ned felt a bit confused.

"Of me, of course. I am the only one who is truly of the nobility, *la haute noblesse*. My parents, my grandparents, all the way back we are of the nobility. Not like Marguerite, whose father is nothing but a musician, a performer. And Antoine, his father and grandfather married women whose families were in trade." She gave a delicate little shiver.

"Delphine," he said carefully, not quite knowing how to put this. "Delphine, don't you think you are being a bit foolish?"

"But no!" She looked at him with wide, innocent eyes. "That is why the vicomte has called me here."

He tried to be patient. "But he also wanted Tony and Marguerite here."

"He will doubtless leave them something. But I am the one who must inherit the chateau. That is only sensible. Antoine would turn it into a factory, and Marguerite thinks of nothing but her music." She looked around with a smile. "But this is the home of my ancestors, and I am the only one who truly belongs here."

Chapter Nine

AT LEAST THERE WAS A PIANO, A DECENT ONE, AND THERE had been a man in the village who could tune it. Marguerite did not think she could have borne it all without a piano.

It was not her own instrument, of course. It was not her beloved Pleyel, the piano her parents had given her when she was sixteen. She needed a piano to match her gifts, her mother had said, and hugged her. Her beautiful Pleyel, with its wonderful sound. She closed her eyes, and she could see her father's smile when he had shown it to her. She remembered the look of pride in his face the first time he listened to her play on it. Would she ever see her Pleyel again?

What was lost—all that was lost—she did not want to think about that.

She had come here—fled here—from the breakfast table. What had she been thinking? Ah, what nonsense. She had not been thinking at all. That was the problem. There was no reason for her to lash out at Lord Edward that way. It was hardly his fault that he had always been safe, protected by wealth, position, family. Was she going to turn into one of those bitter people who hated all who were fortunate? No, she would not let that happen to her.

She caressed the keys gently, playing a soft chord, then another, turning them into a sad, minor cadence as she waited. These days her life was spent in waiting. How she hated waiting.

There was nothing she could do until she knew more—any-thing—about her situation. She had to wait until she heard from M. Villoteau. She had written to M. Canonge also. He had arranged some of her father's concert tours. Perhaps he could arrange something for her.

But until she knew, she could make no decision. They were safe here for the moment, but for how long?

Wondering would accomplish nothing. There was always work to do at the piano. She began a series of Czerny's dexterity exercises, familiar to her since she had been a small child. Even-tually she began to work on the left-handed etudes. These were also familiar, but her left hand was still weaker than the right, and concentration was needed to force herself to work on this.

Half an hour later, the exercises ceased to demand her full attention. Her fingers drifted into Chopin's C-sharp minor etude, its passages of hopelessness all too attuned to her mood.

"It is of no use to let yourself drift into despair." Tante Héloise came in scolding. "And you must not let yourself pay attention to my foolish fits. Did the English aristo take offense? If so, I regret it." She did not sound in the slightest bit regretful, but that hardly mattered.

At the final chord Marguerite left her fingers on the keys and stared down at them. "It is of no importance. I too flew out at him. I have no idea why. There was no need." She lifted her fingers and slammed them down in a discordant crash. "Why do I keep doing that?" she burst out. "What demon is driving me?"

"Ah, little one, I am sorry." Tante Héloise came up behind Marguerite and, putting one hand on her shoulder, rested her cheek on the girl's head. "I am sorry. I had not thought. But he is a handsome one. Even I see that."

"Handsome enough, I suppose, in that English way." *Yes, standing tall and strong as if he feared nothing, as if there were nothing in this world to fear. And with those eyes, brilliant blue eyes, eyes with no shadows behind them. A man who could make you feel safe. Who could make you accept the illusion that there might be safety in this world. The dangerous illusion.* She tightened her jaw and smashed out another chord.

Tante Héloise sighed. "It is not the piano's fault, little one. But you must be careful. Men like him, aristos, they care nothing for people like us."

She shook her head. "But he seems different. He is not arrogant, careless, like those creatures at the concerts in Paris." They had posed no danger to her. For them she felt only dislike. This one, however… He had made her lose control back there in the breakfast room. No man had ever made her lose control. She must not do that. She could not afford it.

"That is simply because the English aristos are so assured of their place in the universe that they need not proclaim it. The French aristos are always uncertain now. They must keep reminding us that they are the powerful ones, lest we forget and believe once more in Liberty, Equality and Fraternity." A corner of Tante Héloise's mouth lifted in a bitter smile. "And lest we bring out the guillotine again."

She wanted to protest, but she knew Tante Héloise was right. "I know I should pay no attention to him. I do know that. But Delphine was prattling on about heroism and glory. Does she not remember what it was like in Paris just a few months ago? Has she already forgotten the misery? The hunger? The fear? Or has she been so completely wrapped up in her own dream world that she never even noticed?"

"*Pfft.* Of course she did not notice. You know she notices nothing that does not affect her, and even then she twists it in her mind."

Marguerite looked off into her memories. "We almost made it. That week in May when the army came in to put down the Commune—it was ending. Everyone knew it."

Tante Héloise put an arm around her shoulders and joined her in the memory. "Yes. The Commune was defeated, the cold and the hunger and the fear were coming to an end. We thought that in a day or so life could return to normal."

Marguerite lifted a hand as if to catch the memory, or perhaps to hold it at bay.

The gunfire in our quartier had stopped. Even the shouting seemed to have come to an end. We were all still crouched behind the furniture, waiting until Papa said it was safe to move. It was so quiet. We were not used to the quiet. All through the quartier people must have been waiting. As if we were all holding our breath.

Finally Papa stood up, ever so cautiously. He stepped into the middle of the room, a smile slowly appearing on his face—the first smile in many months. "I think it may be over," he said. "I think it is over." He opened his arms, and I started to run to him.

And then some fool, some wicked, evil monster of a fool out in the street started shooting off his rifle wildly at nothing. Nothing! Didn't he know it was over? Hadn't there been enough shooting? It should have been over. Except that one of those wild shots came through our window and hit Papa. He just stood there for a moment, the smile fading into a look of surprise, but still holding his arms out to me. His legs just crumpled beneath him. By the time I reached him, he was gone.

The trembling overwhelmed her and she collapsed against Tante Héloise. The older woman held her, rocking her like a child. She would have liked to weep, but the tears would not come. There was only the fear. What was she going to do? How was she going to take care of Delphine and Tante Héloise? And poor, simple Horace?

They could not stay here. Delphine might like to pretend that she would be the lady of the chateau, but was simply foolishness. The invitation from the vicomte had been fortunate...ah, it had been more than fortunate. She had buried Papa in the midst of the nightmare that was Paris, when so many were being buried that she feared the cemeteries would not hold them all. That had been necessary, and she had done it, but afterward? Afterward she'd had no idea what to do.

Finally she pulled herself up.

"You are all right?" Tante Héloise looked at her doubtfully.

"Well enough. There is no choice, is there? One must be well enough." She would have liked to give Tante Héloïse a reassuring smile, but she could not manage that.

The older woman nodded her understanding and squeezed Marguerite's hand before leaving.

Marguerite stared at the piano keys, and pressed down a few notes. Then she straightened up, put both hands on the keys, and slowly, softly began to play. Music. At least there was music. The chords piled upon each other, growing louder and louder until they drowned out all the worries.

A bit of sun escaping from the clouds drew Ned down from his tower. The breeze off the sea was chilly, but it had blown away the fog and for the moment at least the world was bright and clear.

The chateau boasted a surprisingly attractive formal garden, small but neat with its miniature boxwoods and topiaries in stone planters. Even now, with summer's flowers vanished, its straight paths and clipped hedges gave pleasure. He was admiring its mathematical precision—so distinct from all the churning undercurrents roiling the inhabitants of the chateau—when he caught sight of Delphine wandering along the same paths as he.

He had to admit that she made a pretty picture. The ruffles of her dress cascaded below her short cape, and a silly bit of nonsense perched on her curls. She looked delicate and fragile.

Footsteps startled him, and he turned to see Horace looming at his shoulder. Tony's distaste for the fellow seemed more understandable every time Ned saw him. Horace was large, yes, but he didn't give the impression of strength so much as thickness. He was not wearing any unusual amount of clothing, and what he wore seemed to hang loosely. It was as if his body were made up of extra layers of flesh. Combined with the dull look of his eyes and the way his mouth often hung open, his appearance was somehow discomfiting. That discomfort made Ned feel guilty. It was hardly Horace's fault that he was a simpleton.

"Mlle. Delphine is very pretty," said Horace.

"Yes, she is." Ned was not sure this was an appropriate thing for Horace to be saying. The young man might be simple, but he was still a young man.

"I take care of her." Horace smiled proudly. "M. Benda told me to watch over her, and I do."

"You take care of her?" Ned was not sure how a simpleton could take care of anyone. Perhaps Delphine had been told to take care of him.

"Yes. I make sure that nothing bad happens when she is around. Nothing that might upset her."

That sounded marginally like a duty that might be given to a simpleton. "I'm sure that you do an excellent job of that." Ned smiled uncomfortably and patted Horace on the shoulder.

Delphine greeted him with one of her shy smiles, peering up at him through her lashes. "Good afternoon, Edward. You too seek the sunshine. It is pleasant after all these days of clouds and mist, no?"

"Indeed it is. And you are looking quite as delightful as the sunshine." He felt a bit foolish saying that, but she seemed to expect that sort of florid compliment. There could be no harm in indulging her, since she could not be finding life here at the chateau terribly exciting.

She dimpled prettily and took his arm. "They are very foolish who say that the English are cold. You are far more charming and gallant than my cousin Antoine, who thinks of nothing but business. Come, we will explore this so very pretty little garden."

She really was a pretty little thing herself, he thought, and he patted the hand clinging to his arm. "Yes, it is a charming garden, and decidedly unexpected here."

"Unexpected? But why unexpected? A chateau should have a garden."

"Well, the chateau seems very much of the Middle Ages,

very gothic and forbidding, and this garden seems to belong to a later, more frivolous period." He thought perhaps that he needed to explain more since she looked puzzled, but before he could, her face cleared.

"You have not seen the real chateau then." She gave a little laugh. "Come, I will show you where the family lived—not in the fortress the old man has chosen for himself."

She tugged on his arm and drew him along the side of the chateau. As they turned a corner, they encountered a deluge of music pouring down from a window above them. Music so powerful that it had an almost palpable presence. Ned stopped as if he had run into a wall, causing Delphine to stumble slightly.

"What is it?" she demanded crossly.

"The music…" He held up a hand to ask for her silence, but she ignored it.

"That is only Marguerite. She is forever at the piano. One learns to ignore it." She tugged at his arm.

He refused to move. He could not.

The music swept him up, took him to a place he had never been, arousing emotions he had never known, teaching, tempting, tormenting. It swirled, rose and fell. One moment there was joy, and then it tumbled toward despair. But always it rose again, never quite surrendering, ever hopeful.

It filled the world. There was nothing but the music. It wrapped around him, obliterating everything, overwhelming him.

He stood spellbound until the notes exploded in a final inevitable conclusion, leaving him bereft. He longed to reach back, to return to that place where the music had been everything.

At a sound behind him—half groan, half sigh—he turned and saw that Horace too had been listening, mesmerized. The fellow looked as awestruck as Ned felt himself. For the first time he felt a kinship with Horace, and shame for the distaste he had felt earlier.

"There. She is finished. May we proceed now?" Delphine vibrated with irritation.

He shook his head in amazement. "I had no idea. I mean, I knew she played, but...but I had no idea." When she played the harpsichord—that had been good, impressively good. But this? This was music of a different order.

"Of course she plays. That is how she earns her living." At the look of confusion on his face, she sighed impatiently. "She played with her father in concerts, in people's homes and on public stages. You can imagine the humiliation for me." She shuddered theatrically and pulled him down the path.

It seemed futile to protest. Delphine obviously understood nothing of what they had heard. How could she be so deaf? Even poor simple Horace knew that Marguerite's music was something extraordinary. This was not the music of a polite young lady entertaining her guests, or even a professional performance in a concert hall. This was something entirely different, a kind of music he had never heard before. It swept him to places he had never known existed and left him filled with longing.

Chapter Ten

IF HE HAD BEEN PAYING ATTENTION, HE WOULD HAVE REALIZED that Delphine was leading him to the same door he had used when he arrived at the chateau. As it was, he was still under the spell of the music and did not notice where he was until he stood again on the stone floor, with the somber paintings of religious processions looming over him.

He frowned. "I came this way when I arrived."

"Yes, I know." She tossed him a smile over her shoulder. "But no one uses this entrance any more. That is why it took so long for anyone to let you in."

He continued to frown. "But you, you were up there at the top of this staircase." He gestured at the stone staircase that was, he now noticed, an elaborate one of carved granite. Surely this was no servants' entrance. Why had his entrance here been so unexpected?

"Yes, of course," she said, starting up the stairs. "This way we can reach the real chateau, not that dreary part the vicomte chooses to live in now. All those gloomy stone walls. This is where his family lived when all was beautiful and gay. You will see."

Horace held back. "But Madame said we should not go there." He stammered slightly.

"Nonsense." Delphine waved an airy hand as she continued up.

"But Madame said," Horace repeated stubbornly.

At the top of the staircase, Delphine spun around. "Then

do not join us. Go back to Madame. Go!" She waved dismissal.

Horace managed to look both mulish and cowed, with his lower lip stuck out before he turned and shuffled off, muttering, "She said. You know she did."

Ned looked after him uncertainly. "Is this part of the building unsafe?"

"No, of course not, unless you consider dust dangerous. Come along." She waved to him impatiently and vanished down the corridor.

He followed more slowly, feeling uneasy for reasons he did not understand. Part of it was simply that he was a guest here, and had no business intruding on private—or forbidden—areas. No one was likely to reprimand him, of course. Over the years he had learned that few people ever reprimanded the son of a marquess. That made him particularly careful to avoid over-stepping boundaries. He disliked even the possibility that he might be taking advantage of his position.

But was this part of the chateau private? No one lived in these rooms. That much was obvious. Dust there was in plenty, dust everywhere, piled up in corners and covering every surface. The only indication that anyone had entered these rooms in years—possibly in centuries—was the disturbance in the center where footprints and smears could be seen. Small footprints, probably Delphine's. And smears from her trailing skirts. Did anyone else come here?

His first thought, that the building might be physically unsafe, seemed wrong. The floor under his feet was definitely solid, and there seemed to be no danger from the ceiling. The plasterwork and cornices showed no missing pieces, no likeli-hood that bits might come tumbling down. The only possible threat came from the spiders that had spun those webs up there.

So why had Delphine been told not to come here?

"In here. Come." Her head appeared from a doorway and promptly disappeared.

He obeyed.

The doorway was one of those immensely high ones with double paneled doors folded back on each side. And the room itself was…incredible. He turned slowly, drinking it in. Even covered with decades of grime, something of its old glory shone through. It was a ballroom, he supposed. It was too big for anything else. On one side were long windows so coated with dirt that they barely let in any light now, but he imagined that they probably opened onto a balcony stretching the length of the room. On the opposite wall were long mirrors, their frames echoing the window frames. The chandeliers were long gone, only the plaster rosettes and brackets in the ceiling showing where they had once been. Bits of fabric still clung to the window frames, tattered remnants of old glories.

Ned shook his head. It was all incredibly sad.

Delphine stood on the dais at one end of the room, smiling joyously and stretching out her arms. "Is it not magnificent?"

He raised his brows. "That is not quite the way I would have described it."

"Oh, not at the moment, perhaps." She shrugged dismissively. "But when I have restored it, then you will see."

"You are planning to restore it?"

"Not yet, of course. I must wait until it is mine. It will be expensive, no doubt. I will need to find the treasure. He cannot live much longer, and he really must tell me how to find it before he dies." She was looking around the room meditatively.

"You are the vicomte's heir?" She seemed to assume so, but no one else had said anything about it.

"Who else?" She was not paying much attention to Ned. Her attention seemed focused on the windows.

Ned did not know whether to laugh or scold. She had said something of the sort once before. Playing games of make-believe was all very well and good, but she really should learn not to talk that way. "Tony is his great grandson," he pointed out. "And Marguerite is as closely related to him as you are."

She made a dismissive noise. "I told you, they are not truly of the nobility. Not any more. Their blood has been contaminated by their parents' *mésalliances*."

"Delphine!" It was more gasp than protest, more shock than either.

He might as well not have spoken for all the attention she gave him. Her thoughts were directed elsewhere, and hectic red spots appeared on her cheeks. "Tell me, do you think I should have velvet for the draperies or brocade? It must be blue to match my eyes. I may have to have it specially dyed. And I shall wear sapphires in my hair. The guests—they too will be of the ancient nobility, none of these new creations—they will all be struck with admiration for me, and they will recognize my worth. I shall reign over them all." She tilted her head as if in gracious acceptance of the admiration of the crowd.

Ned did not know what to say. Was this just a childish fantasy? He was beginning to doubt it. She looked and spoke as if she seriously planned all this. As if she believed what she was saying.

"Delphine." To his relief, Marguerite came through the door. She approached slowly, almost hesitantly, and spoke in the soothing tones one used for a frightened child or a wounded animal. He had heard her use that tone to Delphine before. "Delphine, I thought…"

"There is no need for you to worry, Marguerite," Delphine interrupted with a regal wave of her hand. "I have not forgotten you. There will be a piano up here on the dais for you, beside the orchestra, and you will be able to play for my guests." She looked at her cousin with a frown. "But if you persist in dressing like a crow, I must insist that you sit behind a screen. I will have no black at my ball."

"Very well, dear, no black. But don't you think…" Marguerite stretched out a hand toward the younger girl.

"Stop that!" Delphine leaped back, out of reach. "You don't believe me. You think I am just being silly. But it will all be true. This will all be mine. Why do you deny it?" Her voice kept rising.

"Calm yourself, Delphine." Marguerite kept her voice soft,

but she looked as if every muscle in her body was tensed.

Ned wanted to help. He hated that he was just standing there, but he did not understand what was happening and he feared making things worse. There did not seem to be any physical danger at least.

"Enough." Mme. d'Hivers' voice was not loud but was decisive. "It is time, Delphine. You will come with me."

Everything seemed frozen. Mme. d'Hivers stood in the doorway, holding out a hand to Delphine, dominating by her very presence. Horace hovered behind her, his head appearing over her shoulder. Inside the room, Marguerite waited, watching Delphine, just watching.

And Delphine? She stood up on the dais, head high, one hand at her breast, immobile while they all stared at her. Finally, she gave a gracious smile and nodded at Mme. d'Hivers. "But of course," she said, and moved gracefully across the dais, down the two steps, and across the floor to the door, where she placed her hand on that of the older woman and allowed herself to be led from the room.

Ned let out the breath he had not realized he was holding and turned to look at Marguerite.

She shook her head. "I am sorry. It is not your fault. Someone should have warned you."

"What isn't my fault? What should someone have warned me about?" His confusion was giving way to anger. "What the hell just happened?"

She was standing there looking coldly emotionless again. Could this possibly be the same woman who had made the music he had listened to not an hour ago? This, this ice queen? She was so pale he could believe that it was ice water, not blood, running though her veins.

"I am sorry," she said again. "It is just that…" She licked her lips—at least that was some sign of emotion. "Delphine…she is very imaginative. There are times when she forgets and gets carried away."

"You mean she lives in a dream world." The brutality of his tone made her flinch.

She held herself up stiffly, however, and persisted. "It has been difficult for her. Her father died, then her mother, then her uncle. My mother. The siege. My father's death."

"I apologize." He felt a guilty flush creep up his face. "It must have been difficult for you as well."

Her shoulders lifted in a dismissive shrug. "I am not so... fragile as she is. And then I never knew her father, barely knew her mother and uncle."

"Now you are responsible for her?" This could not be right. Delphine was...he was not sure what Delphine was, though she was obviously not the sweet, angelic creature he had thought when he first saw her. Something was certainly wrong with the girl. Marguerite could not possibly have such responsibility thrust upon her. She was too young herself, not more than a year or two older, and, now that he looked more closely, too pale and thin, too fragile herself for such a burden.

But she looked away. "I promised my mother. There is no one else."

He muttered an oath and seized her by the arm. "Come with me."

Chapter Eleven

MARGUERITE WAS TOO SURPRISED TO DO ANYTHING BUT GO along with him. Was it surprise, or did she want to go with him? Was she fooling herself? She should not be affected by his touch, but somehow she was unable—no, unwilling—to resist.

In no time, it seemed, she found herself back in the inhabited part of the chateau, seated by the fire in a small parlor. She ought to protest such high-handed behavior, she supposed, but it had been chilly in the music room and the old rooms, especially that ballroom, had been icy. She shivered and reached her hands out to the fire and the warmth. Her fingers tingled as they thawed and the blood returned to them.

"Do you need a shawl?" Lord Edward asked. She found it impossible to think of him without his title, no matter what sort of informality Delphine had ordained. Just now his voice sounded more angry than concerned.

She shook her head. "No, I am perfectly comfortable, thank you." That was not true. She was never comfortable these days. Still, what business was it of his, how she felt?

He did not look as if he believed her, and went to the door to call for a servant.

She stiffened in irritation, not accustomed to being disbelieved. It was even more annoying when she had been lying, or at least suppressing the truth. "I do not wish a shawl," she snapped.

He turned back from addressing the servant and scowled at

her. "Then you shall not have one. But I wish for some tea, and from the look of you, you could use some as well."

She tightened her lips and turned back to the fire. She was cold. Her very bones were cold. There was an icy chill at the very heart of her. A shawl, a cup of tea, even this fire would not warm her. There were times when she thought that she would never be warm again. Her fingers at least were beginning to thaw. She sank into the chair closest to the fire.

At least Tante Héloise had taken charge of Delphine. For the moment she did not need to worry, but the fear at the heart of her gave way to a weariness that swept over her in waves. She was tired, so very tired. And the chair was so soft. She leaned back, sank into it, and closed her eyes.

A sudden clatter made her jump. For a noise to have startled her that way, she must have dozed off at least a bit. Surely she had not fallen fully asleep—that would be too embarrassing. Yet when she opened her eyes, there was a laden tea table in front of her, and Lord Edward was pouring. She straightened up in her chair and stopped her hands from reaching up to make sure her hair was neatly in place. She was not going to fuss about her appearance in front of him.

"Do you take milk and sugar?" he asked. Perhaps he had not noticed her drowsing.

"Neither. Some lemon if there is any."

He nodded as if he had expected that and put a slice in her cup before handing it to her. She took it and nodded thanks. Then he held out a plate of cakes to her. This time she shook her head to refuse, but he did not withdraw the plate.

"Take one and eat it," he said. Ordered, one might say.

She disliked taking orders. "Thank you, but I am not hungry."

"You do not eat enough." He was frowning at her.

She sighed impatiently. "There is enough food served at every meal here to feed an entire village."

"That may well be true, but you don't eat it. You just play with it." He continued to hold out the plate of cakes, and continued to frown.

She was taken aback. He should not have been aware of that. No one else was. Her appetite vanished each time a plate of food appeared before her, but she thought she took enough tiny bites to fool people. Who would have expected him to be the one to notice? She hesitated, then took a small cake covered in white icing, and popped it into her mouth. It seemed easier than arguing. Besides, while her mouth was full of cake, she could hardly be expected to converse.

It seemed that Lord Edward was not inclined to converse either. He put down the plate and sat back, arms folded, to watch her eat. Not until she had swallowed the cake, had a sip of tea, and dabbed her mouth with her napkin, did he give a satisfied nod and speak. "How did Delphine come to be with you?"

That was not quite what she had expected, but upon consideration, it was a question that could be answered.

"It was about five years ago now," she said. "We were living in Paris, and one day Delphine and her mother, Tante Louise, just appeared on our doorstep. The baron, Delphine's father, had died and it seems he left debts and nothing else. Naturally, we took them in. After all, Tante Louise was Maman's sister." She shrugged and took a sip of her tea, glancing at him through her lashes. Surely that was enough explanation. He was listening but did not appear satisfied. Pity.

"What of her father's family?" he asked.

She settled her cup in its saucer. "There was an uncle, her father's brother. He came not long after, and wanted Delphine to go back to the school where her father had put her, with the nuns. Delphine did not want this; neither did my aunt, but her uncle kept insisting it should be as her father had wanted. There were many arguments." She shook her head, but could not shake away the memory of those angry voices and her aunt's hysterical weeping. "It was not a pleasant time."

When she did not continue, he prodded. "Did he give up then?"

"Not precisely. He was not well—we had not realized he was so ill." She shrugged. "He said it was dyspepsia, and he was about to go to a spa, but it was too late. Not long after he died, Tante Louise fell ill as well."

"Rather an epidemic," he said.

"Not really. Tante Louise had been ill before they came. Consumption. That was why she brought Delphine to us—she wanted to be sure she would be taken care of."

He was looking doubtful. "I thought her uncle wanted to take care of her. You said she had been in a school—a convent school, I assume. Would it not have been better for her to remain there, in a familiar place, if her mother was so ill?"

How could she explain? Both Tante Louise and Delphine had grown hysterical at the suggestion. They'd said it had been a truly dreadful and frightening place and they had not calmed down until Maman had sworn to take care of Delphine.

"It was not a good place. Delphine disliked it," she said. "My mother promised Tante Louise that she could stay with us, that we would take care of her. She promised that we would never send Delphine back to that school. Then when my mother was dying, I promised her. Does that satisfy you? Have you asked enough questions?"

Maman! That horrible day. I had turned away for only a minute to look in the window of the milliner, wishing for the pretty, frivolous little hat, when I heard the crashing sounds, the shrieks of the horses, of the people. When I reached them, I had to push through the people.

There was blood, and Maman was lying on the ground, her face twisted in pain. When I grasped her hand, Maman had known me. She looked at me, and managed to speak. "Delphine," she had said. She sounded so urgent, so I said, "Don't worry. I will take care of her."

And then Maman was gone. Just like that. It was over.

She jumped to her feet, abruptly enough to make the tea table before her shake. She was trembling. This could not be allowed. None of this was any business of his. Why was he asking all these questions? More importantly, why was she answering them? She did not want to think about all of that. She did not want to remember. She must be more tired than she had realized to have so little control over her tongue.

It was no concern of his if she was cold, if she did not eat enough. Why was he acting as if it was his concern? Why was he acting as if he had a right to take care of her?

Why did she want to let him take care of her?

Because she did.

She closed her eyes. She must be out of her mind. A handsome young man had done something as simple as lead her to the fireside and hand her a cup of tea, and all of a sudden she was ready to cling to him and tell him all her troubles. All her secrets. And more.

She could not be tempted. She must not. Without another word she fled the room.

He had managed to stand before she ran away, but he hadn't been able to stop her. Should he have tried? Did he even have the right to stop her? The infernal woman seemed quite clear that she did not want any help from him. Not that he knew what sort of help she needed. More than a cup of tea and a frosted cake—that much anyone could see.

She must have been exhausted to fall asleep that way in front of him. And it had been a shock to see her. In sleep she had seemed different—softer, more vulnerable. Her defenses had fallen away. And she looked really quite—not pretty. No. Not that. Even in sleep she was too regal for mere prettiness. But there was true beauty in her face. Her mouth, when it was not pressed tightly into that disapproving line, was soft and delicate. Beautifully shaped. Inviting. He shook off the thought.

There was a mystery here. What was she afraid of? Why did she always hold herself so tensely defensive?

She had her secrets and she had her responsibilities—far too many responsibilities, it seemed—and no one to take care of her. The old man obviously was in no condition to do anything himself, but he should have made some provision for her and Delphine. Or Tony should step in—he was their cousin, after all, even if distant.

It certainly wasn't *his* job to take care of her. He didn't even like her. She was nothing like the pretty and charming—if slightly odd—Delphine.

Marguerite was proud and arrogant and generally unpleasant. She had made her indifference perfectly clear, and that was fine with him. If she wanted to clutch her problems to her bosom, he wasn't going to try to pry them loose. She could play the tragedy queen to her heart's content. It was no affair of his.

She was indifferent to him, and he was indifferent to her.

Fine.

Marguerite managed to get to her room before she began to tremble. She leaned against the door, barely able to stand. What was wrong with her? This woman here in her body—this was someone she did not recognize.

Bad enough she had confided in him—not too much, but she had told him more than anyone but Tante Héloïse knew. It was so easy to talk to him. There he was, so big and strong and solid, and she could lean on him and be safe.

Except that she couldn't.

It was the temptation of him. He made her want things she had never wanted before. Never before had a man tempted her as a man. But he was so beautiful. Whenever he touched her, just a brush of the hand, it was enough to send heat coursing through her. She could feel his touch like a flame.

In the past, there had been men who wanted to tempt her—the theaters and concert halls had been full of them—but they had raised no answering emotion in her. And Louvois had filled her with disgust.

Why did it have to be this man, who did not even like her? He was kind and sympathetic, but it was kindness born of pity. She had no use for pity. She despised it.

It seemed a waste of the vicomte's beautiful plumbing, but perhaps she should start taking cold baths.

Chapter Twelve

THE CHILL OF LATE OCTOBER CREPT INTO THE CORRIDOR when they all gathered once more for their morning audience with the vicomte. Ned didn't know how he looked, but he felt haggard. He had not slept well and that was unusual. All his life he had slept well, and he resented the disturbed night he had just suffered.

She had kept invading his dreams. It was infuriating. She had no business doing so. He didn't even like her. She was hard and prickly and took offense at every little thing. There was nothing soft or attractive about her.

Except…

Except that when she had fallen asleep in her chair yesterday, she had looked so different. Vulnerable. The little frown marks had disappeared, and the tightness around her mouth had softened. The frozen mask she habitually wore had melted away and given him a glimpse of the beauty that lay beneath it.

This was preposterous! If he didn't get hold of himself, he would be writing poetry next. She had no interest in him, and he had none in her—at least, no more than an intellectual curiosity. Puzzles had always intrigued him, and he couldn't help wondering about the secrets she was hiding. It was no different, really, from wondering about the mysteries of the past, why things had turned out as they did, why people had chosen as they had.

It was curiosity that drew his eyes to her. Nothing more.

She was standing a little apart from the others, looking out, wrapped in a drab black cloak, always in black. Perhaps she had gone for an early morning walk. If so, it was sensible of her to keep the cloak on. It was always cold in these corridors, and she was too thin.

Where she was standing, by the slitted window, the light outlined her profile, her surprisingly elegant profile. But she shouldn't be standing by the window—it was even colder there. He moved toward her.

Her hand was at her neck, fingering the brooch that closed her cloak at the collar. It was an odd one—about three inches across, with rounded stones arranged like a rosette in a setting of dull metal.

"An unusual piece," he said.

She jumped, as if startled by his presence. Did she think he had been offended by the way she ran off the day before? He offered what he hoped was a reassuring smile.

"Unusual?" she said. "I suppose so." She offered a polite smile of her own.

"Ugly." Delphine had come up beside them and wrinkled her nose. "It is ugly and unfashionable. You should have sold that instead of my pearls."

The child certainly clung to her resentments. Ned frowned at her, but she paid him no attention.

Marguerite sighed. "I am sorry, Delphine, but my mother gave this to me, and her mother gave it to her. Maman used to wear it to close her cloak, too. It is the only thing of hers that I have."

Antoine joined them and huffed a short, bitter laugh. "Typical. He lies there on all the wealth the family has ever had, and the rest of us cannot touch it. You, at least, have a brooch, however ugly it may be."

Delphine sniffed and turned away with a toss of her curls.

Ned, however, had not lost interest in the brooch. "May I?"

he asked, reaching out a hand toward her collar. She started to pull back but then tilted her head back and held still. He lifted the brooch with a finger and peered at it intently. "I am no expert, but the style is indeed antique. It may be very old indeed. Are the stones real?"

"I doubt it. They are so dull that I have always assumed they are glass." She looked down, avoiding his eyes, and ran her finger over the smooth surface of the stones.

He stepped back but continued to look at the brooch. It intrigued him. There was something about the design. "Glass? Perhaps," he said. "But if it is actually medieval, gems would not be cut with facets and might look dull to the modern eye."

That caught Delphine's attention. "Gems? Is it valuable then? Could the stones be recut?"

"Delphine…" Marguerite sighed.

"If it is a family heirloom, it should be mine. It is my family, after all." Delphine began to reach out for it, her eyes shining.

Ned caught her hand. "Stop that. It is Marguerite's brooch." When she seemed about to erupt, he added placatingly, "Besides, much of the value is in the sentiment, not in the gemstones."

For a moment, Delphine's reaction was uncertain. Then she tossed her head and said, "It is an ugly piece. Marguerite may keep it." She stepped away, ignoring the others.

Marguerite gave a short laugh. "How kind of Delphine to allow me to keep my own brooch."

Ned was not amused, but before he could say anything, the doctor appeared in the doorway to bid them enter. He looked much the same as usual, neither pleased nor displeased. When Antoine asked if there had been any change in his great-grandfather's condition, a slight shake of the head was his only response.

As they all moved toward the vicomte's room, Ned happened to glance up at the coat of arms in the carving over the door and noticed the rosette. It was the same design as Marguerite's brooch—seven petals surrounding three petals around a single center.

That suggested that Marguerite's brooch might really be very old. An heirloom indeed. He would have to tell her.

Marguerite approached the bed feeling uncomfortably shaken. Lord Edward's nearness should not affect her this much. He had barely touched her. A slight brush of the fingers against her throat when he had lifted the brooch—that was all. It should not have felt as if he'd set her skin aflame.

He had defended her against Delphine's silly outburst of greed, but she should not read anything into that. It was the normal reaction of an adult to a childish tantrum.

She should be paying attention to the vicomte and his condition instead.

Was the doctor lying? It appeared to her that change was visible when they lined up as usual beside the bed. The shriveled old man was once more propped up against the pillows, half sitting, half reclining. He was neatly shaven, dressed in a pressed night gown with a cap on his head, but today his mouth was not quite closed and his eyes were not quite open. His hands lay on the brocade of the coverlet with the fingers curled, almost as if he clawed at it.

Every time she saw him there seemed to be less of him, as if he were drying up and shriveling away.

Those hands held her eyes almost hypnotically. Each slight movement of the fingers seemed weighted with meaning. In the silence of the room, the scraping of his fingers on the brocade seemed preternaturally loud.

She forced her gaze aside and tried to think. This could not go on much longer. The vicomte was fading away. Soon he would shrivel up and vanish completely. There would no longer be any excuse for them to be here.

Things were getting more complicated. Lord Edward's presence, his very existence, was making them so. He was a distraction, and she could not afford any distractions. Why did he have to come here? Why couldn't he have stayed in England where she would never have even seen him?

For a while, things had been under control, but not any longer. She had to get away from this place. She had to get Delphine away. The girl was getting worse here. There had to be a way to get them all away.

Antoine gave an irritated wave of the hand that drew her attention back to the presence. His impatience was showing. He seemed to be holding himself still through sheer force of will. "Well, doctor, your patient appears to be asleep. Did you call us in here so that we could bear witness to that?"

"You have somewhere more important to be?" Doctor Fernac sounded dismissive.

Antoine exploded. "Yes, as a matter of fact I do. This pointless daily attendance on a dying man who does not even know we are here…" He halted, shocked into silence when the old man's eyes suddenly opened and stared at him.

Then the vicomte turned those eyes on Marguerite. No, she realized, not on her. On her brooch.

"You have it still, Marguerite." His voice was surprisingly strong.

She was not sure what he meant, but she put up a hand to cover the brooch. Still, a response seemed necessary. "Yes, *Monsieur le Vicomte.*" She never knew quite how to address him. None of them did, really. She could hardly call him uncle. He was a complete stranger to her. Until a few months ago, she had not known that he existed. Antoine referred to him as "the old man" and simply avoided addressing him directly.

The vicomte frowned slightly and one of the hands on the coverlet fluttered slightly. In some sort of protest? Or was it confusion? Did he know who she was? Who any of them were? But he seemed to be speaking directly to her. "You never told me what it means. Do you know? The priest, Abbé Seznec, did he tell you? Where did he hide it?"

She did not know what to say. All she could manage was to stammer out, "I don't know."

He looked away, and his voice grew querulous. "It wasn't my fault. There was nothing I could do. So many of them, and Léchelle leading them. I could not stop them. Everyone feared Léchelle. But he would not tell them, the abbé. Even when Léchelle struck him down. They left then. The others did not like it that he killed a priest."

In the silence it seemed as if everyone was holding his breath. Was he telling them about the treasure? Something a priest had hidden? If the priest had been killed by this Léchelle right after hiding it, then perhaps it really was still hidden. Perhaps there really was something.

Perhaps there would be enough to buy safety.

A wave of dizziness swept over her. She might have fallen had not an arm caught her around the waist to steady her. Lord Edward. He was right beside her, looking concerned, keeping her safe. Again. It was so tempting. She wanted to smile and lean against him.

No! She must not. A polite smile of thanks was all she could allow herself. That, and then she must keep herself erect and rely on no one. Before he came, there had been no difficulty in remembering that. She had to be strong. A few kind gestures could not be allowed to get under her guard.

The vicomte was looking at her again, but he seemed to have mistaken her for someone else. "Did you tell our father before he died? He didn't tell me. Why didn't he tell me? Why won't you tell me? I should have been the one who was told about the treasure. I was the heir. Not you." His voice faded to a whisper. "Not you."

His eyes closed, and the hands on the coverlet relaxed. He was asleep once more. The doctor leaned over to check his patient's pulse, nodded to himself and shooed the visitors out.

They all stood about in the corridor, not quite ready to leave and go about their business. It was an uncomfortable silence.

Delphine spoke first. "I don't understand. He called you by name, but he was talking as if you were someone else."

"I don't understand either," Marguerite said. "I didn't think he even knew my name. He never used it before."

"It was odd. All of it was odd." Antoine tugged at his little beard.

"Is there another Marguerite in the family?" asked Lord Edward.

Antoine and Marguerite shook their heads and shrugged, but Delphine burst out excitedly, "But of course! Our great-grand-mother—his sister—she was called Marguerite. He must have thought you were his sister." Then her face fell. "Why you? Why would he mistake you for his sister and not me? That is not right. I have seen her portrait. She was fair and dainty, like me. Not dark and strange like you."

"Don't distress yourself," said Marguerite in soothing tones. It was so hard to be soothing all the time. "His mind was wandering, and his eye fell on me. I'm sure that's all it was. Doubtless next time he will think you are his sister."

"The brooch," said Lord Edward. They all looked at him.

"That's what he was staring at," he explained. "You said that it was a family piece, an heirloom. Perhaps he recognized it as something his sister owned, and that is why he thought you were Marguerite—his Marguerite, that is."

"Possibly. Quite possibly," said Antoine.

A very French moue appeared on his face, and it amused Marguerite to think that her cousin was becoming more and more French these days. It was a relief to find something amusing.

"He seemed to think she would know where to find the treasure," Antoine continued. "But since she has been dead for half a century, that is no help. It's a pity that he did not tell us something more useful."

"Perhaps he did." Lord Edward looked thoughtful. "He mentioned Léchelle. I know the name. He was one of the more brutal enthusiasts of the Revolution, and he was only in this area for a short time in '94."

"Ninety-four?" Antoine frowned. "That was when the last of the family fled to England—the old man and his sister and their father."

Lord Edward was frowning. "When was that? Do you know?"

"I know," said Delphine, holding out an arm in a dramatic gesture. "It was in February, in the bitter cold. They fled in a small fishing boat, carrying almost nothing with them. *Hélas*, the poor old vicomte was wounded and had died by the time they reached England."

"Fortunately they had sent most of the family fortune to England when the Revolution began to look serious," said Antoine dryly. "They were not among the penniless aristocrats offering to teach dancing to the English."

"I am not certain of the dates, but I think that Léchelle didn't arrive here until January or February," said Lord Edward. "That would mean that the murder of the priest would have taken place very close to the time of their departure."

"I don't see how that is of any help to us." Antoine shook his head.

Lord Edward ignored him. "And not long after that, Léchelle himself was assassinated. It all makes a kind of sense. If the priest died before he could tell anyone where the treasure was, and if Léchelle did not live long enough to find it for himself, it may still be hidden."

"Fine." Antoine still looked disgruntled. "But that doesn't tell us where it is, or even what it is."

Lord Edward's eyes shone with enthusiasm. "Think about it. We do have some clues. The old man said that he saw the priest come out to wherever he was captured, so the hiding place must be somewhere inside the chateau. And it must be someplace where a boy could see what was happening without being seen himself."

"And it must be in the other part of the chateau," said Antoine, straightening up and looking attentive, "because this part was not in use then."

"We will find it. I am sure of it!" Delphine's eyes were shining, and she quivered with excitement.

The others all looked eager to get on with the search. Marguerite feared she was the only one who had difficulty responding with enthusiasm. What was wrong with her? If they found the treasure, surely the vicomte and Antoine would allow her a share in it, even if it was only a small share. Money could buy them some measure of security.

Why did she not share the eagerness of the others? Had worry become so much a part of her that nothing could make her feel hopeful?

Chapter Thirteen

DELPHINE INSISTED THAT THEY ENTER THE BAROQUE—AND uninhabited—section of the chateau through what would have been the principal entrance. As they all trailed along after her, Ned realized that she was the only one who was actually familiar with this part of the building. He, at least, had never been here before.

Traces of the broad gravel drive that had once led visitors to the door were still visible despite almost a century of neglect. The steps were mainly intact, though mossy at present and covered with dead leaves. As for the door, or rather, the doors, a pair of them beneath the lofty marble pediment, they may have been cracked and stained with age, but they still looked formidable enough to keep out invaders.

Ned was about to suggest that they try a different entrance, one that might offer easier access, when Delphine pulled a massive iron key from one of the urns flanking the doors and dealt with the lock. It turned easily, and the doors swung open without a creak of complaint. She waved them to enter with a flourish.

He was about to obey when he realized that Marguerite was not moving. What was wrong? He started to reach out to her, but she didn't seem to see him. Her eyes were fixed on Delphine and her mouth was pinched in annoyance. When she spoke, it was as if the words had to fight their way out. "You said you had not been visiting this part of the chateau. You gave me your word."

"Oh fiddle-faddle. Don't fuss. There is no reason I shouldn't use this door as well as any other."

Marguerite looked as if she would be pleased to argue, but Tony hurried toward the house. "There's no need to make a fuss. Why shouldn't she play in here if she likes? I'm sure it's perfectly safe." He paused in the doorway to look around, then nodded. "Yes. You can still see where the drive must have been. This is where people would have entered. And you have seen to it that the lock and hinges are oiled? Good girl."

Delphine smirked at Marguerite before following him into the building.

The tension between the two women was palpable, but Ned had no idea of the reason for it. There was no point in asking Tony—he understood machinery but had no interest in what made people tick. Delphine was obviously rebelling against Marguerite's authority. Understandable in one way, but he doubted that Marguerite was simply trying to impose her will on the younger girl.

Delphine's flights of fancy, her play-acting—was it possible that these were indications of something more serious than childishness? He'd seen that they were odd and could be tiresome. Was there more that he had not noticed?

Marguerite's hands were clenched tightly at her waist, and a small sound of distress escaped her. Ned could not help himself. He reached out to touch her. "What's the matter? Can I help?"

Immediately her face assumed its frozen mask. "It is nothing. Why should anything be the matter?" She began walking into the chateau, but he refused to let go of her arm, walking beside her.

Something obviously was the matter, and he wished she would tell him what it was. "Would it not be better to tell me what has you upset? It cannot be simply that Delphine has been wandering through this part of the chateau. She might get her gowns dusty, but that hardly warrants your distress."

"I am not distressed," she snapped.

She did not say any more, and he did not ask again. He simply looked his disbelief.

She stopped and drew a deep breath. "Really, it is nothing." Then she turned to look at him, and the frozen mask slipped slightly. "There is nothing you can do. Please do not ask any more."

He waited, but when she said no more, he inclined his head. "As you wish. But please remember, if at any time I can be of assistance, you have only to ask."

"For that I think you." A brief smile slipped across her face before vanishing behind the mask.

He tucked her hand under his arm to escort her into the chateau. At least the stubborn creature did not refuse that much assistance. Pride was all very well and good, but it could veer into danger. If she needed help, and it was fairly obvious that she did, it was foolish not to ask for it. Couldn't she see that he wanted to help her? There was no need for her to shoulder her burdens alone.

Then again—the thought struck him suddenly and unpleasantly—it might not be pride that kept her from confiding in him. It might be that she simply did not trust him. There had been that outburst against aristocrats. Surely she couldn't think that he looked down on her in any way. He refused to believe it.

Did she think he was one of those arrogant wastrels who hovered about in theatrical Green Rooms? His family would howl with laughter at the suggestion. He had never been in a Green Room in his life. At a ball, he was always the one partnered with the shyest young debutantes so they would feel comfortable. He almost laughed, but he held it in. He doubted she would appreciate the joke.

Being mistrusted was a new experience for him. For a moment he toyed with the idea of playing the dangerous rake. It might be fun. Then he remembered something Delphine had said about some French comte who wanted Marguerite to be his mistress. He glanced at Marguerite's tense face and decided that the last thing she needed was someone joking about a situation she had found deeply insulting.

One of these days he might be able to tease her, but not yet. He still needed to earn her trust. Finding out what was troubling her was far more important than playing games.

They stepped through the door into a square room that was large for a vestibule, but too small for a hall. It must have been impressive once, before the black and white tiles on the floor had been turned to a dull gray by the dust, before the ceiling plasterwork and cornices were draped with cobwebs.

Dust also covered the Holland cloth that had been laid over all the furniture. Looking around with fastidious distaste, Tony picked up the corner of one piece of Holland and raised it high enough for them to see that it had been shrouding a table. He started to speak but dropped it abruptly to pull out a handkerchief to cover his sneeze. "Good God! Is the whole place like this?"

"Do not be difficult," said Delphine with a playful smile. "We shall order the servants to clean it, and soon it will be…" She paused, and then clasped her hands at her breast. "Magnificent!" She breathed the word out slowly, a look of ecstasy on her face.

"We will do nothing of the sort." Marguerite spoke with cold finality.

Delphine spun around, ready for battle, but Marguerite ignored her. "First of all," she said, holding up a finger, "bed-ridden or not, the vicomte is master here. He chose to leave this wing untouched. It is not our place to ask *his* servants to countermand *his* orders."

"But he is dying! He will not even know."

Marguerite ignored the protest. "Second, if there really is a treasure hidden here, it will not do to have servants swarming all over the place. If it is here to be found, it must be found without help from the servants. Unless you are willing to share it?"

At the look of horror on Delphine's face, Marguerite smiled sardonically.

Tony grimaced. "I suppose you are right. Secrecy will be required. But this place is enormous. It could take us years to go through it all."

Ned had been wandering around and found himself in the next room. "We might do well to think of this as the starting point. Come look."

He was standing in the middle of a perfectly round room. Curved staircases led to a balcony that circled the room at the level of the next floor. High above, a dome roofed the space, with small oval windows spaced closely at the base of the dome. Dust and grime dimmed the light coming in, but it was enough to see what must have been a magnificent hall once upon a time.

Tony peered up at the dome. "A good piece of construction, that, if it's undamaged after all these years."

Delphine shot him a look of contempt. "That is what you see? Engineering? Look at this." She waved her hand around. "Have you no imagination? Can you not see it filled with people, the cream of the nobility, all dressed in their finest robes, glittering with jewels. Above, where that chain dangles, a chandelier with a hundred candles illumines the space. And I stand at the top of the stairs, to greet my guests." A hectic flush colored her cheeks and her eyes glittered.

"Delphine, if you want to be part of this search for a treasure, you will stop this fantasizing now." Marguerite seized hold of the girl's arm and looked steadily into her eyes. "Right now."

The younger girl pulled back, twisted, and tried to look away. She could not. Slowly she grew calm. Her whole body seemed to droop. With a nod of acceptance, she leaned against Marguerite, who held her gently, murmuring words that seemed to be soothing.

There it was again. Another scene where Delphine began fantasizing and Marguerite pulled her back. In one way, it seemed harmless enough, just a game of let's pretend. But he was beginning to see that for Delphine it was not entirely make-believe. The scene she described, the guests and the chandelier and all—for a moment it seemed that it was really happening.

What Marguerite had done was pull the girl back to the present.

But what if one day Delphine could not be pulled back? Is that what had Marguerite so worried?

Ned gave himself a shake. That was sheer melodrama. He was probably the one who was overreacting. Tony seemed to consider the little scene nothing out of the ordinary. It was possible that, as usual, he had not even noticed it. He was wandering around examining the pillars that held up the balcony. He scraped one with a nail and nodded with satisfaction. "Scagliola. Not just painted to look like marble. A good job, but still plaster."

Why that was something to be pleased about, Ned did not know, so he ignored it. "We may have to search the entire building, but it would be sensible to figure out the most likely places to start. Now, the vicomte said that he saw the revolutionaries come in and encounter the priest. Look around you." He waved up at the balcony. "That's a place where a boy could have hidden to see everything that happened without anyone knowing he was there. And if the door we came in was the main entrance in those days, surely that is the entrance the revolutionaries would have used."

Marguerite opened her mouth as if to dismiss what he said, but stopped. She looked around, dubiously at first, but then with grudging acceptance. Raising her shoulders in a resigned shrug, she said, "It could have happened that way." She thought bit more. "Yes, you are right. If they were revolutionaries, they would have been determined to use the main entrance."

Not precisely boundless admiration, to be sure, but at least an acknowledgment that he was not a fool. He would settle for that at the moment.

"Yes, of course!" Tony sounded positively excited. "This must be where the priest was killed."

"Then all we need to do is search this room." Delphine spun around enthusiastically.

"Not quite." Ned shook his head in regret. "If the priest hid the treasure in this room, the vicomte would have seen it, and he would not be wondering where it is. No, the priest must have come to this room on his way out. Unfortunately for him, he ran straight into the revolutionaries."

Tony's enthusiasm collapsed as quickly as it had risen. "Then that isn't any help at all. We still don't know where he hid the treasure."

"Of course it's a help," said Marguerite with an impatient look. "There must be a dozen ways in and out of this building. If he used this one, the hiding place is probably fairly nearby. And if you seriously believe in this treasure, it would be sensible to begin by checking the rooms closest to this hall. At least Lord Edward has provided you with a place to start."

Ned resisted a desire to preen, though why even a hint of praise from Marguerite should please him so, he did not know. Unless it was simply that she rarely seemed to praise anything.

"True enough," Tony said, growing thoughtful as he looked around the room. "There may be some plans for this part of the chateau. Have you come across anything like that, Ned?"

"Not yet, but I haven't been looking at things that are quite that old. I'll start tomorrow. There are bound to be plans, architect's drawings, that sort of thing."

"But are we not going to begin immediately?" Delphine looked horrified at the prospect of delay. "No, no, there is no need to wait."

She seized the corner of a Holland cover and whipped it off a table. A dense cloud of dust filled the room, leaving them all coughing and choking.

"There is most definitely need to wait," said Marguerite, trying to cover her face with her hands, and stumbling toward the door.

The others followed, and they gathered on the gravel drive outside to cough their throats clear.

"Tomorrow morning, you should begin cleaning the first room off the center hall," said Marguerite.

"What?" Tony sounded outraged.

"What do you mean, 'What?'" asked Marguerite. "It is your treasure, is it not? Do you expect someone else to do all the work for you?"

"Yes, but, but what about Ned? Why shouldn't he help with the cleaning?"

"Because he will be busy looking for the architect's plans." Marguerite sounded as if she were speaking to a slightly simple-minded child.

"And what about you? Aren't you going to help?"

Marguerite made a dismissive noise. "Do you think I have nothing better to do than chase chimeras? A wonderful treasure that will solve all our problems? I have my own work to do."

Before Tony could respond, Delphine wailed her own protest. "But you must help us. You must!"

That won a sigh from Marguerite. "Very well. I will give you afternoons, but that is all. You must wear old clothes, both of you. And Delphine, you will need to cover yourself with a sturdy apron and tie up your hair."

Delphine did not make any objections. However, she did not look as if she intended to obey either. But that was Marguerite's problem. Ned did not see why Marguerite was giving in to Delphine's demands but he was quite happy with his assigned role.

Chapter Fourteen

NED PUT ASIDE THE LETTER WITH A GRIMACE. TWO HUNDRED years ago, a cousin of the Morvans at the court of Louis XIV had taken an unpleasant delight in the humiliation of the Princesse de Conti at the hands of Clermont and Mlle. de Choin. Pettiness and spite were the same in all centuries, and were no help at all to his efforts to learn about the construction of the chateau.

And if there was a family treasure, no one wrote about it.

In need of fresh air, he opened the window of the muniments room and leaned out. For a change, the sun was shining. It felt almost warm on his face. Soothing after still another disturbed night filled with dreams dominated by visions of Marguerite. Dreams he did not want and should not have.

A movement caught his eye and he looked down to see a figure in a black cloak crossing the causeway—and leaving the castle. That was Marguerite's cloak, he was sure of it. Where was she going? She hadn't said anything this morning about leaving the chateau. As far as he could recall, she had said nothing to indicate that she wasn't going to spend the afternoon battling the dust and grime in the deserted rooms.

To be fair, Delphine could be expected to avoid doing any of the work, and Tony had declared himself busy with correspondence. Marguerite could hardly be blamed if she had decided to leave the drudgery behind as well.

In which case, there was no reason for him to feel obliged

to continue the hunt for floor plans or comb through ancient gossip looking for references to a possible treasure.

After a week of this, he needed fresh air and exercise too. Anything to blow the cobwebs from his head.

But where was the blasted woman going? Was she meeting someone? She had never mentioned any friends in the area. Not that she was under any obligation to keep him apprised of her acquaintance. Still, why would she bother to keep an acquaintance secret? Unless it was a less than respectable acquaintance.

He hurried down the staircase of his tower, turning over possible reasons for her secrecy, because it was deliberate secrecy. He was convinced of that, and he was increasingly annoyed by this secrecy. Why should she keep secrets from him? He had never given her any reason to distrust him, had he?

There had been no mail for her recently. He probably should not have noticed that, but he had, so it was unlikely that anyone had appointed a meeting. At least not formally. Such an appointment did not have to be made through the mails. A servant could have passed a message to her privately. That would be the appropriate way to arrange a romantic tryst.

The thought was remarkably unpleasant. The knot in his gut bore a distinct resemblance to jealousy. He knew he had no right to such an emotion, but his rights did not matter at the moment. The idea that she might be, somehow, less than he thought was disturbing. He would not have believed her to be someone who would indulge in a tawdry affair—and one conducted in secret could not be anything but tawdry.

Soon he was on the causeway himself, though not soon enough to see which way she had gone. Still, the choices were limited. When she came to the fork at the top of the hill, she could take the route he had followed when he arrived. As he recalled, that would lead her through mile after mile of forest before she reached anything resembling a human habitation. Pleasant enough, perhaps, on a warm summer day. But in November? Despite the sunshine, the day was chilly.

Besides, she had been walking like someone with a destination, not someone out for a stroll. Of course, now that he thought about it, she always moved like someone with a destination. Delphine might float about the garden, a charming butterfly lighting first on one plant then on another, with no reason other than the whim of the moment. Did Marguerite ever permit herself to indulge a whim? Did she even have whims? He could not imagine it.

So she would not be off for a casual stroll through the forest. When she came to the fork, she would choose the other road, the one that led down to the village of Morvan. He had yet to visit the village himself, so it would be easy to claim that he was simply exploring the area when he turned in that direction. Should anyone ask, he was not following Marguerite.

Not that anyone would ask.

But just in case anyone did.

It was a longer walk than he had expected, and Ned was decidedly irritated by the time he reached the village. The sight of it did little to improve his mood. It was far from attractive. Gray stone buildings huddled behind gray stone walls. On one side, a few lanes led down to the harbor, where a handful of boats in need of paint languished on the shore, with the gray sea stretching beyond them out to the horizon. On the other side, a few more lanes led to fields covered with gray stubble. Over it all hung the aroma of dead fish.

There must be inhabitants in this place—occasional bits of smoke drifted from a few chimneys—but none were visible.

The village did not simply lack charm. It exuded a grim hostility.

What on earth had possessed Marguerite to walk all this way to such a miserable place? A gust of wind sped through an alley from the harbor and tried to snatch his hat. He pulled it firmly down and turned up his collar in defiance of the sudden chill. Where could she have gone?

The largest building in the village—the only one of any

notable size—was the church. Built of the same gray stone as all the other buildings, it boasted a bell tower with a peaked roof soaring well above the other buildings in the town, but its unwelcoming doors were firmly closed.

The one open door he could see belonged to what was apparently the village shop. At least it had a window that displayed some dusty jars and a box of smocks. There was also a small yellow sign, a rare spot of color, affixed to the wall bearing the word *poste*. Like village stores in England, this one also served as a post office. Was that what had brought Marguerite here? That made no sense—mail was delivered to the chateau every day. There was no need for her to walk all this distance for a letter.

Yet that had apparently been her purpose, for there she was, a tall figure in black, stepping out of the shop. He felt a sudden spurt of irritation at her gloomy garb. He knew she was in mourning, but did it have to be such unbecoming mourning? Did every dress she wore have to be stiff and ugly, draining her face of color? Did she have to pull her hair back so tightly that it looked painful and then hide it under that hideous cap?

Why did he care? He shook his head in disgust at himself. It was no business of his that she deliberately set out to hide her beauty.

She stood just outside the door of the shop looking down at the envelope in her hand and turning it over carefully as if she mistrusted it. What the devil was she doing getting letters that she had to collect in secret? Not a letter she was eager to receive, from the look of her. Or perhaps it was only that she feared that it might say something she did not want to hear.

Was it a letter from a lover? The knot in his gut tightened and twisted uncomfortably. A faithless lover? Why else would she be so hesitant to open it? Or an unacceptable lover, who had to be kept secret?

But there was another possibility. Tony. An inner chill seized him. Was she somehow plotting against Tony? Did she know something about the treasure? She said her brooch was a family heirloom, and the old vicomte seemed to recognize it. Did it have something to do with the treasure? Was she trying to steal it?

Or was he simply trying to find a respectable excuse for his feelings?

Secrets. There were too damned many secrets swirling around her. They were infuriating, all these secrets.

So intent was she on the envelope that she did not even notice his approach.

"If you open it and read it, you will know what it says." He had intended that to be a bland, indifferent comment. Even to his ears it sounded snappish.

She stumbled back, stuffing the letter in the pocket of her cloak and staring at him with frightened eyes. "What…" She licked her lips and tried again. "What are you doing here?"

He raised his hat politely, then stepped to her side and took her arm. "Merely taking the air."

Her lips tightened, and she tried to pull away. Unsuccessfully. "You followed me—how dare you!"

He did not bother to answer. She tried to pull away again, but he did not allow it. Instead he drew her toward one of the lanes. If there was going to be a scene, it was not going to be enacted in the middle of the village, deserted though it seemed to be.

"Let go of me!" When she could not pull her arm free, she swung the other at him. It landed a ridiculously ineffective blow on his chest. He drew her around a corner.

The lane he led her into was little more than an alley between two high stone walls. It promised privacy if nothing else. One end led to the empty beach, and he blocked the end leading back to the main street.

She seemed to realize that there was no escape for her and stopped struggling. He in turn let go of her arm.

She rubbed the spot where he had held her and glared at him. "What do you mean by this assault?"

"Hardly an assault." He ignored the way she was rubbing her arm. There was no way he had held her tightly enough to hurt her.

Had he? He would not believe it. "I simply want to be assured that these secrets of yours do not in any way threaten Tony."

"Threaten Antoine?" She looked absolutely flabbergasted. "Are you mad? What could I possibly do to threaten him? And why would I? I did not even know he existed until a few months ago." She turned away from him, still rubbing her arm, and tilting her chin up. This gave him a splendid view of her profile, her absolutely perfect profile.

He had an unpleasant feeling churning in his gut. A new and different feeling. The kind of feeling that said he was making a serious mistake; that he was making a fool of himself. He forced himself to ignore it and seized her arm, swinging her around to face him. "Do not pretend that you are not hiding something, you and your aunt and Delphine. If it does not affect Tony, why all the secrecy? Why are you sneaking down to the village for your letters? What are you hiding?"

"Why, you pompous, arrogant…*aristocrat!* You think that your title gives you the right to spy on me? To poke and probe into my private affairs?" Tears of fury filled her eyes, and she beat at his chest with her fists. "You have no right. No right. Not you and not any aristocrat. None of you has any right to control me."

She was going to hurt her hands, beating at him that way. He was wearing too much clothing for her blows to have any effect on him. She was going to… He couldn't think. He grabbed her by the shoulders and gave her a shake. When he opened his mouth to say something, all he could manage was, "Don't."

In the silence that fell between them, she stopped beating at his chest and looked up at him. The silence stretched out and wrapped itself around them, isolating them. He could not move. Then her hand moved, ever so hesitantly, and she reached up to cup his cheek.

His arms slid down to wrap around her, pressing her against him as his mouth came down on hers.

Chapter Fifteen

THE KISS BEGAN ALMOST GENTLY, TENTATIVELY, BEFORE IT exploded in a blaze of desire. Courtesy and deference dissolved in an overpowering hunger. He had not known he could feel such hunger. He fell on her like a starving man, devouring, demanding. He crushed her to him as he invaded her mouth.

Vaguely he was aware that after a first moment of hesitation she was responding with enthusiasm. Her fingers seemed to have gotten inside his coat, where they fastened themselves on his shirt. His fingers made their way up from the nape of her neck, freeing her hair from the imprisoning pins, tilting her head the better to explore her face with his mouth.

Then she began to make more demands herself. Her hands reached up and tangled themselves in his hair, pulling him down to her for more kisses. He could hear whimpers, moans—her sounds or his? A growl—that was his. But when his mouth moved across her jaw and his teeth nibbled at the soft skin of her throat, the moan—that was hers.

Yes, his body was exulting, yes, this was what he wanted. This was what he needed. His hands explored her body and he thrilled to feel her hands on him. He pulled her closer, crushing the silly wire cage she wore under her dress. It could not impede him. He could feel the roundness of her buttocks and he pressed her to him. That gasp she gave surely meant that she could feel him too.

Her body fit so perfectly against his. They were made for each other. This was what he had been seeking all his life, this closeness, this woman. Time and space vanished. They were alone in the universe.

A raucous cry followed by a metallic clamor and the yowl of an angry cat shattered the quiet, shocking him into consciousness.

It took a moment to recall where he was. With something like horror, he realized that he had pulled up Marguerite's skirt until his hand was on her thigh and he was pressed against her. Good God! He had her pushed against a wall in an alley.

Trembling, he removed his hand to let her skirt fall back into place but wrapped the arm around her waist to keep her close. His forehead rested against hers. Minutes went by while he tried to get his breathing under control. She was trembling as well, and her breathing was no steadier than his. Whether he should take comfort from that was not clear. He could feel her shiver within the circle of his arms. Unless that was his own trembling.

"Well," he finally managed, "that was a surprise." *Oh brilliant, Ned. Could you manage to sound like any more of a fool?* "I hadn't realized…" *Better and better. How romantic. That's the way to woo a lady.*

Perhaps Marguerite was feeling no more articulate than he was, because her response was a little sort of huff, barely a sound, and certainly not a word. When he managed to lift his head enough to look at her, her eyes were dazed, just coming into focus, and aimed at his shoulder, not his face.

"No, I…" She licked her lips and tried again. "I wasn't expecting… I had no idea."

It was good to know that he had not been alone in his failure to realize. But there were certain practicalities that required immediate attention. They were, after all, still in a lane of the village. Quiet, but hardly private.

She untied the ribbons of her cap to replace it on her head, but before she could, he reached out and fingered a lock of her hair that had come loose.

"Pretty. So soft."

Her flush deepened. "You also need to…" She gestured at his disordered neck cloth and waistcoat.

He ought to feel a certain embarrassment, he supposed, but he couldn't manage it. Instead a grin kept tugging at the corners of his mouth. A sense of the rightness of what had just happened buoyed him up. It was unlikely that she would appreciate the pleasure he felt in the realization that she had been an active participant in this, this *tempest* that had swept over them.

She was looking down the alley with some concern. "Oh dear. Your hat…"

He followed her glance. Oh dear indeed. His hat had landed in a puddle. Since it had not rained today and the road was dry, he did not care to think what it might be a puddle of. "I think I shall leave it. Should anyone ask, a determined breeze captured it."

Strange, that he should be able to speak so calmly, and even make a small joke. One that even won him a small smile, though she would still not look him in the face. In fact, she stepped back from him—not far, only a step or so, but still it was a step in the wrong direction.

He reached out to touch her shoulder. "We need to talk, you know."

She nodded, a brief nod, barely acknowledging his words. "Delphine…"

Delphine? Surely she did not think he was interested in her cousin—or perhaps she did. "Delphine is a pretty child," he said, choosing his words carefully, "but she is a child."

Marguerite nodded. "And she must be taken care of."

He was not sure just what she meant.

"She must be taken care of by me," she said, clarifying her position.

"If you wish." They could certainly take care of her cousin, if that was what Marguerite wanted.

"It is not a matter of what I wish. It is the promise I made to my mother as she was dying. Delphine is my responsibility."

Now she looked directly at him, but it was almost a challenge.

"I would be perfectly willing to share that responsibility," he said. "We can take care of her, and of your aunt and Horace as well."

Shaking her head, she turned away. "No. You do not understand."

Chapter Sixteen

His voice seemed to come from far away. He was saying something, but she was not paying attention. She was trying to make sense of what had just happened. And trying to keep on her feet.

It was not possible. It was as if the world had shifted on its axis.

She was Marguerite Benda. She was a musician. She had responsibilities. There were people who depended on her, people she had to protect. She could not…she simply could not.

She did not recognize herself.

How could she have behaved so? Not even like a courtesan. Like a trollop. Like one of the whores who offer themselves on street corners for a few sous. And with this man. This English lord, she reminded herself. An aristocrat, for God's sake. Hadn't aristocrats caused her enough trouble? Had she lost all sense?

What had she been thinking? Obviously, she had not been thinking. She must have lost her mind. She could very easily have lost her virtue—that was certain. Lost it? She would have thrown it away gladly. What she had done was simply horrifying.

Oh, but it had been wonderful.

She couldn't deny it. Never had she experienced anything like that embrace. She had found herself—no, she had *lost* herself in a maelstrom of sensations. When he stopped and drew back from her, she had wanted to weep from frustration.

She had felt bereft.

When he had dragged her off to feed her tea and cakes, and their hands had touched, when he had admired her brooch, and his fingers had brushed her cheek—she should have known where she was heading.

The heat rose in her face as she remembered. She should be ashamed of herself, and she was. But that was not all. It was not shame she felt, or not only shame. It was also delight, a heady joy that was all-powerful and at the same time terrifying.

Madness. That's what it was. She had lost her mind. There was no doubt about it. Nothing else could explain it. She could not have such feelings—it could not be permitted. She had responsibilities.

Could she possibly be more confused?

A stumble sent her not quite into his arms, but it was only because his arm caught her that she did not end up sprawled in the street. That would have been all she needed to complete her humiliation.

He was holding her arm. It felt like a possessive gesture, and now that she thought about it, he had been holding her arm for quite a while. She had actually been leaning on him. This was not good. They had left the lane and were already out of the village, and she hadn't even noticed. This was definitely not good. It was as if she had put her trust in him, and she must not do that. She dared not trust anyone, and above all it would be lunacy to trust an aristocrat—and an aristocrat who threw her into such turmoil.

Ah, how she longed to be able to trust him!

Suddenly panicked, she pulled her arm away. "Where are you taking me?"

He seemed taken aback by her question, but answered calmly enough. "I thought we might find some privacy down by the shore."

"Privacy?" Her panic increased. "Why do we need privacy?"

He looked at her with amusement. "To talk. Just to talk. And we must talk, Marguerite. You do see that, don't you?"

He was speaking to her in a soothing tone, as if she were a child. Irritation vanquished the panic. Of course they needed to talk. She looked around. He was not, perhaps, a complete fool. Of course he was not. Pretending that he was foolish would do nothing to ameliorate the situation. It would not even salvage her pride.

This was a good place for a private discussion. The road led along the shore, and only some dunes and outcroppings of rock separated them from the water's edge. If they moved off the road, closer to the rocks, they would still be visible, but the noise of the waves would make it impossible for anyone to hear them.

"Very well. We will talk." She set out toward the nearest rocks that looked likely to provide a place to sit. She hoped he was following her, but she didn't look back. He might still be smiling that amused smile, and she didn't want to see it.

Ideally, she would be striding proudly across the sand, but the sand wasn't cooperating. To her annoyance, it kept shifting under her feet, and the narrow heels on her boots kept slipping and turning. A helping hand from the gentleman behind her would actually be helpful, but she would be damned before she asked for it. She gritted her teeth and concentrated on getting over the dunes to the rocks without actually falling on her face.

As soon as she crested the dunes, the breeze blowing off the sea caught at her cloak, making it flap around her. It wasn't a fierce wind, but it came in sudden unexpected gusts. Cold gusts that made her shiver. Good. That would help her to keep her mind on reality.

When she finally reached the rocks, she was relieved to see several flat spots and sat down on one. It had not looked damp, but it was cold, with a chill that penetrated right through all the layers of her clothing. She pulled her cloak closed against the wind and fingered her mother's brooch, drawing strength from it.

Lord Edward was right behind her, but instead of seating himself on the rock across from her, he remained on his feet, positioning himself to block the wind from her. Why did he have to be so considerate? Why did he have to look at her with those kind, smiling eyes? Why couldn't he behave like an arrogant, privileged aristocrat? He was just making everything more difficult.

"Is it too cold here? I had not realized how windy it would be on this side of the dunes."

"Not at all," she said, turning slightly to avoid looking at his eyes. "I am not, after all, some delicate flower." *Like Delphine.*

"No," he agreed, though it sounded more like a question than agreement.

"What happened before—it will not happen again." She kept her tone firm.

"No?" There was no doubt about the amusement this time.

She flashed an angry look at him before turning away again. "No. That was an aberration, a mistake. It must not be allowed to happen again."

"An aberration, was it? A mistake? I don't…"

"Yes, an aberration. You may find this amusing, but I do not do things like that. I cannot. And I cannot permit it to happen again." She pushed herself to her feet and glared at him. He was too close, but at least while she was standing she felt at less of a disadvantage.

"My dear, I fear you are mistaken." He took hold of her hands, lifted them to his mouth and kissed them. "It was not an aberration but a revelation, and I think I can promise you that it will happen frequently in the future."

"No!" She tried to pull her hands away, but he held them firmly in his. "No. That is impossible. I am not that sort of woman. Nothing like that has ever happened before." She had to make him understand that this had been some sort of insanity that had overcome her. "I do not behave that way."

"No more do I," he replied. "I know you seem to think that this sort of behavior is something aristocrats indulge in all the time, but I assure you that I do not. And I also assure you that what happened between us back there is something I have never experienced before."

She looked at him uncertainly. Now that she looked, he also seemed shaken. Far less sure of himself than she had thought at first.

"Never before," he repeated. "It seems we have both been caught up in something outside of our usual experience."

Outside of her experience, certainly. She turned away to look at the sea. It was not truly stormy, but rough enough so that white crests topped the waves. She shook her head. "This must not happen again."

His had cupped her cheek and he turned her to face him. "There is no way we can assure that. I don't think we even want that. I know I don't." His face was serious as he looked at her. "I think the most sensible thing for us to do is marry as soon as possible."

She was unable to move for a moment. Then her legs collapsed under her and she sat back down abruptly. "Have you lost your mind?"

"No, I think it quite possible that I have just found it." A bemused smile tugged at the corners of his mouth.

"You are a madman," she said, trying to sound calm. "You are an English aristocrat. Such as you do not marry women like me."

"Only if they are extremely fortunate."

Would he never stop smiling? "Do you not understand? I am a musician, not one of your aristocratic ladies. I perform before the public. I do not simper and giggle and hide behind a fan. I go out on a stage and play before an audience."

He nodded. "And judging by what I have heard of your playing, you do it brilliantly. As for me, I am a scholar, and I spend my days in dusty rooms surrounded by dusty volumes, much as I have been doing here at Morvan. Do you mind? It's not terribly exciting, I know, and many find it dull and boring, but it's what I do."

She stared at him in bemusement. Did he understand

nothing? "My lord…"

"I wish you'd stop calling me that. Only strangers do, you know. My name is Edward, and my friends all call me Ned."

"My lord," she repeated firmly, ignoring his sigh, "you do not seem to understand the difference in our stations. You are an aristocrat…" She held up a hand when he wanted to interrupt. "I know you possess only a courtesy title, but your father is a marquis, and an important nobleman in England. Young men of such families may enjoy brief associations with actresses and such, but they do not marry these women."

"For heaven's sake," he burst out, "you talk as if all artists are no different from courtesans."

"In the eyes of the world, that is precisely true. Your family would be horrified by such an alliance."

He grinned at her. "On the contrary, my mother and sisters would be ecstatic at such an alliance. They haven't said anything, but they have been terrified that I would bring home a pretty but brainless ninny." He paused and ducked his head sheepishly. "Like Delphine."

She ignored that last comment. "And your father?"

"He would be ready to burst with pride at your accomplishments." Ned paused briefly and cocked his head thoughtfully. "Now, my oldest brother, Pip, he tends to get a bit stuffy, but the rest of the family will soon set him straight."

"How have you survived so long, to the ripe old age of what, twenty-five?"

"Twenty-eight," he said stiffly.

"Forgive me, twenty-eight, with no notion of how the world works?" She shook her head.

"No, forgive me, but you are talking nonsense. 'Such as you, such as I'—where do you get such antiquated notions? Unless…" He stopped abruptly. "You must forgive me. I had not considered that there might be someone else."

Now she was confused. "Someone else?"

"That letter—the one so secret that you had to retrieve it

from the village rather than have it delivered to the chateau."

The letter? She reached into her pocket and felt it there, a bit crumpled but still there. She had forgotten all about it. How could she have forgotten? She began to laugh. He thought it a letter from a lover? As if there had ever been room in her life for love affairs. Especially now, when everyone depended on her.

She pulled it out of her pocket and stared at it, her laughter fading. So much depended on what it said. If it was bad news, what could she do? How could she take care of them—not just Delphine, but Tante Héloise and Horace?

And this arrogant lord thought she had nothing more to worry about than a clandestine love affair. She thrust the letter at him. "Here. Read it yourself."

Chapter Seventeen

HE TOOK THE LETTER. REALLY, HE HAD NO CHOICE, THOUGH he would much rather not. He handled it gingerly, as if it were a serpent.

Was this a test of some sort? What he would like to do was burn the damn thing. He was chagrined to realize how much it bothered him that this letter should matter so much to her. After that kiss he knew that nothing mattered to him as much as she did, and he wanted her to feel the same way. He could hardly say that, but he needed some explanation of his reluctance. He dredged up a schoolboy sense of honor and said, "It is addressed to you. I should not read your private letter."

"You should if I give you permission to do so. If I insist that you do so. It will be much easier for me to explain things to you once you have read it."

The letter seemed to grow heavier in his hand. He stared down at it. Did he really want to know what was in it? The writing was French—hardly unexpected, since they were in France—and a man's handwriting. Not, he thought, a young man. Was that better or worse?

"Are you sure? I have no right to pry into your private affairs…" His voice trailed off as she gave him a mocking look. No right, perhaps, but they both knew that he wanted very much to pry. What else had he been doing when he followed her here to the village in the first place? For days now, weeks even, he had been trying to discover her secrets. If that wasn't prying, what was?

He set his face and tore open the envelope.

Ma chère Marguerite…

His jaw tightened. It was in French as he had expected. His accent might leave much to be desired, but he could read the language with no difficulty. Still, *My dear Marguerite?* That was a more familiar salutation than he would have liked to see.

He glanced over at her, but she was looking off into the distance, tensed, as if fearing to hear what the writer had to say.

He returned to the letter with a scowl, but that soon tempered into confusion. "He says that Paris is still difficult. Louvois has apparently made his views known, and his influence is enough to frighten people." When he looked at her with a question in his eyes, she simply nodded, as if she had expected nothing else.

"He goes on to say that Paris is not the only city in Europe. He has written to Liszt, who remembers you well." He looked at her, startled. "Liszt? Franz Liszt?"

Her face softened, almost into a smile, and her eyes widened in amazement. "He remembers me?"

"It seems that Liszt is outraged on your behalf, and says that he will sponsor a series of concerts beginning in Weimar, where he is teaching at the moment, and continuing to Vienna and Prague." He paused to look at her. "I don't understand."

The soft expression stiffened. "But Delphine told you, did she not? I am a performer. I go out on stage and play for the entertainment of the audience."

He gave an angry snort. "Do not talk dismissively of yourself. I have heard you play. But even so, Liszt?"

"Yes. Liszt. He was a friend of my father, a good friend, and at my father's request he invited me to play for him." The memory was obviously a happy one, judging from her expression. "Just to play for him was an honor, you must realize. I am not as good as Clara Schumann, he said, but perhaps one day I will be. Oh, that lovely, generous man! To say he will sponsor me. And in Weimar, Vienna. A whole series of concerts. We are saved!"

She collapsed back against the rocks, like a marionette whose strings had been cut. But she was smiling. "We are saved," she repeated softly. "Louvois cannot touch me now."

That name again. "Louvois?"

She shook her head. "I do not want to think about him. Not now. Did Oscar say anything else?"

"Oscar?"

"In the letter." She pointed at it impatiently.

"Oh." He had not looked at the signature. He did not know the name. "Who is Oscar Villoteau?"

Her impatience seemed to be growing. "I don't know what you would call him. He publishes music, and he arranges concerts, engagements for musicians. A manager? But he does not have a concert hall of his own. What else did he say?"

Little the wiser, Ned nodded and quickly scanned the rest of the letter. "He says he knows you did not ask this, but he was so impressed with your sonata that he sent it to Liszt, seeking his opinion. The Maestro was more than enthusiastic. He said he would be pleased to introduce it, but thought it would be better if you did yourself. Liszt said it will make your concerts an instant success."

"He said that?" She held her hands to her throat, as if holding up her head. "Truly?"

"Read it for yourself." With a smile he held out the letter.

"You don't understand. You cannot know what it has been like." Shaking her head, she clutched the paper to her. "I've been so afraid. But now we'll be safe. If I can get concert engagements, I will be able to support us."

"Have you been worried about that? But why?"

She looked at him incredulously. "Why? Only an aristocrat would ask such an idiotic question. Are you so insulated from reality that you do not know that is what most people worry about all the time?"

He could feel himself flushing. "But your father was a famous musician. Surely he left you provided for. And here at your family's chateau, you are perfectly safe."

"You know nothing," she snapped. "Have you forgotten that we just had a war? Paris was in chaos. Everything was in chaos. We came here, yes, but out of desperation. Do you think I would willingly choose to live on the charity of relatives who disowned my mother? Am I allowed to have no pride because I am a woman?"

He snapped back. "And am I allowed no pride? Do you think I am unable to provide for my wife's family? Or do you think so poorly of me that you think I would not do so?"

She closed her eyes and shook her head. "Oh, you foolish man. Can you not get it through your head that you cannot marry me?"

Oh lord, he thought, she was back on that subject. "Unless you already have a husband, I do not see the problem."

Suddenly she was on her feet, and thumped him on the chest. "I do not see the problem," she repeated in a singsong tone, and thumped him again. "If you do not see the problem you are a blind fool. Tell me, if I married you, what should happen with that concert tour Oscar wrote of? What do you propose?"

"Why, I suppose it would not be necessary."

"No?"

"Well, you will not need the money." He spoke cautiously, suspecting some trap here.

She shook her head. "You see? You do not understand at all. Tell me, have you ever known a professional musician? Not one of your aristocratic ladies who plays her little Mozart minuet for her guests. But a professional."

He shook his head.

"Of course not," she said. "But that is what I am. Do you not understand what those concerts mean for me? It is not simply the money, though those worries would have been enough! But the honor of it! Liszt himself thinks I am good enough. *Liszt!* And my sonata, *my* sonata—he thinks it is good. And you would have me give up all this? You would let me play for your family and friends, I suppose. Like a caged bird. That is what Louvois wanted to do to me. You might as well kill me." She flung a dismissive hand at him, turned and began walking back to the road.

Flummoxed. That was the word he wanted. He was flummoxed.

He had the horrible feeling that she was right.

He had heard her play and thought she was excellent, but he hadn't thought of it as something more than, well, a pastime. Ladies often played. She just played exceptionally well.

Though if he actually had thought about it, he probably would have realized that no one plays that well, with the practice required, merely as a hobby.

He didn't know what to think, except that, obviously, he was an idiot.

If she had been a man, would he have dismissed her music so casually? After all, he didn't think of Tony's obsession with steel factories as nothing more than an amusing little curiosity. And he knew how offended he could be when people did not take his historical studies seriously.

How insulting he had been without even realizing it. No wonder she was furious.

And that piece he had heard her playing, that magnificent, soul-wrenching piece—*she* had written it? He had been stopped in his tracks by it. Not only was her playing superb, but she had actually composed the piece. That was not talent; that was... that was *genius*.

He tried to picture her playing at a musicale, in some London drawing room, where half the guests were not even listening.

It was ridiculous. Ludicrous.

Of course she did not belong in such a cage. He would never try to put her in a cage. That would be criminal—worse than criminal. Any attempt to constrain her would be infamous. He could never be guilty of such iniquity.

Could he?

No, not now that he realized—had been forced to realize—

that she was right in one sense. They did come from different worlds. He had only begun to see some of the differences.

This was not going to be simple. The road ahead was not a straight, smooth path. Instead, it was all too much like the road he had ridden to get here—twisted, treacherously muddy, and shrouded in fog.

But he would not, could not give her up, not when he had just discovered her.

This was not what he had thought love would be like. He had always imagined his future wife as someone soft and sweet; not a cipher, not really, but someone gentle. They would live in the country. He would have to travel from time to time, of course, for his research, but he would come home to a smiling wife, surrounded by their brood of children.

It was difficult to picture Marguerite in that setting. No, not difficult. Impossible.

Well, not completely impossible. He could imagine her with children. She would be as fiercely protective of them as she was with Delphine and Horace and Madame. Not indulgent. Not obsessive, like those women who thought of nothing but their children. Protective. A tigress.

A tigress should not be caged.

But if he would never try to cage her, neither would he give her up. He did not know how they would manage it, but there had to be a way. They would find it. On that he was determined.

She had already passed out of sight. He hurried across the sand to catch up with her.

Chapter Eighteen

"Who is Louvois?"

He had appeared at her side halfway through the village and had remained with her, matching her step for step. They had left the last of the houses behind them and now they were climbing the hill to the road that would lead them back to the chateau. In all this time, he had not said a word, and now he asked about Louvois? Marguerite shook her head. The ridiculous things men decided to pounce on.

There was no need for Lord Edward to concern himself with Louvois. "He is no one of any importance," she said.

He caught hold of her arm to halt her and then turned her to face him. "Your correspondent said that Louvois' influence frightened people. Who is he? Some sort of criminal?"

A wild desire to laugh seized her. "If only he could hear that! How I would love to see his face when he hears that you suspect he is a criminal. A street thug, perhaps?"

But Louvois was no laughing matter, not for people like her. "No," she said, "he is not a criminal. Rather, an aristocrat. He is the comte de Louvois, a wealthy and powerful man who wields considerable influence in Parisian society."

Lord Edward looked puzzled. "What has he to do with you? Why should he wish to make Paris difficult for you?"

She shrugged. She was tired, so tired of Louvois and the problems he had caused. Why not tell Lord Edward? Perhaps it would help him understand what nonsense his talk of marriage was.

Louvois had made no secret of his interest in her, after all. Half of Paris knew of it—and that was probably why he had been so difficult. He was annoyed when he did not get what he wanted. Worse, he must have been embarrassed when people realized he did not get what he wanted, and that—naturally—made him even more vicious.

But she did not want to look at Lord Edward while she told him. The way he spoke of the world—he was a naïve innocent. How could he understand how Louvois made her feel soiled just by looking at her? The way his touch filled her with disgust?

She turned to look off to the side before she spoke. "Louvois decided that he wanted to have me for his mistress, and he considers himself entitled to have whatever he wants, whenever he wants it. For a while, Papa managed to discourage him, telling him I was too young, making excuses. But after Papa died, we found ourselves in financial difficulties. Everything was in chaos, banks had failed, records had been lost. The building with our attorney's office had been burned to the ground. Everything was in ashes."

He reached out for her, but she shrugged him away before continuing. She was not asking for comfort. "The comte renewed his attentions, assuming that under the circumstances, I would be grateful for his protection. When I turned him down again, he was…he was furious. He said he would make it impossible for me to find any work in Paris. No concert engagements anywhere. And his patronage was important to the theaters. All at once, there was nothing for me, not even work as an accompanist."

"What?"

The look of outrage on Lord Edward's face almost made up for the humiliation of Louvois' pursuit. It comforted her enough to enable her to manage at least a twisted smile.

"You will understand that the invitation from the vicomte to come here to Morvan was very welcome. It provided a refuge precisely when we needed one. But this is a respite, not a solution."

"Forget about that. I want to know about this blackguard of a count. Who the devil is he and where can I find him?"

She could not quite identify her feelings at the moment. Amazement, perhaps, at his anger. It was ridiculous of him to react this way, of course. He had not even known her when Louvois threatened her. Many people thought that she was a fool to turn the comte down. He was, after all, a wealthy and powerful man. But to have Lord Edward champion her this way—even Papa had felt obliged to be circumspect in his discouragement.

And his assumption that he could actually do something, that he did not feel powerless. That was what it was to be an aristocrat, then. How strange it must be to think yourself so safe and protected as all that. How strange to be one of the powerful and never need fear them.

"It is over, my lord." She put a hand on his arm. "Do not distress yourself. It is all in the past now."

There was a look of icy determination on his face. He grasped her by the shoulders as if to shake her. "Never," he said, "never again will anyone offer you such an insult."

She tried to smile. "Many would have said it was no insult at all, that it might even be considered a compliment."

His face softened as he looked at her. "I never said there are no fools in the world. Both you and I know that it was a gross insult, a demeaning slander. I will never allow such a thing to happen again."

"My lord…" Before she could say any more, he put a finger to her lips. She didn't pull away. She didn't want to.

"Hush now." He cradled her face in his hands and covered her mouth with his. He did not embrace her. Only his hands on her face touched her, his hands and his lips.

This was not the passion of that earlier kiss. It was not the wild firestorm that had swept over them. This kiss was gentle, tender, soft and full of promises—promises of something lasting.

His lips were warm, and she melted beneath their warmth.

Her head was swimming. She knew she should not surrender, yet she could not help it. It was foolish to believe in tender promises, but she wanted so badly to believe, to trust. She lifted her hands to push him away, but somehow they ended up clinging to his coat. Had she not been clinging to him, her knees might have given way beneath her.

When they came apart, they looked at each other, trading silent questions.

He put his arm around her shoulders and turned with her to resume their journey. "It's getting chilly. We'll talk later."

It was chilly, especially once they reached the crest of the hill and began the walk down to the causeway. Here there were no trees to break the wind. The low sun was disappearing into the clouds and offered only a gray light. His arm around her shoulders sheltered her in a way that meant far more than the warmth it provided.

Whether the road was long or short, she could not have said. She walked as if in a dream, aware of nothing so much as the man beside her. Aware, but bewildered. His nearness promised safety, permanence, to say nothing of pleasure. She could not forget the whirlwind that had swept her up in that earlier kiss. She could so easily surrender herself to him. She could so easily fall in love with him.

He was a hundred times more dangerous to her than any Louvois could ever be.

So lost in her worries was she that it was only when his arm fell from her shoulders that she realized they had reached the chateau. The door closed behind them, and he stood there, looking down at her and fingering the brooch at the collar of her cloak.

"More than an heirloom, I think," he said. "A talisman?"

She nodded.

He dropped a kiss on her forehead. "May it keep you safe when I am not here to do so."

Chapter Nineteen

"I do not understand." Tante Héloise was frowning at her. "You tell me that Oscar sends wonderful news. Liszt himself will give you his support. There is nothing more to worry about. Yet you are looking positively tragic. What is the matter with you?"

Marguerite forced up the corners of her mouth and hoped that it looked like a smile and not a grimace. "It's just so sudden. I can't seem to take it in. All these weeks and weeks of worry—I can't make myself believe that it's over."

Tante Héloise sniffed. "It's not any too soon. We allowed ourselves to be intimidated by that accursed Louvois."

"It was not just Louvois."

"Ah, my little one." The older woman was suddenly contrite. "Of course it was not. So much has befallen you so quickly, so suddenly. Your mother dies, and so soon your father dies. All at once you are responsible for Delphine, Horace, and even me. Too much responsibility. Too many burdens."

Marguerite did smile now and reached out to grasp Tante Héloise's hand. "You were never a burden. You were the one who kept us all steady. I don't know what I would have done without you."

She flushed and patted Marguerite's shoulder. "Well, that is all past now, and you need not worry. I will write to Oscar and he and I will work out the schedule for your tour. Liszt—who would have believed it? At least now that he has taken minor orders and is known as Abbé Liszt, we don't need to worry about what he might expect as an expression of gratitude."

"Tante!" Marguerite was shocked.

The older woman shrugged. "It is not as if he didn't have women throwing themselves at him all the time. He came to expect it."

"But we are talking about music. He would never compromise about music."

"If you say so." That was accompanied by another shrug. "In the meantime, we can stay here, no? It would be foolish to try to find another apartment in Paris when that is not where you will be playing. Unless you want to move to Weimar immediately?"

Marguerite hesitated. Should she do that—just leave? It might make things easier with Delphine. Paris had not been good for her, and neither was the chateau. Both places fed her fantasies. All around her were relics of the aristocracy she was convinced was her rightful milieu. Perhaps in Weimar, where she knew no one, she would grow calm.

What was she thinking? Marguerite shook her head. Weimar would have the court of the grand duke. It would probably be worse than Paris. She doubted there was any place on earth that could discourage Delphine.

As for her own fantasies, running away would solve nothing. Did she really think Lord Edward would vanish from her mind if she fled to another country? She could barely recognize herself. Never had she reacted this way to a man. It was as if that kiss in that gloomy little alley had dissolved the armor that protected her and left her defenseless against this man.

She had always been able to look at her admirers—and there had been more than a few—with a cold eye. They had meant nothing to her. Less than nothing. An annoyance at most. Now she could not stop being aware of him. It was as if a flame was burning deep inside her. Rather, she thought wryly, like a case of indigestion.

She realized that Tante Héloise was still waiting for a response. "No," she said. "We don't know when I will be playing or where or how much I will be able to earn. It is best to stay here. Now that I know we will be able to leave, it will be easier. I can feel like a guest, not a beggar." *And I can meet Lord Edward with my head high.*

"You and Delphine have always been invited guests. Horace and I, on the other hand…"

"Don't be foolish. How could I manage Delphine without you?"

"You would do as you always do. You would find a way. But now, at least, the way ahead is clear."

Marguerite watched as Tante Héloise bustled off to write her letters. Now that she had said they would stay here, she was having second thoughts. It was infuriating—she did not think she had ever been so uncertain in her life.

Should she move them all to Weimar after all? It would be difficult. She had been there years go, when she was still a child and her father was playing there. That did not mean she was familiar with the city. Nor did she know anyone there, except Liszt, and she did not even know if he was in Weimar at the moment. He was giving master classes there, but he was often in Budapest or Rome. Besides, she could hardly ask Franz Liszt to find a house or apartment for her. One did not ask the king to wash the dishes.

Then there was the question of money. She quite simply did not know how much she had. Her father had accounts in various cities, but she did not know where. Those accounts could be found, but she did not know whom to ask. Papa's attorney would straighten it all out eventually, but he was not a particularly courageous man. If delays would please the comte de Louvois, he would not be in any haste. In the meantime, she had to remain in uncertainty.

Her piano. She had forgotten all about the difficulty of moving her piano. If all was well, and she was doubtless foolish to hope that anything was well, her piano was being housed at the Paris Conservatory. Their old apartment had been right across the street, so moving it there had not been too difficult. But she was not in Paris, and had not been for many months. Who knew what might have happened?

No. She would trust that all was well with her Pleyel. Even so, suppose she moved it to Weimar and then they decided they did not want to remain there? She would have to move it again.

That would be foolhardy. She could not drag her beautiful Pleyel piano all over Europe. There was always the danger that it could be damaged, and she could not risk that. Not when it had been her parents' gift, tangible evidence of their belief in her and in her talent. It would be difficult enough to move it once, so she must wait until they decided on their permanent location. If she played the violin, like her father, or better yet the flute, it would be easy to wander. A pianist needed a permanent home.

In one way it might be sensible to move to Weimar immediately. That would put some distance between herself and Lord Edward. She could concentrate on her music then with no distractions.

That was a lie, of course. It would not matter how much distance she put between herself and Lord Edward—she would be unable to banish him from her mind. She did not even want to. That was the problem.

Marry him. What a preposterous notion. Even if his family had no objections—and no matter what he said, she could not imagine a marquis having no objection to his son's marrying a professional musician. Her own mother had been disowned for doing so by her family, and they ranked much lower than a marquis.

But even if his parents had no objection, how could she marry him? He would expect her to stay at home, running the household, caring for the children. Her parents had had Tante Héloise to take care of those things so that they were not distracted. Without a Tante Héloise, there would be no time for music.

Even if Tante Héloise remained with her, what about concerts? What aristocrat would be willing to allow his wife to go traveling around Europe giving concerts?

And how could she bear the notion that someone could allow or not allow her to do what she wanted to do—what she had to do?

It was impossible.

What she needed to do now was assert herself, to make him see that she was not merely someone who needed to be protected. If she was not yet someone of importance, she would be in the future. Liszt himself thought she had talent.

She went over to the cheval mirror to take a good look at herself. She knew that black was a becoming color for her—she always wore it when she played—but not this bombazine she had on now. The finish was so dull that it drained all color from her face. Or maybe it was not just the fabric. The worry of the past months had not helped.

She was thinner than she had been. Lord Edward had been right when he said she played with her food instead of eating it. During the siege, she had thought that she would give anything for a full plate of food, but since Papa's death, her stomach had been tied up in knots. This dress hung on her. She needed to look at her old concert gowns. One or two of them had been too snug for comfort. They might fit now.

And her hair. She had been wearing it pulled back tightly into a bun. It made her look like a nun, an angry nun. She could not dress it herself as elaborately as a good lady's maid could, but she could manage something better than this.

Yes. She would stop trying to vanish into the shadows of this chateau. She was not some helpless creature in need of protection anymore. Admittedly she had had some moments of doubt, but no longer. She was fully capable of protecting herself and those who depended on her.

Tonight she would go down to dinner with her head high, and Lord Edward would see what Marguerite Benda was really like.

Ned leaned back in the tub, letting the steam rise around him. He probably should have asked for a cold bath, but even if he had the heat from his body might have been enough to set the water boiling.

He had demanded a bath, rather to Clivers' surprise, because he needed to think, and the bathing tub was the one place he could be certain of no interruptions. He had long ago convinced his valet that he did not need anyone to help him bathe. Although now that he thought about it…

No. That was not what he needed to think about. Not just now, at least. He needed to try to understand what she would need from him before she would agree to marriage.

It was a bit humbling to have her dismiss his proposal so easily. He had never thought of himself as particularly vain, but most of the women he met considered him a matrimonial prize. He might not be the heir to the marquisate, but he was the son of a marquis and wealthy enough in his own right. Families frequently pushed their daughters in his direction.

But those were families in the upper reaches of English society. If she married him, Marguerite would have entrée to that society. Unfortunately for him, that did not appear to be a society that appealed to her. And also unfortunately for him, he had no connections, no influence in the musical world that mattered to her.

What could he offer her?

He paused in his ablutions, sponge in hand. Offer her? Was he really thinking that way? As if he was planning a purchase? He leaned back and slipped under the water. He was an idiot. Did he have anything she wanted?

Passion. He remembered that kiss. Her response had been as overwhelming as his. Passion was something they shared equally.

Shared. He rolled the word around in his mind. Was that the clue he sought? Was the idea not that he should offer her his life or that she should let him share her life but that they could share a new life? One that had room for the things they both valued?

The water was cooling, so he got out of the tub but wrapped himself in a towel and sat down on the stool. He needed to think in a new way.

What was there about his current life that he would not wish to change?

He had rooms in London, near the British Museum, though they were mainly for convenience. He spent a good bit of time in the Reading Room, but he also traveled around to various libraries and collections. Now that he thought about it, he probably spent most of his time at Penworth Castle, where he could study and write undisturbed.

He realized that it did not really matter where he lived. If Marguerite wanted to live in France or Italy instead of England, he would have no objection. He could study and write anywhere. Books were easily transported. And aside from making their home any place she liked, he could accompany her whenever she was on tour, giving concerts.

That could be done. It sounded odd, put that way. It was not the kind of life he had ever imagined for himself, but it could be managed. Now that he thought about it, such a life sounded appealing. Traveling around the world—how could anyone object to that?

Now he needed to convince Marguerite.

Chapter Twenty

NED COULDN'T MOVE. ALL HE COULD DO WAS STARE AS MARguerite made her entrance into the drawing room with Mme. d'Hivers hovering behind her. Tony had been expressing delight that his digestion had finally recovered—he was turning into a caricature of a Frenchman, obsessed with his digestive system—and Ned had been listening. He had even been listening attentively—really he had—until Marguerite appeared.

Her beauty was enough to strike any man dumb. He had caught a glimpse of it when she'd fallen asleep by the fireside, but that had been only a hint of this glory.

She had changed. Her hair seemed softer. She glowed, where he could have sworn she used to drain the light from the room. Yes, she was still dressed in black—he understood that. She was still in mourning, and he could not ask her to deny her loss. But this evening her gown was of some sort of silken fabric that gleamed in the candlelight and rustled as she walked. It no longer made her melt into the shadows.

Even her walk seemed different. The tension seemed to have left her—or some of the tension, at least. She was no longer a warrior on guard. There was still a challenge in her stance, but it was the challenge of a woman to a man. A challenge to him.

Now there was a challenge he longed to accept. He could feel his body rising to the occasion and was grateful that his trousers were not too snugly fitted.

Walking away while Tony was switching to his usual lecture on the shortsightedness of those who failed to see the superiority of the Siemens-Martin method for producing steel, Ned moved to her side. Anyone who was watching him might have said he prowled toward her. He certainly felt like a lion, not stalking his prey but affirming his claim to his mate.

"Good evening, Marguerite." His words came out somewhere between a purr and a growl. He took her hand and lifted it to his lips.

She tilted her head at an arrogant angle and reclaimed her hand. "Good evening, my lord."

Her determined formality made him smile. "I think we know each other well enough for you to call me by name. If you find Ned too difficult to pronounce, I do not mind being called Edward."

She did not answer, but neither did she refuse when he offered his arm to lead her in to dinner. He seated her in her usual place, but did not sit next to her. Instead, he chose the seat opposite, where he was free to look at her.

Delphine sat beside him, exuberant as usual. Her nonsensical chatter required no more than the occasional murmured response, leaving him free to concentrate on Marguerite. He was pleased to see that she was actually eating her dinner this evening, not just playing with her food. Her restored appetite probably had more to do with the assurance that she would be able to support her little family than with him. Still, he was pleased to see that every time he caught her eye, the color rose in her face.

He could look at her forever, and he had every intention of doing so.

He had just lifted his glass to take a sip of wine when he realized that Delphine had asked him a question. Possibly more than once, since her tone had shifted from playful to impatient.

"I apologize. I seem to have been woolgathering. What did you ask?"

She blinked, then changed the motion to a fluttering of her eyelids. "It was nothing important." But then her eyes narrowed as her glance shifted to Marguerite. Ned was startled to see something like malevolence in that look.

Marguerite could feel his eyes on her as she ate her meal. She tried to concentrate on the food in front of her and ate almost mechanically. It did not help. She tried to converse with Antoine, but he was distracted by his food. The tournedos Rossini, complete with shavings of truffle, were certainly worth eating. Antoine, freed at last from his diet of boiled fish, seemed ecstatic to indulge in rich cuisine.

No matter what she did, she was only too aware of Lord Edward. Even when she kept her face turned away so she did not meet his gaze, she could feel him looking at her. It was a physical sensation, almost like a caress on her cheek, on her shoulders—she might as well have been naked, the way she could feel his look on her body.

This was not good. The heat rising in her body was not good. She could not afford any involvement like this. Certainly not with a man who was making her feel things she did not dare feel.

She had thought that her concert gown would serve as a sort of armor, making her feel more like her old self, in command of the situation.

Ha!

She had been lying to herself. What she had wanted was to show Lord Edward that she was not the dowdy crow Delphine proclaimed her to be. She wanted to impress him, fool that she was, and that was the last thing she should want.

He should be the kind of man she thought he was when she first met him—a bland and brainless aristocrat, kind and courteous enough, but one who cared about nothing but the cut of his coat and saw nothing that did not contribute to his own pleasures. That's what he was supposed to be. A pleasant dinner companion at most. Such a man would have been no problem at all. Even a man as tall and handsome as this one. She could have admired his fine features the way one admires a fine painting.

Instead he was a problem.

She caught his eye and could feel the color rising in her cheeks. He saw too much. How had she ever been fool enough to think those blue eyes of his were innocent and guileless? He did not see everything because he did not know everything, at least not yet. But he saw far too much for her comfort.

Taking a deep breath, she tried to distract herself by mentally going over the tricky fingering in the Bach F major fugue. It was a piece that always seemed to soothe the vicomte. The prelude was easy enough for the listener, but the simplicity of the fugue section was misleading. Keeping her hands in her lap, she went over the fingering. And then went over it again.

When she was calm enough to look up, she saw that Delphine had managed to distract him. Good. But then Delphine looked across the table at her. The fury in the girl's look knocked her back in her chair. Why? What had happened to infuriate Delphine so? She quickly ran through the usual causes of temper, but there had been no reason to deny any of the girl's requests lately. No one had even insisted that she help in the dusty business of searching for the treasure.

Marguerite gave a mental shrug. She would doubtless find out soon enough.

As it turned out, she found out as soon as the ladies reached the drawing room after leaving the gentlemen to their port.

With a toss of her head, Delphine sneered at Marguerite. "You are a fool if you think you can take him from me. He may dally with you, but that is all."

"Take him from you? What are you talking about?" Marguerite could scarcely believe it. Surely the child wasn't still indulging in the fantasy that she was going to marry Lord Edward.

"Oh, I will permit that he have his little affairs. He is a man, after all." Delphine was in her grand lady mode at the moment. "I am not the sort of *bourgeoise* who would expect fidelity from her husband. But I would expect you to have better taste than to throw yourself at my betrothed."

"Your…? Delphine, stop this. You are not betrothed to anyone. Certainly not to Lord Edward." Marguerite was getting worried. Delphine's fantasies did not usually last this long.

"If you choose to think so. But you do not know everything." Delphine had a sly smile on her face.

"I know that you are talking nonsense," Mme. d'Hivers said firmly. "You must calm yourself."

"Marguerite should be practical. If she is going to be someone's mistress, she would do far better to accept the comte de Louvois' offer." Delphine ignored the gasp that her statement drew from Marguerite.

"Delphine!" Mme. d'Hivers spoke sharply. "You are overexcited and overtired. You had best go to bed."

"And you, old woman. You know nothing!" Delphine sneered and snapped her fingers.

Mme. d'Hivers caught the girl's hand and forced Delphine to look at her. "To bed," she said in a low voice.

Delphine stuck out a rebellious lower lip but slowly collapsed in surrender to the older woman's command and departed in a flurry of ruffles.

With a shake of her head and a deep sigh Mme. d'Hivers turned to Marguerite. "She is right, you know. A blind man could have seen that there is something between you and the Englishman. The air positively crackled between you. What is going on?"

Marguerite's throat suddenly felt dry. "I don't know. I don't know what it is."

"But something is?" Mme. d'Hivers' eyes grew wide. "My God, have you lost your mind? He's an aristocrat."

Marguerite raised her hands in a helpless gesture.

"You cannot… Marguerite, child, you know that nothing good can come of involvement with such a man. You will lose everything you have worked for."

"I know." Marguerite could barely get the words out.

Mme. d'Hivers covered her mouth with her hand and closed her eyes. "There is nothing I can say that you do not already know. I will go take care of Delphine."

Indeed, that was perfectly true. There was nothing Tante Héloise could say that Marguerite did not already know. The problem was that she seemed to forget it when Lord Edward—Ned—was present.

Penworth Castle

"My goodness!" said Lord Penworth, staring at the letter. He had been the first one down to breakfast this time.

His wife looked up in alarm. "What's wrong?"

He looked up with a smile. "Not to worry. Nothing is wrong with Ned. I was just surprised. It seems that one of Tony's cousins turns out to be the daughter of Matthias Benda."

"The violinist? Really?" Lady Penworth looked intrigued. "How very surprising that Tony should have artistic relations. I always thought of him as terribly practical and hard-headed. Such an unusual friend for Ned to have."

Lord Penworth turned back to the letter. "Well, it sounds as if she's in rather a fix. After they managed to survive the war with Prussia and the siege and the Commune, her father was killed."

His wife frowned. "It seems to me that I read something about that. It was one of those pointless tragedies—he was killed by accident or some such."

"Yes, and what with all the disturbance, it seems the daughter is having financial difficulties. Ned wants to know how he can find out what happened to her father's money. There's sure to be some, I think."

Lady Penworth smiled indulgently. "Is the girl Ned's damsel in distress?"

"No, this is the other girl, the stern one. He says that she's a musician, too, like her father."

"Really?" Lady Penworth looked a bit uncertain.

"Things are pretty well settled in Paris now. Alphonse de Rothschild has had his hands full raising the money to pay the indemnities, but he can probably spare a clerk to look into this for me. It's a minor matter, but Ned wouldn't know how to go about it himself."

Lady Penworth was not listening. She was thinking. "Did he say anything else about this Benda girl? What's she like?"

Her husband looked up from the letter. "What's she like? He

doesn't say much of anything. Here. You can read it for yourself."

She did, and frowned over it. Obviously this Miss Benda wasn't the pretty damsel in distress her son had mentioned in earlier letters, but she might well qualify for the position. Her father was dead, presumably making her an orphan, and she was having financial difficulties.

But there was nothing about how lovely and charming and delightful she was. Or the reverse. Ned had nothing at all to say about the girl personally. Nothing at all.

This was not Ned's usual pattern. As a rule, they could expect several weeks of paeans to golden curls and a rosebud mouth. Silence was something new.

She did not like this.

When her children started behaving in unaccustomed ways, Lady Penworth knew it was time to pay attention. Careful attention. And her sons were far more of a problem than her daughters. The girls were all, at bottom, hard-headed realists. The boys were romantics, especially Ned.

Chapter Twenty-one

FOR THE NEXT WEEK THEY SEARCHED THE DESERTED ROOMS in a desultory way. They would sweep up enough dust to be able to move around a room without choking, and then open chests and cabinets, searching drawers, feeling cushions, even turning chairs upside down on occasion.

Their efforts were not entirely fruitless. They found a chest full of gowns from an earlier century. It was not a chest that had been left behind when the family fled. These gowns belonged to a still earlier generation, a generation that had gloried in its finery and made no pretense of simplicity.

Delphine was ecstatic.

She insisted that the chest be carried to her room, and she pressed one of the maids into service. They set to work on the gowns, cleaning and mending them and altering them to fit.

Marguerite worried that Delphine might slip further into her fantasy world but Tante Héloise pooh-poohed the notion. "Just be grateful that she is distracted," the older woman advised. "So long as she is absorbed with gowns, she cannot be causing other difficulties."

"I hope you're right," Marguerite said, but she was not quite at ease with the notion.

To complicate her life still further, she kept encountering Ned in deserted hallways or in empty rooms. It was not deliberate. She was certain it was truly accidental. But every time they were alone together, she ended up in his arms.

This had to stop. It was far too dangerous. But it happened again.

She was trembling, barely able to stand. If she had not been leaning against him, clutching his coat to keep herself from falling, she would have been a little puddle on the ground.

Since her cheek was pressed against his chest, she had no difficulty in feeling the rapid beat of his heart, a match for her own. His ragged breaths came just a half beat after her own as they gasped in counterpoint.

His voice was as ragged as his breathing. "That, you see, is why we must marry. And soon."

Chapter Twenty-two

NED STOOD UP AND RUBBED THE BACK OF HIS NECK TO RELIEVE the stiffness and grunted in frustration. He had gotten nowhere with the archives, at least as far as any treasure was concerned. The Morvan family was there, alive in every word they had written in letters and diaries, their loyalty to the crown and church, their loyalty to the village that shared their name. Indeed, there were times when it was difficult to know if Morvan referred to the family or the village.

All of that was fascinating, and a month ago he would have been thrilled at the chance to turn it into a book. And he would do that, he vowed. Just not yet. Today all he felt was frustration. His obligation to Tony meant that the treasure had to be found before he could turn his attention to the things that mattered to him. To Marguerite.

The past week had brought him no closer to convincing her to marry him. His need for her seemed to increase every minute. Why did she refuse?

It was not indifference to him that held her back—of that much he was certain. Whenever they managed to steal a private moment, she melted in his arms and returned his kisses with a hunger that matched his own. But she was still afraid. There was something gnawing away at her, and he needed to know what it was.

Meanwhile, there was still no sign of any treasure. He was

beginning to doubt that there was any such thing. Could the old man have imagined the whole thing? But his descriptions of the scene had been so vivid—the old priest, the angry revolutionaries, the violent confrontation. Would a boy have imagined all that? Well, perhaps, but it didn't sound like a child's fantasies.

He walked over to the ceramic stove and held his hands out to the warmth. Even though the stove kept the fire enclosed, he didn't dare let it get too hot. Not with all the fragile old paper here in the tower room. But numb fingers were also a danger, so he made frequent trips to the stove.

The sound of wheels on gravel distracted him, and he went to the window. A slightly shabby coach, pulled by four horses, had pulled up at the door. Probably hired, he guessed. But who would be coming here? Was there another cousin come to join the hunt?

After a brief wait, during which no servant appeared to greet the arrival, the groom who had been sitting beside the coachman got down and opened the carriage door. A gentleman descended. He was far from shabby. A gleaming silk hat, pristine yellow gloves, a silver-knobbed walking stick—the visitor's trappings exuded wealth, and the tilt of his head proclaimed arrogance.

Ned was curious. Extremely curious. It was time to descend from his tower.

The footman coming down the hall—Louis—was looking slightly perturbed. This was surprising because Ned had never seen any of the servants in the chateau display any emotion whatever.

"Do we have a visitor?"

Louis stopped—willingly, one would have thought. "He said Mlle. Benda was expecting him, but she did not mention anything about visitors. And she does not like to be disturbed while she is at the piano."

"Did the visitor give his name?"

Louis held out the tray on which the visitor's card lay. Ned picked it up. "The comte de Louvois?" *The bastard who had persecuted Marguerite—terrified her, though she would not admit it.*

Louis nodded and hesitated. "I have put him in the yellow sitting room."

The comte had obviously not made a good impression on the young footman. All the rooms on the ground floor were chilly, the yellow sitting room more so than most. In addition, the door to the larger room next to it did not close well, so there was a curtain to keep out the draft. Anyone standing behind the curtain could hear everything being said.

"Very good, Louis," Ned said with an understanding smile. "There is no need to worry. I will keep him company while we await mademoiselle."

Looking relieved, the footman went off to find Marguerite. Ned decided that he wanted to meet the comte. Actually, what he really wanted was to give the comte a thrashing. It seemed unlikely that he would be given the opportunity, but one never knew. There was always a chance that the comte would give him an excuse to do just that. He flexed his fingers, just in case.

The door to the yellow sitting room was standing open, ensuring a draft strong enough to flutter the draperies. When Ned entered, the comte was examining a painting, one of Bouguereau's idealized peasant girls.

Louvois himself was as fashionable as he had appeared when Ned spotted him arriving. Fashionable, but not, Ned was pleased to see, particularly attractive. His beard was neatly trimmed and still brown, as was the hair on his head. At least, what was left of it was still brown—his hairline had receded to the rear of his head. He wore a formal black frock coat and a matching waistcoat with a heavy watch chain draped across his paunch.

Since his entry had not attracted the comte's attention, Ned cleared his throat and spoke. "A remarkably clean and attractive peasant girl, is she not?"

"One would hardly wish to have a filthy peasant in one's home." Louvois shrugged. "Personally, I prefer Bouguereau's classical subjects."

Ned smiled, unsurprised. "Yes, I would have expected you to prefer nude females."

At that, Louvois turned to Ned with a frown, as if uncertain how offended he should be. "And you are…?"

"Lord Edward Tremaine, at your service." A slight inclination of his head served as a bow. "And you are Louvois. I must say, you are something of a surprise. Not quite what I had expected."

Still uncertain, but increasingly distrustful, Louvois said, "I do not know you. Why should you have had any expectations regarding me?"

"One hears things," Ned said, waving his hand vaguely. "I can see that you are hardly love's young dream, but I'm sure you know that. There are mirrors, after all." Ned ignored Louvois' hissed intake of breath and continued, "Still, you seem prosperous enough. I would have thought you would be able to lure a woman to your bed—given adequate recompense, of course—without having to threaten her. Threats are hardly becoming behavior in a gentleman."

Louvois looked ready to explode. "How dare you speak to me in such a way, you presumptuous puppy!"

"Would you care to challenge me to a duel?" asked Ned hopefully.

Just as Louvois took a step toward him, glove in hand, Marguerite burst in. "Ned, what are you doing?"

"Just chatting with your visitor here, my dear." He smiled innocently. "I say, did you ever seriously consider an alliance with this fellow?"

"No, of course not." She dismissed the notion with a grimace before turning to the comte. "Monsieur le comte, what brings you here?"

His color still high, the comte turned to her. "Marguerite, my poor girl, have you been forced to associate with shabby riff-raff like this?"

"Riff-raff!" Ned put his hands to his head in mock horror. "Dear me, my parents would be mortified to hear me spoken of in such terms."

"Ned, stop it." Marguerite closed her eyes and took a deep breath. "Ned, please excuse us. I must speak to Louvois."

Suddenly serious, Ned paused, then nodded. "Very well. But if you need me…"

She looked at him with a challenge in her eyes. "Yes, I know. But I can manage."

He didn't want to go. Yes, she could doubtless manage, but she should not have to. He wanted to manage for her. He wanted to protect her. Hell, what he wanted was to smash the pompous bugger's face. But it seemed he wasn't going to be allowed to do that. Pity. "As you wish." He bowed slightly and left the room.

The last time Marguerite had seen the comte, she had been terrified. He had uttered his threats and she had felt trapped. Doors had been slamming shut all around her and she did not know if she would be able to find a way out. Even when they left Paris and came here to the chateau, she had brought that fear with her. This had been a hiding place, but not a solution.

Now things were changed. Oscar's letter assured her that she could support them all. They were not in danger of penury. The burden of that terror, that enormous terror, had been lifted.

There had been a more important change. Ned had kissed her, and she had kissed him back. More than once. The embrace in the village had been followed by stolen kisses whenever they had a moment of privacy—surprisingly rare despite the size of the chateau. Nothing could come of it, no matter what he chose to say. But now that she knew what it could be like to be with a man, she could never, never allow a swine like Louvois to touch her.

So it was that she could face Louvois calmly and with her

head high. "Again I ask, M. de Louvois, what brings you here?"

He snorted dismissively. "There is no need to play games. Your audience has departed. Were you amusing yourself by leading that puppy on? That was beneath you, Marguerite."

"You may address me as Mlle. Benda."

He actually seemed surprised. "What is this nonsense? But if you will, it makes no difference. Are your things packed?"

It was her turn to be surprised. "Packed?"

"It does not matter. We can send for them later if there is anything you truly want." He eyed her dress scornfully. "It is obvious you shall need a new wardrobe. I do not like to see you looking like a crow."

She stared at him. Whatever was he talking about? Did he think she was leaving here?

"Were you afraid I would not forgive you? Foolish girl." He pulled out his watch and looked at it. "It is too late for us to get back to Paris this evening. We will have to spend the night in Brest. Fortunately, there is a decent hotel there."

She finally found her tongue. "Are you mad? What makes you think I would go anywhere with you?"

He snapped about to stare at her. Without taking his eyes from her, he carefully closed his watch and replaced it in its pocket. "Do not attempt to play games with me. I have forgiven you much, but that I will not tolerate."

His icy glare drove her back a step, but she recovered quickly. "I am not playing games, but I have no intention of accompanying you to Brest or anywhere else."

Moving more quickly than she had expected, he seized her arm so tightly that she gasped from the pain. "You think you can write to me, asking me to take you away, and then change your mind? Have you forgotten who I am?"

She tried to pull loose, but he twisted her arm behind her. "You are mad. I never wrote to you."

He barked out a laugh. "No, you had your cousin write for you. Do you think that matters? The pimp often arranges matters for the whore."

Her eyes opened wide with fury, and something snapped in her. Pulling her free arm back as best she could, she swung it to strike his smug face with a satisfying crack. It was powerful enough to stagger him. Unfortunately, it was not enough to loosen his grip on her arm, and his free hand turned into a fist that smashed into her cheek just below the eye.

She must have cried out—she was not sure. The scream might have been just in her head. But the fist that was coming at her again suddenly flew up in the air, and Louvois staggered back, letting go of her arm.

The release was so unexpected that she stumbled and fell to the floor, disoriented. *What…?* Still furious, she pulled herself up to her knees, ready to fly at Louvois, and fell back in surprise.

Louvois was up against the wall and Ned drove a fist into his midsection. He doubled over with a grunt, but before he could finish the sound Ned had twisted his hand in the comte's neck cloth.

Ignoring the older man's gasping protests, Ned tightened his hold and growled, "You bastard. You blackguard. You unmitigated swine. If you ever come within a mile of Marguerite again, I swear I will kill you."

Her fury began to ebb, though it was not replaced by anything resembling forgiveness. It would doubtless be more ladylike of her to swoon, but Marguerite found herself positively exultant at the sight of Ned pummeling the comte. She was more bloodthirsty than she had realized. However, Louvois was turning a rather deep shade of red, and it would be awkward if Ned actually killed him.

She stepped over to Ned and put her hand on his arm. "That's enough, Ned."

He immediately let go of Louvois, allowing him to slide down to the floor. The comte made various croaking and gasping noises which Ned ignored. His attention was fixed on Marguerite. He lifted a hand to hover over her red and aching cheek. A feral growl escaped his throat and he started to swing back to Louvois.

She caught his hand. "No. It's all right."

"It's not all right." He ground out the words. "It's not all right. We must get you to the doctor."

She started to say that there was no need, but her cheek hurt, and she felt suddenly weak, barely able to stand. She started to sway, and the next thing she knew, Ned had lifted her up and carried her through the door.

"Louis," he called out to the footman hovering in the hall, "throw that piece of offal out of here. His carriage must be around somewhere."

Up the stairs they went, with her cradled in his arms. She was trembling. Even with her arms around his neck and her face buried in the soft wool of his coat, she could not seem to stop shaking. "You do not need to carry me," she said, but her voice, even muffled by his coat, was trembling as well.

His only answer was to tighten his arms around her.

Chapter Twenty-three

"FETCH THE DOCTOR," HE SNAPPED AT A MAID HOVERING IN the corridor. "And ask Mme. d'Hivers to come."

He managed to lean over and open the door of her room without dropping her and laid her carefully on the bed. She was too thin. She was a tall woman and should not weigh so little. Did no one ever take care of her?

His hand hovered over her cheek. The mark was darkening, and she would have a black eye. "There is a bit of blood. His ring cut you." He tried to keep the anger out of his voice.

"It's nothing, truly." She tried to smile but winced at the movement.

"Right, nothing. You'll be fortunate if he didn't break a bone." He sat down on the side of the bed and took her hand, caressing her fingers gently.

A corner of her mouth lifted. "Ah, well. He was angry. Men like him, they do not like to think someone has played them for a fool."

He gave a dismissive snort. "No one likes to be played for a fool. Decent men do not react by using their fists on a woman."

She gave him one of those looks of hers that made him feel like a naive idiot. He tried to ignore it. "Anyway," he said, "what made him think his arrival would be welcome? I cannot believe you invited him."

"Of course not. It was, I think, Delphine."

"Delphine? What about Delphine? What has she done now?" Mme. d'Hivers came hurrying in. After one look at Marguerite's face, she began making clucking noises. Moving efficiently, she poured water into the washbasin and soaked a cloth. Her glare made Ned get up. Only after she had sat down in his place and held the cloth against Marguerite's cheek did she speak again. "Tell me what Delphine has done now."

"Louvois said she had written to him. Ah, the cold feels good." Marguerite closed her eyes.

"A cold compress? Yes, that is good." Doctor Fernac arrived to take over. Ned found himself pushed out, told he would just be in the way.

He resented the dismissal, though it was quite possible that he would be in the way, since he had no idea what to do about Marguerite's injury. But he was too angry and frustrated to do nothing.

Delphine. He recalled what Marguerite had said. Delphine had written to Louvois? Whatever for? She had to know that her cousin feared and loathed the man. Why was she trying to create difficulties for Marguerite?

He charged off to confront her.

After slamming his way through half the rooms on the main floor of the chateau, his temper began to cool. Still, he needed to talk to the girl. When he finally found her in the green sitting room, she was standing, arms akimbo, staring out the window at the drive, where the comte's carriage was just disappearing, and tapping her foot impatiently. And, of all things, she was in costume. She was wearing one of those silly gowns she had found. It didn't quite fit, and was trailing on the ground.

Once the carriage was out of sight, she let out a disgusted *humph* and flung herself into a chair. When she noticed Ned's arrival, she burst out, "She let him leave without her. How could she be so foolish?"

"Foolish! You think she is the one who was foolish?" He heard his voice rising, so he took a deep, calming breath and began again. "Is it true? Did you write, asking him to come?"

"But of course." She waved a hand dismissively. "Marguerite, she does not write herself. She does not have the sense to see that he is the best she could hope for. I think to do her a favor. He will come, she will see that he is still interested, and *poof!* She will go off with him."

"What are you talking about?" He could not believe what he was hearing. "Do you realize that he struck her?"

Delphine shrugged. "She should not have angered him. At her age she should know better how to deal with a man."

This was utter nonsense. He felt as if he had tumbled into a topsy-turvey world. Had Delphine lost all sense of reality? Taking still another deep, calming breath, Ned tried again. "She does not want to deal with Louvois. You know—she has told you—she does not even like the man."

"Bah, *like!* What has liking to do with it? She must be re-alistic. He is a comte, not perhaps the highest of the high—it is only a few hundred years old, that title. But still, he is of the aristocracy, and he is rich. She will mingle with people she could never hope to meet otherwise, and she can stop always pinching the pennies. He will buy her decent clothes, so she does not always go around in black, like a crow. And if she uses her wits, she should be able to get some good jewels from him."

It was getting increasingly difficult to keep a rein on his temper. Yes, she was very young, but even a child should have more sense than this. "Delphine, don't you understand? He wanted to make her his mistress."

"But of course." She looked at him as if he were the child. "What else could such as she hope for? Ah, I know she has her eye on you, but your family is also of the aristocracy. They would never allow you to marry a performer."

"You cannot be such a fool. Marguerite is hardly a music-hall performer. For heaven's sake, you've heard her play, you've heard her music. She has an incredible talent, and my family—any family—would be honored to welcome her."

She turned on him in fury. "Music, music, music! That is all I hear from her and her father. As if anyone of any importance cares! And the humiliation for me. Imagine it to yourself. I am of the true nobility, *la noblesse ancienne,* and I must stand by while my cousin displays herself on the common stage."

Ned lost his temper completely. "Have you lost your mind? You must be mad to think that your childish pretenses are of any importance compared with Marguerite's gift."

There was silence while she froze and stared at him. Then she erupted into a whirlwind, shrieking and attacking him with her hands curved into claws. "I am not mad! I am not! You are wicked to say such a thing! Wicked!"

Caught off guard, never having expected such a frenzy, Ned stumbled back, holding up his arms to keep her from scratching his eyes out since that seemed to be her goal. He didn't want to hurt her, but she had turned into some sort of demonic creature. "Delphine…" He should probably say something to calm her down, but he didn't know what would work. All he really wanted was to get away from her.

"Delphine!"

Mme. d'Hivers' voice carried over Delphine's shrieks. Ned had never been so glad to hear it.

"Horace, come help me."

While he was ducking and fending off Delphine's attack, he caught glimpses of the pair of them—the companion and the servant—coming up behind the girl. Horace caught hold of her from behind, pinning her arms to her sides, and Mme. d'Hivers stepped in front of her to administer a sharp slap to her cheek.

"Enough of that, Delphine!" The older woman spoke sharply, and to some effect. Delphine's shrieks subsided to sobs, and she sagged against Horace.

Mme. d'Hivers took the girl into her arms, rocking her gently and making soothing noises.

"He said…he said I am mad…" The words came out between sobs and hiccups.

"No matter," said Madame. "Come along now, you need to rest."

The two women walked slowly from the room, the older supporting the younger while she murmured soothing words.

Ned felt in need of support himself. He had no idea what had just happened. Surely a scolding—and a well-deserved one at that—should not have brought on such a tempest.

He turned to Horace, who was regarding him reproachfully. "What was that all about?" he asked. Then he wanted to laugh at himself for asking a simpleton for an explanation.

Horace shook his head. "You shouldn't get Mlle. Delphine upset. It's not good to get her upset."

Not good to get her upset? He stared at Horace, though the statement seemed to have been made in all seriousness. For God's sake, the girl had created a situation where Marguerite had been attacked, struck in the face by that bloated bastard, then she had flown into an hysterical temper tantrum at a perfectly justified reprimand, and he was being blamed for upsetting her?

Were they all mad?

Chapter Twenty-four

REFUSED ADMISSION TO MARGUERITE'S ROOM—THE DOCTOR had given her laudanum and insisted she needed to rest—Ned headed for the library. There, he knew, he could find a decanter of brandy. Perhaps that could subdue the combination of fury and fear churning through him.

Slamming into the room, he snatched up the decanter and poured a healthy portion into a tumbler. He downed half of it, refilled the glass and carried the decanter with him when he seated himself beside the fireplace. Evening was drawing in and the lamps had not been lit, but that bothered him not at all. The fire burned brightly enough, and he stared into its flames.

This was not what he had expected love to be like.

Oh, he wasn't an idiot. He knew nothing in life would be all sunshine and roses, and that included his future with Marguerite. Her musical career, composing, concert tours—he was still trying to understand what it meant to her, what it required. He did understand that it would require accommodation. Especially from him.

But these were practical problems, and could be dealt with. He knew himself to be perfectly competent when he had to be.

What he hadn't expected was this *pain*. She had been hurt—punched in the face! He had been right there in the next room and had still not been able to protect her. His failure tormented him.

Should he have ignored her when she told him to leave?

She thought she could manage, but obviously she had not been able to do so. Should he have insisted on staying?

He had no right to insist. Not yet. He wanted that right—he needed it.

Another gulp of brandy burned its way down his throat. It didn't burn nearly as fiercely as his need to protect her. Once they were married, he could stand between her and creatures like Louvois. But until they were married there was always the danger that his protection would be misunderstood. He certainly didn't want to make her life any more difficult.

Why wouldn't she agree to marry him? Her stubborn refusal made no sense. He knew perfectly well that the problem was not indifference to him. He could feel her vibrate whenever they touched—whenever they were even near each other.

Had he failed to convince her that he would not interfere with her musical career? What more could he say? No, he thought he had made her believe him.

That nonsense about his family not approving? Would he have to drag her to Penworth to meet them before he could convince her that they were nothing like Louvois?

Or was there something else? There must be—he was certain of it. Some secret she still kept hidden.

He could help her. Whatever the problem was, he could help her. Even if he could not eliminate it—and he was not such a fool as to think all problems could be solved—he could share the burden so that it did not fall so heavily on her shoulders.

His meditation was interrupted when Tony burst into the room and began pacing back and forth in front of the fireplace.

Ned carefully centered the decanter on the table. "You are creating such a breeze that you could blow the furniture over."

Coming to a halt and looking around at the heavy mahogany tables and oversized chairs, Tony snorted dismissively. "This furniture? A tornado would be needed to lift it an inch, and even that might not be enough. A nice big explosion—that's what's needed to obliterate this ridiculous monument to the past." He slammed his hand against the carved escutcheon over the fireplace. This caused no damage to the stone but brought a grimace of pain to his face as he shook his hand.

Ned dragged his thoughts away from Marguerite long enough to peer at his friend. Was Tony actually looking ill again or was he just in a rotten mood? Ned couldn't tell—he seemed to be having a slight difficulty focusing—so he asked. "Has something happened?"

Tony flopped down on the sofa with a snort. "Happened? Of course not. Nothing has happened here in years. Decades. All that old man can think about is something that took place a century ago. Will he listen to reason? Will he consider the future? No. All he can think about is that blasted treasure." He leaned back with his arms under his head and stared at the ceiling.

Ned thought about that for a minute, then drank some more brandy. "He's an old man. Very old. He hasn't much future to consider."

Tony turned his head just enough to glare at Ned. "That's right. Be reasonable. No one else around here is."

They sat in silence, each one meditating on his own problems. Eventually, Tony roused himself to speak. "Am I as mad as the rest of them?"

Ned thought some more. "Marguerite's not mad," he said with finality. "Determined, driven, yes, but not mad."

"That's because her mother escaped," Tony said. "But the rest of the family? Mad as hatters, the lot of them. Do you realize that Delphine grew up in England but had to be taught English by a governess? That whole branch of the family is so obsessed with their noble blood that they have spent the past eighty years waiting for the restoration of the monarchy, and a constitutional monarchy was not enough for them. They spend their lives pretending they are living under the *ancien régime*. They even refuse to speak English."

"That's mad. But it does explain Delphine. A bit." Ned considered, then shook his head. "They must be mad. Ignore them."

"But should I ignore the old man as well?" Tony brooded in silence. Finally he shook his head. "To hell with them all. Pass the brandy."

Penworth Castle

The weather had turned, and there was no sunshine streaming through the window to greet Lady Penworth that morning. There was, however, a letter.

"There's another request for you, my dear," she said when her husband arrived. She was frowning at the letter.

Her husband was just pouring himself a cup of coffee and looked over in concern. "Is that from Ned? Is something wrong?"

"Yes and no. Do be careful."

He caught himself up and stopped just before the coffee overflowed his cup. He waited until he had settled himself at the breakfast table with bacon, toast, and coffee before speaking again. "I meant, is something wrong with Ned?"

"I don't know." Lady Penworth spoke slowly and handed her husband the letter. "He asks if you know anything about a French count named Louvois who has been causing difficulties for Miss Benda. But he doesn't say anything about what kind of difficulties and he still doesn't say anything about Miss Benda."

Lord Penworth read through the letter quickly and then read it again more slowly. "He wants to be prepared in case the fellow causes any more trouble? That doesn't sound like Ned. I mean, I know you worry about it, but his villains are usually the obvious kind. The sort he can send off with a raised eyebrow or a black eye or two. He doesn't normally ask for help in dealing with them."

Lady Penworth stirred her coffee as she looked off into the distance. "That's not what bothers me. It's this Miss Benda."

Her husband glanced over the letter again. "But he doesn't say anything about Miss Benda, except that Louvois made problems for her."

"That is precisely what bothers me. Usually when Ned meets a young woman, he can't stop talking about her. There are three or four letters enumerating all her beauties and virtues and talents, and then she is forgotten. But there has been nothing about

Miss Benda except that she is a musician and she appeared on stage with her father." Lady Penworth shook her head. "We know nothing about her."

"Perhaps he doesn't think she's important," he said.

She shook her head again. "More likely he thinks she is too important to discuss in a letter. And that worries me."

Lord Penworth gave his wife an amused look. "Ned is not a child, you know. And there may be things in his life that he does not wish to tell his mother."

"Of course." She fluttered a hand at him. "I know that. Really I do. But I can't help worrying. He is, after all, asking for your help with her problems, and he would not do that if she is someone he would not want us to know about."

"There is that," he said slowly, frowning down at the paper.

"Ned is so trusting," Lady Penworth continued. "All those other girls were no threat to him because they were essentially empty-headed fools. What if this one is clever? Too clever for him."

Chapter Twenty-five

IT WAS STILL TOO EARLY FOR LUNCH, BUT MARGUERITE HAD not been able to concentrate on her music. Her cheek no longer hurt, at least not badly, but she kept touching it, and that did hurt. She gave up the pretense that she was practicing, and retreated to the drawing room. It would be warmer there.

She was standing hunched over by the fireplace when Ned and Tony came in. Tony was puffing angrily on a cigarette. When he noticed her, he held it up and asked, "Do you mind?"

It was, she thought, less a question than a demand, so she said, "No, of course not." Tobacco smoke in the drawing room was the least of her worries.

"He's a bit upset," said Ned apologetically.

"So I see." She sat down to wait for an explanation. Hearing about someone else's problems had a decided appeal.

While Tony paced around the room, Ned sat down next to her and spoke in an undertone. "He heard from his partner, Georges. A man they were counting on for financing has backed out."

"But that is not right." She frowned in concentration. "Tony and Georges have already committed themselves to a site, haven't they? How can this man just leave them in the lurch that way?"

Tony threw his cigarette into the fire and laughed bitterly. "It seems he can do it quite easily. He hasn't signed any formal contract yet. We were foolish enough to trust his word." He leaned on the mantelpiece and stared into the fire.

"I know you didn't want me to, but I can ask my father," Ned said. "It's the kind of thing he invests in all the time—new methods, new factories."

But Tony shook his head. "No, he's done enough for me. There were all those years you took me home with you for school vacations—he was like a father to me. And when I wanted to study engineering, he convinced my family to let me study in Paris at the Ecole Centrale." He managed to quirk a smile at that. "My grandfather did so want a proper gentleman in the family, one who went to Oxford and didn't learn anything. And he was down on France since my own father had died before he could provide my mother with proper title."

"Well then, why not let him invest in your factory?" Ned asked.

But Tony shook his head decisively. "No. I can't become dependent on him."

He pushed himself away from the fireplace. "There's only one thing for it. We have to find that blasted treasure."

"What?" Marguerite protested. "We don't even know if it really exists." She waved her hands about as if to shape something. "I've been thinking of it as a distraction to keep Delphine occupied."

"The old man is convinced that it exists. If we can find it, or find out what happened to it, he'll provide the funding for the factory. It's the only solution."

Ned looked dubious. "How far have you gotten with the search so far?"

"Not very." Tony grimaced.

"It's not his fault. We uncover a piece of furniture and start to examine it, and the first thing we know, Delphine has turned it into a little drama." Marguerite lifted a shoulder. "And I find it simpler to let her do so. I have not been treating it as a serious search."

"But I need you to do so. Please, Marguerite. And you too, Ned. Have you found anything in the archives that might give us a hint?"

"Not yet. I'm not sure there is anything there to find."

Tony turned away, looking frustrated.

"How much time do we have?" Ned asked.

Tony lifted his shoulders and his hands, suddenly looking very French. "I don't know…a few weeks, perhaps a month. Yes, we have a little more than a month—until the first of the year—to come up with the rest of the money for the site."

"All right then," said Ned. "We need to go about this more systematically. In the mornings, I will work on the archives, and Marguerite, you will work on your music." Tony started to protest, but Ned cut him off. "No, she must have time at the piano. You can use the mornings to make a plan of the rooms and note any furniture that should be searched. Then in the afternoons we can proceed methodically, crossing things off as we complete the search."

Marguerite stared at Ned. He had realized that she needed time at the piano? Only her father had realized that. Even Tante Héloïse did not truly understand.

Ned was looking at her with a worried expression. "Is that manageable? Can you spare the afternoons for the search?"

Her throat had dried up, and she was unable to move her mouth, so she nodded. She must have looked like some sort of idiot, sitting there bobbing her head, because his worried expression didn't go away. She tried a smile. It must have worked, because his expression eased.

"Afternoons. Only afternoons." Tony was grumbling to himself quite audibly. He took out his cigarette case and struck a match to light another. He inhaled deeply and blew the smoke out in a slow stream. "It would be a damned sight easier if I had some idea what the size of this thing is. A thimble? A horse?"

"A horse would be difficult to hide." Ned looked relieved to have a chance to smile. "And I doubt an elderly priest would be able to carry anything too big."

Tony was too busy thinking to be amused. "The walls. Most of them are paneled, so there could be a secret compartment.

We haven't checked the walls at all, so even the rooms we've looked at have to be looked at again. I'll start in the morning as soon as it's light." He discarded the cigarette in the fireplace and left, too deep in thought to bother saying good-bye.

Marguerite barely noticed. She was still trying to come to terms with the fact that Ned thought her time at the piano was more important than the search for the treasure. Tony was his friend, had been his friend for a long time, and needed the treasure for his steel factory. Despite that, Ned thought her music was more important.

He had put her first. Her desires, her needs came first.

No one had ever put her first before. Papa had understood about the music, but of course his own music came first. And Mama had always put Papa's music ahead of everything.

She was very near to crying. Now, wouldn't that be ridiculous? She didn't cry. No matter what happened, she didn't cry. Tears were for the likes of Delphine, who could bring up tears whenever she wished. Tears were for those who expected someone to come to the rescue, not for those who had to save others.

Except…except Ned had come to her rescue. Tony would have expected her to devote all her time to the search, and she would have had to fight for time for herself. He would have been angry and no one would understand that she needed that time to practice. She needed music.

It had not been necessary to explain that to Ned. He understood.

She could feel him beside her on the sofa. He was not close enough to be actually touching, but close enough for her to feel the warmth of him. It wasn't a physical warmth, or at least it wasn't entirely a physical warmth. But somehow, his being there wrapped her in comfort and safety.

Delphine showed renewed interest in the search. The problem

was that what she wanted to do was dress up in the gowns and direct the rest of them. Tony found this exasperating, and Marguerite had her hands full keeping the peace.

She pointed out that even if Delphine stood by while the others searched, the beautiful gowns with their elaborate embroideries and intricate flounces would get hopelessly soiled. This Delphine could see would be most undesirable. She consented to wear her usual gowns and even to cover herself with an apron.

"One would not wish to cause excessive work for the servants, is that not so?" Delphine smiled sweetly.

Marguerite never quite trusted Delphine's sweetness, but she agreed.

Of course, Delphine could not be expected to work in silence, so before they had finished tapping even half the panels in the first room, Delphine had begun to chatter about the way it would be decorated once the treasure was found.

Tony, like the idiot he could be, refused to ignore her.

"You're being ridiculous," he told her. "If there is a treasure, it would be idiotic to waste it on restoring this pretentious pile. The old man and your relatives have spent far too much time living in the past. It's high time to think about the future."

Marguerite groaned.

Delphine's head snapped up. "What are you saying? You cannot mean you would use the treasure for your factory."

"Of course. My factory and others like it will give France and its people a future."

"But a factory is ugly." Delphine looked horrified.

Her reaction simply made Tony grin. "It will not look ugly to the people who work there when it means they can earn a decent living."

Fortunately, Tony then turned away to peer down another corridor, so he did not see the look of venom Delphine sent after him. Marguerite was able to get a good grip on the girl, preventing her from flying at him.

Penworth Castle

When Lady Penworth came into the breakfast room, her husband was already picking an envelope out of the mail. This one had a French stamp on it—she could by now recognize a French stamp in an instant.

"Ned is writing again? So soon?" She was definitely getting worried. Ned's usual pattern when he was traveling was three letters in the first two weeks, then nothing until a telegram saying when he would be returning. Something was going on. Something definitely unusual.

"Yes," said Lord Penworth as he scanned the brief missive. "Not a great deal to say this time. Just another request for information." He gave his wife a crooked smile. "It seems our son thinks I have nothing better to do with my time than conduct investigations for him."

She sat down stiff-backed and shook out her napkin. "Another request for aid for Miss Benda?"

He shook his head. "No. This time it's Tony who needs help. It seems that one of their big backers has suddenly changed his mind without any explanation. It might be for a purely personal reason, of course, but Ned wants to know if I've heard anything."

Lady Penworth examined her husband. "You're worried."

"No, no… Well, yes, I am a bit. It seems rather odd. First Miss Benda is having financial problems, and now Tony is. They're cousins, admittedly not close, but still… It's giving me an uncomfortable feeling."

"Right." She nodded decisively. "We'll be off to Paris then. You can have your secretary make the travel arrangements, and I'll supervise the packing and see that there are no loose ends dangling around here. We will, of course, drop by to see Ned while we are in France."

"Er… Just drop by? In Brittany?" He smiled. "Of course. May I finish my breakfast first?"

"Certainly, my dear. I wouldn't want to rush you. But I want to see this Miss Benda for myself."

Lord Penworth put his hands on her shoulders and turned her to look at him. "Anne, my dear, aren't you over-reacting a bit? There is nothing to suggest that Ned has lost his head over this young woman. And even if he has, what of it? Are you going to object to a musician in the family?"

"No, not that. But what if she is taking advantage of him?"

He considered, and then shook his head. "Possible, but unlikely. Ned may be a bit of a romantic, but he is not a fool. Have you ever known anyone to take advantage of him?"

Lady Penworth set her shoulders firmly. "Perhaps not, but there is always a first time."

Chapter Twenty-six

MARGUERITE AWOKE IN THE DARK FROM A DREAM OF NED. This was happening far too frequently. They were not unpleasant dreams—far from it. But they were disturbing nonetheless.

Ned. She was thinking of him as Ned now, and not Lord Edward. That was probably not wise. She laughed to herself. Of course it was not wise, but she was beginning to think that the time for wisdom had passed. Wisdom, prudence, caution, good sense—they all vanished, *poof!* the moment he came near her. She was as addled as Delphine, it seemed.

And she didn't care.

She was not foolish enough to think he could marry her. That was his foolishness.

She had seen enough of the world to know that aristocratic families, no matter how liberal in their thinking, did not welcome an artist into the family. An artist might be a friend, might even be invited to dine, though that implicitly assumed that one way or another the artist would perform to entertain the other guests.

Her parents had frequently been invited in just that way. They had been greeted, included in the conversations, treated with every courtesy, but sooner or later came the moment when they were expected to perform, to sing for their supper, so to speak. Papa had joked about it, but Maman had been less amused.

An artist could never be considered an equal, part of the

family. Her mother's parents had taught that lesson. Delphine might sound ridiculously arrogant, but her attitude had some basis in reality.

Even if there were no chasm of class separating them, the fact remained that she could not marry anyone. Not while she had Delphine to care for. She was bound by the promise she had given her mother, her dying mother.

Did that have to mean she must deny herself any chance for love and passion? Did it mean she had to live like a nun for the rest of her life? That was too cruel.

But perhaps, just perhaps, there was something she could do.

Because she was an artist, she had more freedom than many women. Almost by definition she was not respectable. At least, people assumed she was not respectable. Therefore, she did not need to protect her reputation in the same way other women did.

She would not sell herself, or even become some man's mistress. That would make her dependent on a protector's whims—a humiliating form of bondage, with less freedom than a wife had.

But she had to do something.

What she could do was take a lover, a lover of her own choosing. She would be discreet, not flamboyant. Even if it became known, it need not harm her. Many knew, or at least suspected, that Brahms had long been Clara Schumann's lover, and no one thought any the less of either of them.

What was important was that it had to be her own choice. And her choice was Ned.

They could be lovers.

Nothing less could ease the fever that was consuming her. Every waking minute of the day she longed to be in his arms, to feel his touch. And at night, in her dreams—she woke from those dreams in a turmoil of frustrated desire. For them to become lovers was the only solution, at least for her.

A problem remained. That Ned desired her was unmistakable. She was not the only one who was left shaken by their kisses. Even without that, she could see the hunger in his eyes when he looked at her, just as he could no doubt see the hunger in her eyes. The problem was that he was too honorable to offer an irregular arrangement. He was insisting on marriage.

If she wanted him in her bed—and she did—she would have to seduce him.

She swung her legs out of the bed, lit the lamp, and went over to the dressing table. Her first look in the mirror almost sent her straight back to bed. Anything less like a seductress would be hard to imagine.

The livid bruise that had circled her eye and covered half her cheek had faded. Almost a week later, it was now yellow and blue. These were not her best colors. She would have to go to him in the dark, lest the sight of her frighten him.

Then there was her nightgown—her nice warm nightgown, buttoned up to her neck and with ruffles at the wrist to cover her hands. Very comfortable, very practical, but hardly seductive.

Now that she thought about it, she had no seductive nightwear. She had never needed it. Quite proper of her, no doubt, but of no use at the moment. She would simply have to leave it off.

She also took off her nightcap, and undid her braid. Loose hair, flowing down to her waist, was almost certainly the appropriate way to approach a lover. Or so she had heard. She brushed it out thoroughly and drew some of it over her shoulder so that it could shadow her cheek.

She unbuttoned the nightgown, drew it over her head, dropped it on the floor, and looked at herself in the mirror. The heat of her blush made her feel as if she were on fire. Never had she seen herself completely naked like this. No one had ever seen her like this. But this was what a lover would want to see.

She snatched up a robe and wrapped herself up in it. The wool felt scratchy on her skin. She huddled in it for a long minute before she lifted her head, turned down the lamp, and went to the door.

She could do this.

Chapter Twenty-seven

MARGUERITE CLOSED THE DOOR OF NED'S ROOM CAREFULLY behind her. The slight click did not seem to have disturbed him. The fire had almost burned down—only a few embers still glowed—and she shivered in the cold. She hadn't worn slippers so she would be able to move silently down the hall, but the stone floors of the corridor had been icy. Still shivering, she waited until her eyes had grown accustomed enough to the dim light for her to reach the bed without bumping into anything.

His arm was on top of the covers. His bare arm. The faint glow from the embers was enough to illumine the hairs on that arm.

Lord Edward—Ned—did not wear a nightshirt.

Was that a good omen or not? Good, she decided. It might make this easier.

Dropping her robe on the floor so that she was as naked as he, she lifted the covers and slid in beside him. He gave a short grunt, but did not otherwise seem to notice the intrusion. Ah, the warmth felt so good. Even before she touched him, she could feel the heat radiating from his body. He even smelled warm, if that was possible.

Hesitantly she lifted her hand. It hovered for a moment and then skimmed gently along his side, barely touching him, from hip to shoulder. His skin was smooth, but underneath he was hard and solid. Her breath grew shorter and her caress became bolder. He moved slightly into her hand and gave a soft moan of pleasure.

The nearness of him excited her. Hardly able to breathe, she moved her head into the hollow of his shoulder and pressed a kiss on his neck. In response he leaned over her, inserting his knee between her legs. "Marguerite," he murmured her name softly, almost a prayer. A moan escaped her lips.

His eyes opened wide with shock, and he sprang away from her. "Marguerite!" This time her name was an expression of anger, not longing. "What the devil do you think you're doing?"

Horrified, she snatched at the sheet to cover herself, although there was nothing that could hide her hideous embarrassment. She had obviously made a mistake of grotesque proportions. Shame wrapped itself around her, and tears stung her eyes. "I am sorry," she whispered. "I thought…I thought you wanted me."

"Oh my God." He fell on his back and closed his eyes. "Of course I want you, you idiotic creature. But…" He still sounded angry, but not quite so much. "What do you think you're doing?"

"I thought, perhaps, we could be lovers." She spoke carefully, cautiously.

"Lovers!" He covered his eyes with his forearm. "Marguerite, you are going to be the death of me."

"I don't understand," she said. The tears were too close to falling. "You say you want me but you do not."

He made a noise that was something between a growl and a groan and rolled over. Propped up on one elbow, with his hand cupping her face, he stared down at her for a long minute. "Want you? Want you?" he whispered. "I am dying for you every second of the day and night." He snatched up her hand and pressed it against his erection. "Does this feel as if I don't want you?"

She gasped in surprise, or perhaps in shock. She had known in theory, but she had not realized quite how large it would be. Not just large, but warm. She spread her fingers to explore, just a little. No, not warm. Hot.

His voice was a definite growl now, just before his mouth came down on hers. Immediately the heat flared between them, as it always did when they kissed.

Yes! This was what she wanted! She wrapped her arms around him, arching up to press her body against him. *Yes!*

He pulled back. *Again* he pulled back. With an angry cry, she swung her hand and hit him on the arm. "Why?" she demanded.

He lay on his side, turned to her but not touching. "This isn't right, this sneaking around in the dark. Hiding. I don't want some tawdry affair. I want to stand beside you in front of all the world. Proudly and for all time. I want you to be my wife."

She lay back on the pillow and stared up at the ceiling. "I do not believe this. A naked woman comes to your bed and offers herself to you, and you act as if you are the frightened virgin." She stopped abruptly and looked at him. "Are you?"

It was too dark to be certain, but she could almost see a flush rising in his face. "No, I'm afraid not," he said. "But it is probably best that one of us knows what to do."

"Then why?" She lifted herself to face him, unable to believe how frustrated she felt.

He pushed her back down and loomed over her. "You know why. Because I don't want a night's pleasure with you. I want you beside me every day, every night for the rest of my life. And you want that too. Can you deny it?"

The tears were threatening again. "It is not a question of what I want. You are not a fool. Delphine has the right of it. Your family would never accept such a one as I."

"It is your cousin who is a fool. More than a fool—she's mad as a hatter. Her insane notions are straight out of another century."

A sudden chill went through her. "You mustn't say such things about Delphine."

"Why not? Her ideas of who can marry whom are preposterous. My family would consider them a pathetic joke. And they will adore you."

She tried to shake her head. She knew she should be sensible and practical and tell him he was talking nonsense, but she couldn't.

Her hesitation must have been obvious because this time when his mouth came down on hers, she could feel his smile. Then his lips moved, his tongue—all her thoughts vanished.

When he lifted his head again, she heard the whimper that came from her. His hand was caressing her side, and then her thigh, coming closer and closer. Her whimper grew louder.

"Marry me," he said.

She shook her head helplessly.

"Promise that you will marry me," he repeated.

She moaned and pulled herself together as best she could. "I will marry you, if…"

"No *ifs*."

"Yes, there must be this *if.*" She seized his wrist to keep his hand from further encroachment. "If your family does not object, I will marry you. But I will not allow you to be disowned."

He chuckled softly. "In that case, we will be married as soon as I can arrange it."

His hand escaped from her grip and slid between her thighs once more. She yelped. Why couldn't she make a more attractive noise? "With your family's approval," she gasped. *What was he doing? Oh, that felt…Oh!*

"That's my girl." His voice was smug with satisfaction, but his hands, his clever hands were doing such things… She let herself sink into the extraordinary pleasure of it. And then it was not only his hands that slid between her thighs. Yes. This was what she had wanted. Yes!

Ned woke up with hair tickling his nose. Marguerite's hair. Who would have thought that a tickle could be such a delight? But this was Marguerite's hair. He turned his head slightly to rub his cheek against its silky softness.

She was his now. There would be no more secrets between them. He would protect her and keep her safe. He had the right.

He tightened his arm around her, pulling her snugly against him. Yes, this was how he wanted to awaken every morning, with Marguerite at his side.

But it could not be just yet.

The blackness of night was fading to the pale gray of dawn. He had to get her back to her room before any of the servants were up and about. He leaned over to nuzzle her neck. Her response was a purr of pleasure.

No. This was probably not the best way to awaken her. Not for either of them. In the future, yes, but not today, he realized with regret. With a gentle shake, he whispered her name.

She wrinkled her nose and muttered something before her eyes fluttered open. Then her eyes opened wide and she stared up at him.

He wasn't sure what the expression on her face was—surprise? fear? distress? He certainly hoped not. "Marguerite?" he asked uncertainly.

Then her face softened, and a tiny smile tugged at the corners of her mouth. "It happened then, did it?"

His worry eased. "Yes, it happened. Are you all right?" When she didn't immediately answer, a bit of worry crept back. "You're not sorry, are you?"

"No, not sorry. I…it's strange, that's all." Her eyes slid away from him. "I do not quite know what I am supposed to do now."

A rush of tenderness swept over him. She looked vulnerable in a way he had not seen before, and he had to lean over and kiss her, not passionately this time, but tenderly. It was not a long embrace, or perhaps it was, but when he lifted his head again she no longer looked uneasy.

"Come," he said. "We need to get you back to your room before the servants are up."

They moved down the corridor to her room, quickly because the stone floor was cold under their bare feet, but his arm stayed protectively around her.

Chapter Twenty-eight

NED WAS HAPPY. NO, NOT JUST HAPPY. EUPHORIC.

It was all he could do to keep from shouting for joy.

She was his! Marguerite had given her word—she had promised to marry him. He laughed aloud when he thought about her worry that his family would not accept her. They would adore her. She was intelligent, talented, independent—all the things his parents and sisters admired. Even his brothers would approve.

Clivers appeared, prepared to give Ned his morning shave. Ned was perfectly capable of shaving himself, and of dressing himself as well. He would actually prefer to do for himself, especially this morning, but that would leave Clivers without a job, and Clivers supported a wife and child back at Penworth. Or was it children?

Ned leaned back in the chair while Clivers tucked a towel around his neck. "How many children do you have now, Clivers?"

"Three, my lord." The valet stropped the razor impassively.

Ned blinked. He had forgotten *two?* "You must miss them. And their mother, of course."

Clivers lathered the brush in the shaving mug, still impassively. "I know they will always be safe at Penworth while I am away." He held the brush toward Ned. "If you please, my lord."

Ned closed his mouth and allowed Clivers to get on with the shave. Silently, as always. The valet never had much to say.

Of course, Ned had never asked much about him. He did not really know much about Clivers, and that was probably his own fault. He could excuse himself by claiming that he did not want to pry, but actually, he had never been particularly interested.

When he and Marguerite were married, they would certainly not live with his parents at Penworth. A country estate in Dorset was not the ideal place for a concert pianist. Or was it? Ned did not know. Perhaps a home in the country was precisely what she would want when she was not on a concert tour.

But it wouldn't be Penworth. They would need a home of their own—a base, so to speak. Perhaps Clivers' family would not mind relocating to wherever he and Marguerite settled. But that might not even be in England. He also did a good bit of traveling himself, though in his case it was to various libraries for research.

A sudden qualm crossed his mind. "Clivers, do you mind that I drag you away from your family so often?"

"Your service is not precisely onerous employment, sir." The valet permitted himself a slight smile as he removed the towel and allowed Ned to stand. "And there is a certain interest in visiting different places and encountering different people."

Hmm. "Clivers, what do you make of the ladies' maids here?"

"The French ladies, do you mean?" Clivers looked disapproving. "They did not arrive with maids of their own."

"No?" Ned halted in the middle of tying his neck cloth, but recovered quickly. "No, probably not. They went through a bad time of it in Paris, with the siege, and then the death of Mlle. Benda's father."

"Dreadful, I'm sure." Clivers held out a woolen waistcoat for Ned.

"But surely one or two of the maids here have been assigned to them."

"The young lady, Mlle. de Roncaille, makes use of one of the parlor maids. The other two ladies do for themselves." Disapproval dripped from his tone.

"They do?" That did startle Ned. He was not sure his mother and sisters actually knew how to get themselves dressed without assistance. Perhaps…perhaps that would be a bit of luxury he could offer Marguerite. There was so much about her life that he did not know.

He shrugged his shoulders to settle his coat as Clivers whisked off an almost certainly nonexistent bit of lint, just as he always did. Ned nodded his thanks, Clivers nodded his acceptance, and Ned stepped out into the corridor.

Near the top of the stairs, he hesitated. Had Marguerite already gone down? He thought he could hear sounds of movement coming from her room, so he waited. Moments later, he was rewarded when Marguerite stepped out.

She was still dressed in black, a plain dress with none of the ruffles and ribbons that decorated Delphine, and her hair was still dressed simply, though not pulled back as tightly as it had been in the past. Somehow she looked softer. Perhaps it was because a bit of color had replaced the pallor in her cheeks.

Perhaps it was because the minute she saw him, a smile lit her face until she glowed.

He basked in the pleasure of that smile until he came to himself again and held out an arm for her. She took it, and they descended the staircase together, not needing any words.

Laughter was coming from the breakfast room, and he could hear Delphine's teasing voice: "Come now, you must take your medicine."

"It tastes foul," Tony protested.

Ned and Marguerite halted in the doorway. Delphine had the bottle of Tony's tonic in one hand, and was holding a spoon to his mouth. "Do not be a baby," she admonished. "You know your stomach has been bothering you again."

Ned heard Marguerite suck in a breath and her fingers dug into his arm. Startled, he turned and saw a look of horror on her face. Before he could ask what was wrong, she flew at Delphine, knocking the spoon aside and sending the medicine splashing onto the tablecloth before she snatched the bottle from the girl's hand.

They all stared at her, startled into silence. The first to move was Delphine, who flew at her cousin with a shriek, her hands curved into claws. Curses, mostly in French, spewed from her lips. It had never occurred to Ned that Delphine might know such words.

Marguerite, her face a pale, frozen mask once more, simply stepped back to avoid the attack, leaving it to Ned to grab hold of Delphine.

Tony remained in his seat, looking utterly confused. "I don't understand," he said finally. "It's just the tonic Dr. Fernac gave me."

"I think that perhaps it does not really agree with you," Marguerite said, still with no expression on her face. "You seemed to be doing better when you were not taking it."

Delphine sagged against Ned and began to sob, but when he loosened his grip on her, she broke free and ran from the room.

"Let her go," said Marguerite, never even looking at her cousin. "It does not matter."

"Well, if it doesn't matter, I think I'll be off." Tony threw his napkin down on the table and scowled at Marguerite. "I don't know what the problem is with you and your cousin, but I don't feel well and I don't much care for all these dramatics at breakfast."

Ned put his hand on Marguerite's shoulder. She seemed immobile, but he could feel a tremble, as if it was deep inside her. "What is it?" he asked. "What's wrong?"

With a faint shake of her head, she turned aside.

"Marguerite, you must tell me." He turned her to face him, but she kept her eyes lowered. "Tell me," he insisted.

Still refusing to meet his eye, she said. "You do not want to know."

"Of course I want to know. You are upset. How could I not want to know?"

"I may be mistaken." She looked up at him then. "You must understand that. I may be mistaken."

He nodded. "I understand. You may be mistaken—but about what?"

"It was just…" She bit down on her lower lip. "I told you that her uncle died."

"The one who wanted to take her back to the school?"

"Yes. He had pains in his stomach, you see. Difficulties. Much like Antoine. And one day, I saw Delphine giving him his medicine. It was just like today. The same gestures. The same words." She looked away again.

"I can see that it might be a sad memory, but…"

She shook her head vigorously. "No, you do *not* see. He swallowed the medicine. And by evening he was dead."

"You can't possibly mean… You can't think…" Ned shook his head in disbelief. "Even if she could do such a thing, why would she?"

"Her uncle wanted to take her back to the school where she had been. She did not want to go. She was quite passionate about it. But she began fussing about his health. I thought she was trying to convince him that she should stay with us."

She chewed on her lower lip for a moment before she continued. "Antoine had been feeling better, remember? But then he began feeling ill again. After he said that if the treasure is real, the money will be used for a steel mill, not to restore the chateau. She was very angry."

Ned's knees suddenly would not hold him up and he collapsed into a chair. "Is it possible? Are you sure?"

With an angry swing of her head, Marguerite snapped, "No, I am not sure. How can I be? Her uncle was ill—that is probably all it was. And there is no reason why Antoine could not be suffering from the same illness. Delphine is so young—little more than a child. How could she possibly do such a thing? I think I must be imagining it all. Then I will glimpse a look in her eyes, see an expression on her face when she doesn't know anyone is looking. And I am afraid."

Ned rose to his feet. He now understood the fear that had always hovered around Marguerite. It was not just worry about how she would support her little family. It was fear that her cousin might actually be dangerous—mad and dangerous.

How had she managed such a burden? He pulled her into his arms and held her so that she could lean against him. She was safe with him, he hoped she knew. With one hand he cradled her head, resting his cheek against her hair.

At first she was trembling, but gradually she grew still. Ned, on the other hand, found himself growing increasingly uncertain. To comfort Marguerite by holding her was one thing. To know what to do about Delphine was another. Assuming that something needed to be done about Delphine, and that Marguerite was not tormenting herself needlessly.

No, probably not needlessly, at least not entirely. Marguerite was not given to wild imaginings. His own initial impression of Delphine as sweet and angelic had not survived for long, and for some time he had been thinking that there was something odd about the girl.

But this? Poisoning? Yet her reaction to Marguerite's interference was so violent... And there had been other times when her reaction had been out of all proportion.

The memory tied an icy knot in his gut.

He had to think. Marguerite's trembling had stopped, but they had to decide what to do now.

"We need to know," he said. "One way or the other, we need to know."

Marguerite shook her head hopelessly. "And how is that to be accomplished? Delphine will deny everything, and I have never been able to tell if she is speaking the truth."

The tonic bottle was still clutched in Marguerite's hand. He took it from her. "Perhaps this can tell us."

A look of panic crossed her face. "You are not going to drink it!"

"Hardly. But it seems to me that I saw a chemist's shop—a *pharmacie*—in the village. Perhaps the apothecary can tell us if something has been added to Dr. Fernac's tonic."

Chapter Twenty-nine

DARK CLOUDS MOVING IN FROM THE WEST THREATENED A storm, or at least rain, so Ned insisted that they take a carriage. A resigned horse pulled the ancient cabriolet, his plodding gait more suited to a plow than a carriage. Ned called it an equipage more suited to a bonfire than an outing but, he said, it did possess a hood should they be caught in the rain. And it was small enough to fit through the village streets.

Sometimes Ned's aristocratic standing was very obvious. The thought gave Marguerite a bit of amusement. She would never have even considered commandeering her host's horse and carriage, no less disparaging it. Walking was her normal mode of transportation—easy enough in Paris. The city was not so big that it was difficult to get from one place to another on foot—at least in the areas she frequented. And here at the chateau, it would never have occurred to her to request a carriage to take her to the village.

Not that she was objecting. She was so shaken by the fear that had attacked her when she saw Delphine with Tony that she might not have been able to make the journey without hanging on to Ned for support. That, she did not want to do. She had to remain strong.

Especially now. He did not seem to have realized. She had to make the situation clear to him.

The carriage, which was indeed showing its age, bumped

across the causeway. The hood helped to break the wind, which was tossing the sea into frothy whitecaps, but in combination with the noise of the waves it made conversation impossible.

Once they were in the woods, however, things were quieter. Even leafless, the trees kept out the wind. The tang of the salty air was replaced by the musty scent of dead foliage. The scent of dead dreams. Foolish, foolish dreams.

"You see now why marriage between us would be impossible." She did not look at him as she spoke, but kept her gaze fixed on the path ahead.

The carriage jolted as the horse jerked suddenly. Ned must have pulled up on the reins. She closed her eyes. He should not have been surprised.

But he obviously was. He gave an exasperated sigh. "Really, Marguerite, you say the most idiotic things."

"It is necessary to be realistic."

He laughed, that low, amused laugh of his. "I think you must spend too much time at the theater. You do see melodrama everywhere."

"And you close your eyes to problems." It was not fair of him to make light of this.

He pulled the horse to a halt and turned to face her. "Listen to me." When she kept looking straight ahead, he reached out and turned her to face him. "Listen," he repeated. "We do not know for sure that there is anything wrong with the tonic."

"Even if there is not, you cannot deny that there is something wrong with Delphine."

"Something *wrong*?" He gave that laugh again. "Is that the polite way to say she's off her head? Mad as a hatter?"

"*Yes!*" She spat it out angrily. "Yes. She is mad. Does it satisfy you to hear me say it?"

His hand reached out and covered hers. When she looked down, she realized that her hands were clenched so tightly that her nails were digging right through her gloves. She carefully unclenched them and let him wrap his own around them.

"Marguerite." He said her name softly, and when she looked into his face she saw only gentleness there. "This is nothing new, is it?"

Lowering her eyes, she shook her head.

"That school her mother took her from, the one her uncle wanted to return her to—it wasn't really a school, was it? It was a lunatic asylum."

A small sigh escaped her, and she nodded. "But I heard my aunt telling my mother about it. It was a terrible place. The way they treated her. My mother promised that Delphine would not have to go back there. And now I have inherited that promise."

He tilted his head, considering. "You know, it is possible that an asylum could be the best place for her."

"No. Absolutely no. You have no idea—they put her in a bath of ice water, and they tied her up so she could not move her arms. And—you will think this is silly, but it is not. They would not let her wear her own clothes. They made her wear ugly smocks." She looked at him beseechingly. "You know Delphine. For her, this would be the worst punishment of all."

She could see that he did understand, but he was not convinced. "If she is dangerous…" he said.

"But most of the time we manage, Tante Héloise and I. You have seen how she calms down when we insist."

Her hand was on his arm, and he covered it with his own. His mouth tilted into a half smile. "There is no need for us to make any decision right now. We still don't know if there is anything wrong with the medicine. But I must warn you, if she is dangerous, I do not want her to share a house with our children."

She closed her eyes and took a deep breath. "Lord Edward, you do not seem to understand. There can be no children, there can be no marriage, if it is as I fear. You cannot introduce a dangerous madwoman into your family."

"Oh, I don't know. My sister Emily married a fellow with some decidedly odd birds perched on his family tree. And there are some cousins we do our best to avoid." He grinned at her. "You have to learn to stop worrying. If she's a serious problem, we can always set her up in a house of her own with a caretaker or two, and let her play queen of the realm to her heart's content."

"But…but the expense of such an arrangement would be enormous."

"Another thing you don't seem to understand is that my family is rich. There's not much we can't afford. And we can certainly afford to take care of our relatives."

He reached over and lifted her chin to close her mouth before giving the reins a shake to start the horse on its plodding way.

He did not understand. But sooner or later he must. She had to make him see the impossibility of it all. How could he think that money would solve this problem?

Ned hadn't been to the village since the day he had followed Marguerite. It was odd—that day had been bright and sunny and today a storm was threatening, but even so, the village seemed to have lost some of its oppressive grayness.

He looked around. No, it was still gray—gray stone for the walls, gray slate for the roofs. There were even gray clouds overhead. The village had not changed. He had changed, and the reason for that change was sitting beside him.

Sitting tensely beside him.

Her hands in their black gloves were clenched on her lap. She was enveloped in her black cloak and another ugly black hat was perched on her head. The only touch of color was the brooch at her throat, fastening her cloak. Her dark eyes, her beautiful eyes, were shadowed again.

If he did nothing else in this life, he would drive those shadows away.

He stopped the carriage in front of the church. It was the only place where the village street was wide enough to leave the carriage without completely blocking the way. It was also the only place with a fence to which he could tie the horse. Morvan was a place where people traveled on foot.

By the time he had looped the reins around the fence, Marguerite had descended from the cabriolet. He shook his head. Couldn't she even allow him to hand her out of a carriage? Did she have to be so independent all the time?

At least she was willing to take his arm as they entered the *pharmacie*. It was a surprisingly modern shop, with porcelain apothecary jars in rows upon the shelves behind a polished counter. Everything was immaculate, and an antique brass scale, which seemed to be more for atmosphere than for use, gleamed brightly.

The chemist, who appeared from the rear of the shop, was also a surprise, and not a welcome one. Ned had expected a dusty, grimy shop, overseen by an ancient, trembling apothecary. A part of him had clung to a hope that if there was something wrong with the tonic, it had been a simple mistake made here, not a deliberate poisoning.

Unfortunately, the chemist was a young man, not more than thirty or so, neatly, almost elegantly, dressed—as well turned out as his shop. He did not look the sort to make a careless mistake. This might be tricky.

Formal introductions were a desirable first step. "I am Lord Edward Tremaine, and this is Mlle. Benda. We are staying at the Chateau Morvan."

A faint smile appeared on the chemist's face, as if he had been well aware of who they were, even if he had not known their names. He inclined his head in courteous acknowledgment of the introduction. "François Seznec, at your service. How may I help you?"

"We have a rather odd request to make of you," Ned said.

Marguerite held out the bottle. "There is this tonic that Dr. Fernac gave to my cousin…"

Seznec took the bottle and sniffed it. "Ah yes. Dr. Fernac's special tonic." He smiled. "Do you require more of it?"

"No," said Ned. "We were wondering if there might be something wrong with it."

"With this?" The young man laughed. "It is utterly harmless. A bit of calcium, and bit of magnesium, and some peppermint for flavor."

Marguerite licked her lips nervously. "I need to know if something might have been added to it."

At that Seznec reared back, his expression cold. "I assure you, mademoiselle, that all medicines that leave this shop are prepared with the greatest care and caution."

"No, no!" She raised a hand in protest. "I did not mean that. Not at all. It is just that—I wondered if something might have been added to it later."

"Accidentally, of course," Ned put in. He kept his face expressionless, as if defying the chemist to question him.

"Accidentally," Seznec repeated, looking at them with icy eyes. "Of course." He looked down at the bottle, and then looked back at them. "Tell me, what sort of symptoms do you think this *accidental* contamination might have caused?"

After a deep breath, Marguerite spoke carefully. "Digestive pains and increasing distress. Vomiting. Dizziness. Then difficulty breathing."

The chemist looked at her steadily. "And then?"

"Death."

He looked at her and then at Ned. "You realize that these symptoms could have any number of explanations. I am not a doctor, and even if I were, I could not give a diagnosis."

"We realize that," Ned said. "We were hoping that you might be able to tell us if our fears that the tonic might have been… contaminated…are groundless."

"*Accidentally* contaminated." Sarcasm dripped from Seznec's tone. He stared at them with stony eyes. Then he shrugged. "I do not have a real laboratory here, you must understand. I do not have a great deal of equipment. But I will see what I can do."

Marguerite sagged in relief, and managed a smile of gratitude. "Thank you. That is all I could hope for."

Seznec's expression softened as he looked at her, and he inclined his head with what was almost a smile.

Only after they were in the carriage and on the way back to the chateau did Marguerite ask, "Do you think he realized I was asking about poison?"

"Of course," Ned said. "He is not a fool, more's the pity. But his name, Seznec. I've heard it somewhere recently, but I can't think where."

"Seznec?" Marguerite frowned in thought for a few moments. "Ah, yes. That was the name of the priest the vicomte was talking about. The one who was killed."

Chapter Thirty

By the time they reached the causeway, the wind was driving the waves against the rocks, sending the spume flying. The ancient carriage shook so violently that Ned was afraid it would fall to pieces before they made it across. Even the phlegmatic horse seemed to notice the turbulence, though not enough to bolt or even increase his speed. Instead he seemed to hesitate with each step before he put a hoof down.

Ned would have gotten down and dragged the beast along but he didn't dare leave Marguerite. Not that he could do anything to keep the carriage from being blown into the sea if the tempest decided to brush them away. Why hadn't he taken a good look at the weather before they set out? Or before they'd left the village, at least.

No, he'd been so damned proud of himself, telling Marguerite what they should do, making her see how she needed him. Ha! What an arrogant fool he was. He'd be lucky if he could get her back to the safety of the chateau in one piece.

How could he have been such an idiot?

He glanced over at her. One hand was gripping the edge of the carriage and she was staring out at the sea, but she didn't look frightened. She didn't even flinch when a wave crested the rocks and sent water rushing across the road, twisting the carriage wheels into a skid.

That forced him to concentrate on his driving, and he leaned to the side in an effort to keep the carriage upright. The mangy excuse for a horse needed to realize that if it picked up the pace, it would get out of this weather and into a dry stable a lot sooner. It was hard to tell if the creature could even hear the crack of the whip over the roar of the sea, but Ned's urging finally produced some movement. It wasn't a canter, or even a trot, but the blasted nag did manage something approaching a walk instead of a stroll.

He stole another look a Marguerite. She had not changed her position, nor had she said a word. Not that he would have been able to hear her over the wind and waves if she did speak. He could not tell if the drops running down her cheek were tears or sea spray. If he did not get her to safety soon, he would—he did not know what he would do.

At last they were across. No sooner had they reached the shelter of the trees than the horse resumed its accustomed plod. Marguerite seemed to relax as well. At least her hand let loose of the carriage and fell down into her lap.

He took one of her hands and lifted it to his mouth. "Forgive me. I should never have dragged you to the village when the weather looked so risky."

"Dragged me?" She squeezed his hand. "No, you were right. We must know, and the sooner the better. Besides…" She looked back where glimpses of the raging waves could be seen through the trees and breathed a sigh. "Besides, I like the storm. I welcome it. Can you understand that? I only wish it could blow me—everything—away. Far, far away."

"Marguerite!" He could barely manage that protest. An icy fear had seized him.

She looked startled by his voice, and then smiled gently. "No, no. There is no need for you to worry. I am not longing for death. Just for—I don't know. Escape? Peace?"

"If it is in my power, you shall have it—peace, safety, whatever you want."

She squeezed his hand again. "Yes, I know that. But…" She

waved a hand at the horse, which had come to a complete halt now that it was out of the wind.

With a silent laugh at himself, he gave the reins a shake. The horse responded with a snort, but resigned itself to movement and eventually they did reach the stable. Inside, out of the wind, the quiet was almost a shock. There was, mercifully, a groom to take charge of the horse. Ned wanted to get Marguerite in out of the rain as quickly as possible, and get her warm and dry. And this time she allowed him to help her down.

By now the rain was coming down in torrents. He started to apologize again, but she placed her hand over his mouth. "There are things that are out of our control. The weather is one of them, and what is or is not in the tonic is another. If M. Seznec finds nothing wrong with it, then I was just making mountains out of molehills. And if he finds there was something wrong—" She shrugged. "We will see what must be done then. In the meantime, I think we both need dry clothes."

The door under the porte-cochère was the closest, and they ran for it, splashing in the mud even as they realized that running was really pointless. They could hardly get any wetter. They ran anyway.

Once inside, they leaned against the door when they finally got it closed against the wind, catching their breath and dripping on the stone floor. "This is where I came in the day I arrived," said Ned, looking around. "It must be the most unwelcoming entrance hall I have ever encountered."

"I don't think it is normally used," said Marguerite. She went over to the table in the middle of the room and lit the oil lamp that stood there. With a bit of adjustment to the wick, some of the shadows were dispelled. "But now, see? It is not nearly so gloomy. It was only the darkness that made it seem so."

"It's not just the darkness. It's these paintings." He gestured at the enormous canvases hanging on the walls and went over to examine one more closely. "Look at this. It's positively grue-some. All these people are marching along carrying a head on a platter. And it looks as if they have gilded it."

Marguerite came over for a better look, carrying the lamp. Then she laughed. "That is not a head, at least not a real one. It is a reliquary. You know. For holding the relics of a saint. They are made in all sorts of shapes. And on the saint's feast day, the people carry it in procession. They still do this in many country villages. This is not a custom in England?"

"Not since Henry the Eighth, anyway." Ned looked at the painting again. "I should have realized. They don't really look as if they are celebrating an execution."

"Well then, come along. We still need to get dry." She started toward the staircase.

"Just a minute." Ned spoke abruptly. "Bring the lamp back for a minute."

Marguerite did so, a slight frown on her face.

He took the lamp from her and held it up near the center of the painting. "The reliquary, look at it."

"It seems to be a gilded bust, studded with jewels." She shrugged. "That is not unusual. They are often very richly decorated."

"Look at the collar around the neck. The jewels in the center."

She looked again, more closely, and sucked in a startled breath. Her hand went to her throat, where her cloak was fastened. "It looks like my brooch," she whispered.

"Yes."

"But how can that be?"

He waited while she thought about it.

"Is that what the treasure is, do you think?" She turned to look at Ned. "The reliquary?"

"That would make sense," he said. "That would explain why the priest was hiding it—the Republicans would have simply destroyed it once they pulled off the jewels. And it would explain why he gave that to your great-great-grandmother to show to her father, who would doubtless have recognized it."

"So we know what we are looking for. A reliquary."

"Possibly." Ned felt a bit hesitant about asking for the next piece of information, but it might be relevant. "Tell me, when the old man talks of the treasure, does he say *le trésor des Morvans,* the treasure of the Morvans, the family, or does he say *le trésor de Morvan,* which could mean the treasure of the chateau or of the village?"

After a moment's thought, Marguerite said. *"Le trésor de Morvan.* A reliquary would belong to the church and to the village." Marguerite stared at the painting. Her lips curved up slowly into a smile, which eventually parted to let out a burst of laughter. "Oh goodness me. Delphine will be furious."

"Well, I might be wrong," Ned said, "so there's no point in setting her off just yet. Besides, I have another idea."

Marguerite looked at him expectantly. He felt a trifle self-conscious, but continued. "When I first looked at your brooch, I noticed the stones, but when we were waiting outside the vicomte's room, I noticed the carving over the door. It's the same design. And I'm reasonably sure I have seen rosettes in that design somewhere in the other part of the chateau."

"Hmm." Marguerite narrowed her eyes to slits and looked at the painting. Then she opened them wide and said, "Yes! There is a room—we have not searched there yet, but it is paneled and there are rosettes like that in the borders." She paused. "On some of the furniture as well, I think."

Turning to Ned, she said, "You think that the brooch was a clue not just to what the treasure was but to where it was hidden?"

"It could be. After all, if it was the reliquary that he hid, Abbé Seznec would not have wanted it lost forever. He knew the family was escaping. It would have made sense to give the girl the brooch to show her father, who would understand what it meant. The design must be of some importance to the family to appear on their escutcheon and in so many other places. Unfortunately, her father did not survive to reach England, and she only knew that it was somehow important. And so it has been passed down to you."

She unpinned the brooch and stared at it, lying in the palm of her hand. "So I have been wearing a brooch that belongs to a saint." She smiled gently. "No wonder it has always given me comfort."

Chapter Thirty-one

THE STORM RAGED THROUGH THE NIGHT, COVERING ANY NOISE Ned might have made on his way to Marguerite's room. It wouldn't have mattered. Nothing could have kept him away.

They made love slowly, giving of themselves freely. There was no need now to persuade or convince. Afterward, they lay wrapped in each other's arms, discovering the time for sharing confidences.

Ned had always thought of himself as an easygoing, cheerful sort of fellow. If he had been asked, he would have said he was made for comedy, not tragedy. But he was amazed by the depths of emotion he was now experiencing.

He lay on his side so he could enjoy the sight of Marguerite's face. She looked softer, the tightness of the frozen mask she wore too often smoothed out. Tenderly, he caressed the side of her face. "There has been very little sorrow in my life and probably far more than my fair share of happiness. Most people would say I have lived a charmed existence. But I have never known the joy I feel with you."

She turned her cheek into his hand. "Is that what it is, this feeling? It lifts me up and carries me to—I don't know where. To some place I have never been."

"You are not afraid, are you?"

"No, not at all. It is as if I have arrived at the place I always longed for even though I did not know it existed."

It was not dark enough in the room to hide the shadows in her eyes, the shadows he was determined to dispel. He made his voice cheerful. "Tell me what our home will look like."

"Our home?" She sounded as if she had never given the matter any thought.

"Yes." He was determined that she would think about it. "Where shall we live? Would you like to live in England? In the country or in London?"

She gave a surprised little laugh. "I never—I always lived with my parents. They were the ones to decide, you see."

"Ah, but now you will be the one to decide."

She laughed again, a little more amused now. "I thought it was always the man who made such decisions."

He loved to hear her laugh. She did it so rarely that he was quiet for a moment, savoring it. He was going to make sure that there was plenty of laughter in her life from now on.

"No," he said, poking her gently. "You will have to do some of the deciding yourself. First, country or city?"

He watched the look of incredulity start to fade. She was drifting into consideration of the idea. He kept very still, not wanting to disturb her imaginings.

"I've never lived in the country." Her voice was almost a whisper. "Not until I came here. The quiet—the quiet has been good. But it's so enormous, and all the stone—so cold."

"There's a start. Quiet, but nothing as big and cold as a medieval castle." He kept his voice cheerful.

She laughed again, but there was regret in it now. "You are being foolish, you know. I must live someplace where I can find work, where I can give concerts. All I need is an apartment with a room big enough for my piano, my Pleyel."

"Now you are being foolish. Spending these past months in this medieval pile has made you forget that we're living in the modern age. Railroads speed us all over the continent in no time at all. You can leave home today and tomorrow be in Paris or Rome or Vienna or Copenhagen or Prague or whatever city you are to perform in."

"Yes, but…" She was frowning. He could almost feel the worry sneaking in. "But traveling is so complicated."

"Now that's where a husband comes in useful," he said smugly. "I can make all the arrangements, see to it that you get to the train and the hotel and the concert hall on time, and there will be nothing for you to worry about." Most of that would actually be done by servants, he thought, but did not mention. He suspected that having servants around all the time was something she would need to get used to.

"A husband." She took a deep breath, as if she was about to start that nonsense about how they couldn't possibly marry, so he kissed her until she melted in his arms.

"Sleep, my love, and dream about our home to be," he whispered.

In response she gave a little wordless murmur as he tucked the blankets around her.

By the time Marguerite awakened, it was quiet—quiet enough for her to hear the thuds and rustles of the maid laying a fresh fire on the hearth. She felt a delicious contentment all through her and stretched out a hand. Sadly, it encountered nothing, not even a bit of residual warmth from Ned's body. Still, she had the memory of him and of his body imprinted on her. She also had the promise that he would return to her bed every night.

He made her believe that a future including both of them was a real possibility, and not just a delicious fantasy. Imagine talking about houses! Still, even if their present idyll could not last, she was determined to be happy. She could store up enough happiness from the time she had with him to last her for a lifetime if necessary.

The glow of contentment was still keeping her warm when she left her room and saw Ned waiting for her. She was not in the least surprised, and took his arm as if it was the most natural thing in the world.

"What should we say to them?" she asked as they descended the stairs.

"That you have made me the happiest man in the world by accepting my proposal?"

"Do not be foolish." She could feel the blush heating her cheeks. "I meant about the treasure. Should we tell them it is a reliquary, and not a treasure of jewels and gold?"

"No, I think not. They might stop searching." He came to a halt on the steps and sounded almost hesitant. "I may be wrong, but if I am right, I feel as if we owe it to that priest to find it. He was willing to give his life to protect that relic."

"Yes. You are right. We owe it to him."

"However, I think I will tell them my idea about the rosette design. There's the one on the escutcheon over the vicomte's door as well as your brooch, and the way he carried on suggests that it means something." He grinned. "If nothing else, it will keep them busily searching."

They arrived in the breakfast room together, as they had the day before, but today there were no dramatics. The scene of the day before might never have happened.

Antoine was dipping his brioche into his bowl of café au lait with no sign of digestive discomfort. Delphine was smiling sunnily at him as she spread raspberry jam on her own brioche. A narrowed glance at Marguerite was the only sign that there might have been some lingering resentment on her part.

Marguerite attributed that look less to resentment than to the fact that her hand remained on Ned's arm longer than was strictly necessary, and as he seated her at the table, his hands brushed her more frequently and more lingeringly than might be considered proper.

If Delphine objected, *tant pis.* So much the worse.

Marguerite was beginning to think that it did not matter what Delphine thought. She was no longer willing to arrange her life to accommodate Delphine's whims and fancies. She saw before her a future that was her own. She was willing to take Delphine's care into account, to watch over her, but she was not willing to sacrifice herself for her cousin. Was this selfishness on her part? Perhaps, but she no longer cared.

Ned's hand brushed hers and she turned to smile at him. If Delphine did not like it, that was too bad. Marguerite was happy, when for too long the best she had hoped for was the absence of fear. She would not let Delphine spoil this with her fits and tantrums.

Tony glanced out the window. "The storm seems to have finished, and we are all here." He shot an annoyed glance at Ned and Marguerite. "If you can spare us the time, we will be able to return to our search."

"About that…" Marguerite looked up. "Ned has an idea."

Tony immediately looked interested. "You found something in the archives?"

"Not there, but I was thinking about the old man's reaction to Marguerite's brooch," Ned said. "It is the same design that is carved on the escutcheon over his door, and it seems to me that I saw a carving of a rosette in that shape more than once in those rooms in the other part of the chateau. Either on a piece of furniture or in the paneling."

Tony's eyes lit up. "Yes—that could be the clue we need! They were clever, those old craftsmen. They created hidden drawers in the furniture and panels in the walls for patrons who trusted no one with their secrets. A rosette is an excellent way to disguise a latch."

"That must be the answer!" Delphine leaped from her chair, bouncing with excitement. "We will find the treasure, and who knows what else besides."

She was so like a child much of the time, Marguerite thought with a smile. With a child's artless enthusiasm, and with a child's ability to create an imaginary world. Had she made a terrible mistake? Had she seen something sinister in Delphine where there was only childishness?

"Come along," Delphine said, pulling on Marguerite's arm. "Why are you just sitting there?"

Marguerite lifted her cup. "I am just sitting here because I have not yet had my breakfast. And neither has Ned. Then we must pay our morning call on the vicomte, and Ned and I both have work to do. If you wish to begin without us, go right ahead."

"We will join you this afternoon as usual," Ned said, helping himself to brioche.

Delphine stomped her foot angrily. "You are impossible! How can you be so unhelpful?" With that, she flounced out of the room.

Marguerite shook her head. Yes, Delphine had a child's enthusiasm, but also a child's selfish impatience and inability to see anyone else's point of view.

Ned had thought it would be fairly simple. They would find the room with the rosette carved into the paneling, Tony could figure out how to open the secret compartment—he was good at mechanical contrivances like that—and they would have the "treasure" to show to the old vicomte. Then he could take Marguerite to meet his family, they could be married, and all would be well.

Ha!

Once they started looking, they discovered rosettes everywhere. There were carved rosettes, marquetry rosettes, and painted rosettes. There were rosettes on furniture, on picture frames, on walls and ceiling, even in inlaid patterns on the floors.

That blasted rosette must have been some sort of badge or talisman for the Morvan family. They used it everywhere.

The first day they spent on the floors. Marguerite had gone into the linen room and found a pair of heavy aprons for her and Delphine, and they tied kerchiefs over their hair. Tony and Ned removed their coats, waistcoats, and neck cloths and rolled up their sleeves. Armed with dustpans and brooms, they went to work.

Once the dust of decades had been swept up, to the accompaniment of almost constant sneezes, they found a rosette in the center of the circular hall's marble floor. It proved to be perfectly solid. Then they found a series of rosettes bordering the parquet of a sitting room. One of these was less than solid, but the weakness proved to be nothing more than insect damage.

Filthy and aching from the unaccustomed physical exertion, they retired to their rooms to soak in hot tubs before dinner. No sparkling conversation accompanied the evening meal. Grunts and groans were the order of the day. Ned had always thought of himself as a reasonably active fellow, fit for a game of cricket or a bruising gallop over the fields. This evening he could barely lift a spoonful of soup to his mouth. He didn't know how housemaids managed.

He managed to stay on his feet long enough to get to Marguerite's room once everyone had settled down for the night only to discover that Marguerite had also settled down and was sound asleep. She lay on one side of the mattress, her hair spread over the pillow, and her arm reaching across the bed. Reaching for him? He smiled at the thought.

Since she had left a lamp burning, he knew she had expected him. There was room on his side of the bed—after one night, it was already his side— so he took off his clothes, folding them neatly this time, and slipped in beside her. When he put his arm around her to draw her near, she made a small noise, almost a purr, of contentment and nestled against him.

His last waking thought was that this must be one of the joys that marriage provided—sleeping in the arms of the one you loved even when you were too tired to do anything but sleep.

On the second day they found a tall secretary-cabinet covered in elaborate marquetry and brass decoration. Tony leaped on this, and his excitement energized them all. It was, he said, almost certainly the work of Daniel Roentgen, an eighteenth-century cabinetmaker noted for the ingenuity of his hidden shelves and drawers.

Delphine had to be forcibly held back when she tried to claw a drawer open.

"If you break the mechanism we may never get all the compartments open," Tony scolded.

"All of them?" she asked.

"All. There could be hundreds in a piece this size." At Ned's incredulous look, Tony retreated. "Well, dozens anyway."

That was enough to keep Delphine from physically attacking the cabinet, but she simmered with impatience as Tony carefully examined it. Gently he caressed the wood. "Magnificent," he said softly. "Look at this craftsmanship." With a finger he traced the inlaid portrait of a musician with a lute. "So perfectly done that even after all these years of neglect, one cannot feel the join."

"But how do you open it?" Delphine practically screamed the question.

"Gently, gently." Tony smiled at the cabinet. "You have secrets within secrets, don't you?"

He fingered a rosette at the top of a narrow band of carving, pushing gently first at its center and then at its sides. A push at its left was rewarded with a soft click. The panel to the left sprang open, revealing a stack of four drawers. Marguerite clutched Ned's arm as she leaned forward to look, but the drawers proved to be empty.

A large rosette unlocked the slanted cover of the desk. The rear compartment had numerous small drawers and pigeonholes, but when Tony turned a knob on the bottom drawer, the center section retreated, exposing a further compartment on each side behind the drawers. All of them empty.

His exploration of the secretary and its secrets went on for hours, to his fascination and everyone else's frustration. Often the release of a catch was greeted by a groan as long-unused mechanisms were awakened. "Yes, yes," he murmured, "I know, my sweet, you want a bit of oil here to ease the passage."

"Tony," Ned said, "remember where you are."

Tony blinked, recalled to his audience, and then grinned and patted the secretary. "She is a beautiful piece of work, isn't she? But she resents having been neglected for so long."

"Couldn't we just smash the thing?" Delphine demanded.

"That would be criminal." Tony was truly shocked. "This is a mechanical marvel."

Delphine was not impressed, but held her tongue.

As the afternoon wore on, Tony uncovered dust, dead insects, and even a mummified mouse, but nothing that could be considered a treasure. Then he discovered a drawer with a hidden compartment beneath it. They hovered over his shoulders as he lifted the false bottom of the drawer to reveal some papers, tied together with a ribbon, and a brooch.

Delphine snatched at the brooch with a cry of satisfaction. Almost immediately, her delight turned to a grimace. "What is this?" She held it up between her fingers.

Ned took it from her and smiled. The small oval, surrounded by pearls, was a miniature painting of an eye. "I have heard of these," he said. "It's a lover's token. A secret one. Instead of an entire portrait, only the eye is shown. The lover knows whose eye is shown, but others will not."

Delphine dismissed it with a *humph*, but Marguerite took it in her hand and gently rubbed the dust off. "How charming," she said.

Tony sighed with disappointment. "I suppose that explains these." He waved the papers. "Love letters."

"I should be the one to read them." Delphine reached out a hand for them. "They belong to my ancestor."

The others were quite willing to resign the letters to her because they kept her occupied for the next two hours while

Tony completed his examination of the cabinet.

From time to time they could hear Delphine murmuring things like, "Ah, that is a pretty phrase there," and "Yes, he does indeed love me." Marguerite cast worried glances at her cousin, but Ned gave her shoulder a reassuring squeeze.

"What does it matter if she imagines herself the recipient of love letters? It amuses her," he said, "and there is no danger."

Marguerite was not so sure. It always worried her when Delphine withdrew into her fantasy worlds, and it seemed to be happening more and more often.

Finally, Tony announced that he was finished. He had measured carefully, and there was no space for any additional hidden compartments. Still, he gave the cabinet a regretful pat. "You are a beauty. I promise I will give you a good cleaning and oiling so that all your gears turn smoothly."

That ended their second day of searching.

As they returned to the inhabited part of the chateau, Marguerite spoke softly to Ned. "Do you suppose there might be other things hidden? Besides the reliquary, I mean."

"Who knows? If your ancestors fancied furniture like that secretary, they might have made hidey-holes all over the place."

Chapter Thirty-two

ON THE THIRD DAY OF THE SEARCH, THEY REACHED THE paneled room.

It was an odd room, Marguerite thought—not terribly wide, but long, with a curved recess at the far end. The only windows were there, on the sides of the recess. Something had been torn from the wall between the windows. The scars were still visible.

In the rest of the room, the paneling went about halfway up the walls. Above there were pilasters that led to arches across the ceiling. The ceiling had been painted in panels between the arches and with a large painting covering the center, but decades of grime made it impossible to see what the subject matter might have been.

The paneling must have once been enchanting. Underneath the dust and dirt, the wood had been painted white with the decorative carvings picked out in gilt. But with only the two windows at the far end to let in light, the room would still have been dark. It must have required masses of candles even in the middle of the day.

They all looked around, slightly confused. No, she realized. Not all of them. Ned was standing there with a look of satisfaction.

"The chapel," he said. "This must have been the chapel. You can see there." He pointed at the damaged wall. "That would be where the altar was. It was probably destroyed during the Revolution."

"They had their own chapel?" Marguerite couldn't quite imagine it.

"Of course we did," Delphine said. "You could hardly expect us to travel down to the village." She looked around with an air of pride.

Marguerite did not like the way Delphine was saying *we*, as if she had actually attended Mass here.

Tony also looked all around the room, but with less enthusiasm. Arms akimbo, he glared at the walls. "Damned rosettes. They're all over the place. It will take forever to examine them all."

"Well, the sooner we get started, the sooner we'll finish," Ned said. Marguerite feared he was getting a bit irritable himself. Trying to work with Tony and Delphine could have that effect. Ned had managed to avoid much of the earlier searching by shutting himself up with his documents.

Then also, the day before had been frustrating, not just because they'd found nothing—or at least nothing of importance—but because Tony had been the only one who knew how to examine the cabinet. She and Ned could only watch. Today, however, Ned was taking charge.

"But look at it!" Tony waved an angry hand at the pilasters, each one with rosettes at the top. "The ceiling must be twenty feet high. How are we going to manage?"

"Be sensible, Antoine," Marguerite said. "It is most unlikely that the priest had a ladder with him. If he hid anything in here, it must be somewhere that was within his reach, and so will be within ours."

"I suppose so." Tony still sounded grumpy, but resigned.

This must be the room Ned had been thinking of when he first fastened on the idea of the brooch and its design as a clue. He seemed on edge, more focused than he had been the past few days. "We need to do this systematically," he said. "Each one of us will take one wall. Examine every rosette you find, large or small. See if it pulls out or turns. Try pushing it in, and not just from the middle. Try each petal."

"That will take forever," Tony muttered.

Ned turned on him. "You are the one who wanted to embark on this search. You are the one who decided it was vitally important to you. You are the one who asked for help. You..."

Tony put up his hands in surrender. "You're right, you're perfectly right, and I apologize." He offered a shamefaced grin. "And I actually am grateful for your help, even if I don't sound it."

Ned responded by clapping a hand on Tony's shoulder. Then he noticed Delphine standing in the middle of the room, smiling dreamily and hugging herself. "You too, Delphine. Don't just stand there. Get started."

A bit high-handed, but then he is an aristocrat. Marguerite smiled as she headed for her assigned corner. Not so long ago—less than a week ago—she would have thought of the word *aristocrat* with a sneer. Now she was thinking of it as just a rather adorable foible, at least when applied to Ned.

They worked more or less in silence for the next hour. From time to time Marguerite could hear Tony crooning to the rosettes rather the way he had crooned to the cabinet the day before.

"Come, my beauty, give up your secrets," he whispered.

She met Ned's eye and they shared a smile.

A rhythm established itself. First pull, then turn, left, right. Next push, once in the center, once on each petal. Nothing. On the next one. Pull, turn left, turn right, push, move on and pull, turn left, turn right, *click*.

She froze.

Click? Yes, click. She had definitely heard a click.

She pulled back and looked. There was a distinct line, a space, at the side of the panel. She was sure it had not been there before.

Running her finger gently over it, she could feel that the panel was no longer flush against its neighbor.

"Ned?" she called, except that her voice was barely a whisper. She swallowed and tried again. "Ned?"

This time he heard her. Something must have shown in her face because he was at her side in an instant.

"There was a click," she said. "Then there was this." Her finger traced the crack in the paneling.

She could hear his sharp intake of breath.

Tony and then Delphine noticed and hurried to join them.

Horace's voice broke in on them. "Mlle. Benda, he says it is very important."

"Not now, for God's sake," Tony snapped. "Go away!"

"But he says…"

"Truly, Horace, this is not the time for your interruptions." Delphine's imperious tones should have been enough to drive anyone away, but none of the three turned to see if she had been obeyed. They were all focused on the opening, the very slight opening, at the side of the panel.

"Truly, milor', I must speak with you."

The speaker sounded distressed enough for Ned to swing around and see that it was Seznec, the pharmacist, who was invading.

"Not now." Ned sounded as snappish as Tony. He returned his attention to Marguerite. "What, precisely did you do?"

"Here." She put her fingers on the rosette and turned it to the right. Again the click came, and she could see the panel bounce out slightly. Ned caught the edge before it could fall back into place.

Seznec had not gone away. "I must speak with you," he insisted, striding across the room.

Marguerite turned to offer him a quick smile to placate him. "Truly, Monsieur, this is not a good time. You must wait."

"You don't understand, Mademoiselle," he said, his annoyance increasing. "I have identified…" He broke off and stared as Ned pulled the panel open to reveal a space several feet high and wide. Within was a cloth-wrapped bundle.

They all stared at it in silence. Not even their breathing could be heard.

At length, Ned stepped back and gestured at the opening. "Tony, perhaps you would…?"

Taking a deep breath, Tony licked his lips, nodded, and stepped forward. He put his hands on either side of the bundle and lifted slightly to test its weight. He glanced back. "A table. Is there a table…?"

This was the kind of task Horace was accustomed to. He had been hovering on the edge of the group uncertainly, but hurried and snatched up a small but sturdy table. Setting it down at Tony's side, he stepped back with an air of accomplishment. He almost bumped into M. Seznec, who did not seem to know what to do but refused to leave and continued to watch the proceedings, mesmerized.

Tony picked up the bundle and set it carefully in the middle of the table. Although the thing had an irregular shape, it seemed to have a flat bottom and rested steadily on the table. His fingers trembled as he began to lift off the cloth wrappings. Dust fell from the stiff fabric, some sort of heavy brocade, dingy with age.

As the wrappings unfolded, a glint appeared, drawing a gasp of excitement from Delphine, who moved closer. Her eyes gleamed. "Gold," she breathed.

But Tony frowned as he removed the rest of the cloth.

"Not gold. Not really," he said and stepped back.

What stood revealed was a bust, carved none too artistically from wood, dried out and cracked in places. It was covered with gold leaf and studded with colored stones.

Marguerite could not tear her eyes from it. Nor could she speak. It did not matter that this was no great work of art. Something about it overwhelmed her. She clutched at Ned's arm in an effort to remain on her feet.

"But it is ugly." Delphine's angry complaint seemed to come from a great distance. "This isn't a treasure."

For once, Marguerite ignored her completely.

It was M. Seznec who captured everyone's attention. Slow steps carried him close to the carving. He abruptly fell to his knees and blessed himself. "*Mon dieu,* is this possible? Is it truly Saint Mael?" he whispered.

"What do you mean, is it Saint Mael?" demanded Tony impatiently. "What is this thing?"

"I never saw it myself, but I have often heard it described," Seznec said, staring at it in amazement. "It is the Treasure of Morvan. It was not destroyed after all."

"It's a reliquary, very old," Ned said, "made to contain the relic of a saint. One of the saint's bones, or sometimes a bit of cloth belonging to the saint."

"What?" Tony sounded furious. "You mean that old man has had us wasting our time on a bit of superstitious nonsense? I can't believe it."

"No!" cried Delphine. "No, this is not possible. I will not have it. I will not be cheated like this." She ran over and swung an arm to sweep the reliquary off the table.

With a cry, Marguerite reached out to stop her, but Seznec was faster. On his feet again, he caught Delphine's arm and pushed her away. "How dare you," he began, but stopped himself. Turning to Marguerite and Ned, he said, "I apologize, but I could not let the young woman damage it. Not when Abbé Seznec gave his life to protect it all those years ago."

"A relative, I assume?" Ned asked.

Seznec tilted his head up proudly. "One of whom we are most proud. We knew he was martyred by the barbarians who called themselves Frenchmen, but we did not know he had succeeded in hiding Saint Mael. How did you find him?"

It was Marguerite's turn to smile. She reached into her pocket and pulled out the brooch. "Abbé Seznec gave this to my great-grandmother. She did not know what it meant, but it has been passed down from daughter to daughter and it has protected us, I think. Now it can be restored to its proper place."

She inserted it into the hollow at the center of the collar that circled the carving. It fit perfectly.

Ned put his arm around her shoulders and she leaned against him as they silently drank in the sight. "All these centuries it has survived," he said.

"All these centuries," Seznec echoed softly.

Tony was less impressed. "Well, I suppose we need to let the old man know we've found it. If this is what he was talking about." He snorted in disgust. "What a waste of effort. And that fool of a doctor probably won't let us see him until morning." He stamped out of the room.

Delphine was even less impressed. "It is not fair!" She stomped her foot. "It was supposed to be a treasure—gold, jewels. A fortune. It would make all of this beautiful again." Still blocked by Seznec from venting her disappointment on the carving, she uttered a cry of rage and fled from the room.

Marguerite felt herself sag as the weight of responsibility returned to her shoulders. She started to follow Delphine, but Ned tightened his arm around her.

"Let her go," he said. "Let her have her tantrum. It won't hurt her."

She should protest, she knew. She ought to follow, but she wanted to stay right here, with Ned's arm around her. Then she noticed Horace, still standing there uncertainly, and called to him.

He nodded, as if relieved to have something to do. "I'll follow and watch over her. Just like your father said I should."

"See? There will be no problem," Ned said.

"Problem. Yes." Seznec turned away from his contemplation of the reliquary and regarded them with a worried air. "I came here to tell you what I found, what I suspect."

Of course he had. And it would not be good. Marguerite tensed herself.

Ned lost his smile, though he did not remove his arm. "Yes, of course. We should, perhaps, find someplace to sit down."

Chapter Thirty-three

THE PLACE THEY FOUND WAS A SMALL ANTECHAMBER WHERE a number of pieces of furniture had been pushed out of the way. Ned pulled off dusty covers to find a pair of low-armed settees covered in tapestry. Even without the covers, they were dusty, but Ned was not about to worry about that. He just wanted to get Marguerite seated before she keeled over. She had turned pale—a ghastly pale—at Seznec's words.

Ned sat down beside her and took her icy hand in his and chafed it in an effort to restore some warmth to her. They waited for Seznec to begin.

"You must forgive me," the young pharmacist said as he sat across from them, running nervous fingers through his hair, as oblivious to the dust as they. "Your discovery, your miraculous discovery, made me forget the reason I came today. And I forgot as well that what I have learned may distress you."

With an air of determination, he looked Ned full in the face. "I needed to find a way to determine if there was anything wrong with the tonic. I caught a pair of mice." He paused. "Two, you see, in case one was already ill. I gave them a few spoonfuls of the tonic. Both died."

Marguerite's hand clenched Ned's, but she did not speak.

Seznec continued. "As I told you when you came to my shop, I do not have a true laboratory here, not the kind you might find in Paris. I used the Marsh test for arsenic, which would have fit the symptoms you described, but that test was negative. Then I noticed that there was a grainy feel to the tonic. That should not have been."

Ned wished the pharmacist would hurry up and get to the point. His impatience must have showed, because Seznec shook his head. "I will not trouble you with the things I tried, but eventually I sieved out some small seeds that looked familiar. They had an odd, irregular shape. I checked with one of the farmers, and he confirmed it. It was *agrostemme—Agrostemma githago.*" He peered at Ned. "I think in England you call this corn cockle."

Ned shook his head. "I am not a farmer. I know very little of plants." He looked at Marguerite, who also shook her head. With a musician for a father, she had always lived in cities. What would she know of gardens?

"No matter," said Seznec. "It is a common plant that often grows in fields of grain. There have been occasions when its seeds have contaminated flour, usually in such small quantity that little or no harm is done. But when I was a student at the Hôtel-Dieu in Paris there was a case where a small boy died from these seeds. As you can imagine, this impressed me greatly, and I remembered it when I saw the seeds again."

Marguerite was shaking her head. "But you said this plant grows in grain fields. We have no grain fields growing near the chateau. How could this happen?"

"Ah, there is the question," Seznec said. "For the seeds to land in the wheat, this is a tragic but understandable accident. For the seeds to end up in Dr. Fernac's tonic—I do not see how this can be an accident." He sat there with his hands on his knees and a stern expression on his face.

Marguerite did not seem to be listening to him. She was still shaking her head and speaking softly to herself. "How could she know?"

Her question drew the pharmacist's attention, and it looked as if he was about to ask for an explanation when Ned interrupted. "This is a common plant, you say. Have there been other cases in other places?"

"Ah yes. But almost never fatal, and probably often not even noticed."

"And it also grows in England?" Ned persisted.

"Assuredly. It is common everywhere, and has an attractive flower." Seznec's stern expression relaxed. "Children often gather bouquets of it. One touches it with no harm."

"Children…" Marguerite's murmur drew Ned's attention, but she was looking off into the distance.

He turned back to Seznec. "You said the seeds are an odd shape?"

"Yes. Here, let me show you." The pharmacist reached into a pocket and withdrew a small envelope. He opened it to display a dozen or so small seeds, twisted so that they looked almost like tiny seashells. "Touch them."

Ned did so, paying close attention and noting that they seemed to be covered with tiny prickles. "Yes. I will recognize them if I ever see them again."

"Good. And if you see them, you should destroy them. Meanwhile, if there is any more of Dr. Fernac's tonic in the chateau, it must be poured away and the bottle sterilized. You will see to this?" He looked from Ned to Marguerite and back again.

Marguerite was still lost in her thoughts, so it was Ned who assured the pharmacist that the matter would be taken care of. "And we can promise you that there will be no more accidental problems."

Ned and Seznec exchanged measuring looks. The pharmacist gave a short nod. "Good." Then he smiled. "And now, if you will excuse me, I must return to the village and let everyone know that the Treasure of Morvan has been found. You can have no idea what this will mean to us. No idea."

Marguerite felt cold. She could not believe how cold she felt. It was as if she had fallen into a place where all was ice. She was not even sure she could move—she might be frozen in place. She heard M. Seznec leaving, but she could not seem to turn her head to look at him.

With a sudden rush of determination, she pushed herself to her feet. She had to escape these rooms haunted by a dead past. She had to get outside. She needed to be alone. Half running, she almost tripped over the discarded covers, but she recovered. Her cloak was in the next room and she snatched it up as she ran past and down the stairs.

Ned's voice was calling her. It seemed to come from a great distance. She kept running.

"Stop it, Marguerite. You have to stop."

An arm—Ned's arm—wrapped around her and pulled her hard against him. She looked around and realized that she was outside now. The wind whipped her hair free of its pins and strands lashed her face and her eyes. The hair in her eyes must be what was causing the tears.

He pulled her close to him and held her head against his shoulder with one hand while the other gently rubbed her back.

"Stop that," she said, her voice muffled against his coat. "You are treating me like a small animal. A pet." But she did not lift her head. She could feel his smile against her hair. Was that possible?

He did not remove his hands, but he allowed her to pull back enough to stand by herself while he studied her face. "You are feeling more yourself, then," he said.

A foolish remark. Who else could she be?

She tried to turn away, but he turned her face back to him. "It cannot be a surprise," he said. "You suspected... we both suspected."

"But suspecting isn't the same as knowing. So long as it is just suspicion, there is always hope." She closed her eyes. "And until I told you, you did not even suspect."

"Marguerite..." He tightened his hands on her shoulders.

"Did I suspect that she was trying to poison Tony? No, of course not. But did I think that there was something wrong with her? At first I thought she was just childish, but recently—yes, I began to think there was something seriously wrong about her."

"Childish, yes. Delphine is such a child. She may not have realized how dangerous these seeds, this corn cockle, could be. Such a silly name, corn cockle. How could she think it deadly? She may have thought the seeds would just make people ill."

She opened her eyes to see Ned looking at her with pity in his eyes. She hated pity, and lifted her chin, which made him smile.

"That's better," he said. "Now think back. When her uncle died, how did she react? Was she horrified? Frightened?"

The memory came back—*Delphine looking up from her needlework when her mother came to break the news. "Then he cannot make me go back to the school," she had said with a smile, and went back to her needlework.*

"No." Marguerite drew the word out. "No. She was not horrified. She was not even upset. How could we not have noticed how strange that was?"

Suddenly she was furious, at she knew not what. "How could we not notice?" She began to beat on his chest with her fists. "Why didn't we notice? Why didn't we see that something was dreadfully wrong?"

Ned's hands rested gently on her shoulders, and he didn't even try to stop her. He just let her beat away at him until she collapsed against him in tears. "You said it yourself. You all thought she was childish, just as I did. No one would be likely to think anything else. No one would *want* to think anything else."

They began walking. She felt so safe walking with his arm around her shoulders. It was frightening how safe it felt. She did not want to think about how soon it must end, how soon they would have to part, so she put her arm around his waist to be closer.

"The next thing we must do," he began.

She straightened up, not having expected the farewell to

come so soon.

"The next thing we must do," he continued, "is to see if there are any more bottles of tonic floating around."

"Tonic?" That was not what she had expected, and her confusion made her feel a bit stupid.

"Yes. Dr. Fernac may have some on hand, and Tony may have an extra. If the tonic is something the good doctor frequently hands out to patients, the housekeeper may have a few bottles tucked away in the pantry. We can't assume any of them are safe so we need to get rid of any we find."

She stopped, and he looked at her in surprise. Formality. She needed formality. There was no other way she would be able to say what she must say. He would not say it himself, but it must be said. "Lord Edward, this is very kind of you, and I can never thank you enough for the help you have given me, but I think it is time for you to leave."

"Leave?" He seemed confused. Did he not realize that she was setting him free?

"Yes, leave. You have found the treasure for your friend, and he is safe now. No more harm will come to him. You need have no worry on that score."

He folded his arms and shook his head at her. "You really are the most ridiculous creature, Marguerite. You left out the most important thing of all."

Now she was confused. What had she forgotten?

"You forgot your promise to marry me." He took her arm to lead her into the house. "Now we need to get to work and find tonic and then see if your little cousin has a cache of those blasted seeds hidden anywhere."

Chapter Thirty-four

NED HAD TAKEN CHARGE AND SHE HAD LET HIM. MARGUERITE was not entirely sure how this had happened. She should not have allowed it—that much she knew. Delphine was her responsibility, not his.

But it was so much easier when he stepped in. If he asked Tony for any extra bottles of tonic, Tony just handed them over without demanding an explanation. When he asked the housekeeper, she immediately retrieved her bottles from the pantry and gave them to him. Even the doctor said nothing other than that he had no bottles at the chateau.

If she had asked, she would have had to say—what? What reason could she possibly have given for wanting the bottles? Would any excuse have been believable? But all Ned had to do was ask. Was it because he was an aristocrat? Or because he was a man? Or, perhaps, because he was Ned, and they all knew him well enough to trust him.

But Tante Héloise—Marguerite could not believe it.

When they reached Delphine's room, the older woman had just stopped out into the corridor where Horace was waiting, as if on guard. She held up a hand. "Hush. I have just gotten her to sleep."

Leaving Horace by the door, she led them into her own room before she questioned them. "What has happened? She was quite hysterical when I found her, and I could get no sense from her. She seemed to think the treasure had been stolen?"

"The treasure?" Marguerite was taken aback at first. "Ah, yes, of course. It was the treasure that Delphine would have been thinking about."

"But is that not what you have been spending all your time seeking?" Tante Héloise sounded exasperated. "What else would upset the girl?"

Ned intervened then. "Yes, Madame, she would be upset about the treasure. When we found it, it proved to be a medieval reliquary, a wooden bust containing a relic of Saint Mael." He smiled slightly. "It seems it was the treasure of the town of Morvan, not the family."

"Ah!" Tante Héloise was taken aback at first. She had doubtless been making the same assumptions about the treasure as everyone else. Then she shook her head and gave a sad little laugh. "No gold, no jewels—she must have been distressed indeed. It is just as well that I gave her some laudanum. At least she will sleep for a while, and we can hope that she will be calmer when she awakens."

"Unfortunately, her disappointment is not the real problem we face." No one seeing Ned's face could doubt his seriousness.

Tante Héloise shrugged dismissively. "Do not distress yourself. I know how to manage her. When she awakens, she may not even remember her disappointment. I will suggest a new way of dressing her hair, or a new trim for a gown, and she will cease to think about the treasure. It is very easy to distract that one."

"I am afraid that will not be enough," he said. "She has become dangerous."

Tante Héloise made a dismissive noise, but before she could speak, Marguerite interrupted. "She has been poisoning Tony."

The older woman turned in astonishment. "Poisoning…? That is impossible."

"I wish it were."

"The tonic he has been taking," Ned said. "Poisonous seeds were added to it."

"And you think Delphine did this? Impossible. How would she even know? She is just a child."

Marguerite reached out to touch her aunt's arm. "Tante Héloise, do you remember when her uncle came? She used to give him his tonic. The symptoms were the same."

"But he *died.* No. No." The old woman shook her head, but she had grown pale, terribly pale. "She could not do such a thing. You must be mistaken."

"I wish I were, Madame," Ned said, "but the chemist from the pharmacy in the village confirmed it."

Tante Héloise seemed to shrink and age right before their eyes. Ned put an arm around her shoulders and seated her by the fireplace. Marguerite added some wood to the fire. They all waited for the flames to catch.

Tante Héloise broke the silence. "I do not understand how this could be possible. What would she know of poisons?"

"Corn cockle. It was corn cockle, *agrostemme*," Marguerite said.

"*Agrostemme*?" Her aunt frowned. "There was a boy, a few years ago…the bread… It was in all the papers. But that was an accident."

Ned shook his head. "In flour, it could be an accident. But not in the tonic. Madame, we must search her things to see if she has any more of the seeds."

Tante Héloise was staring into the fire. "How could I not have realized?" Her voice was barely a whisper. "I knew there was something wrong. She could be selfish and vain, tiresome… but this?"

"Madame," Ned broke in.

"Yes, yes." She waved a hand without looking away from the flames. "Do what you will. What you must."

※

The search was not even difficult. Horace remained by the door, not questioning their entrance—he never questioned anything—and Delphine herself was immobile in her drugged sleep. They had barely begun to search when Marguerite found the bottle tucked in the drawer that held the girl's stockings.

She held it up and Ned took it from her. He pulled out the cork and poured a few of the seeds into the palm of his hand. They were unmistakable—twisted and covered with tiny prickles.

"She didn't even try to hide them." Disbelief, not fear of awakening Delphine, kept Marguerite's voice down to a whisper.

Ned glanced over at the girl, lying so serenely on the pillows. "I don't know if she truly realized she was doing something wrong." He put the cork back in the bottle and went to the tall window, which opened onto a small balcony. It looked out on nothing but the sea and space. An odd place for a balcony, he thought, but useful for his purpose.

He stepped out, and with one smooth motion he threw the bottle far out to sea. Against the gray clouds it was just a dark patch, rising into the air, then descending to vanish silently into the waves.

It traveled a long distance through the air. So had the tonic bottles that he'd disposed of earlier.

He was much stronger than she had first thought, seeing him in the loose-fitting garments he seemed to prefer. So much of his appearance was deceptive. He was quiet and reserved, almost diffident, until something more was needed. Then he stepped forward to take charge, to take care of everything and everyone in need of care.

She could not believe how much she loved him. Would she ever be able to tell him? Would she dare?

They were on their way to the drawing room when she suddenly realized. "Ned! The seeds, the tonic—they were evidence. Now they are gone. How can I convince people that she cannot be allowed…that she has… The authorities will never believe me. Tony will think I am the one who is mad."

"We are not going to involve any authorities and we are not going to tell Tony anything." He turned her to face him and rested his forehead against hers. "Tony is safe now, but if we tell him she has been poisoning him, we can't be sure how he will react. He may insist that she be locked up in an asylum. We need to take care of her ourselves. There is no need for authorities. If she poisoned her uncle…"

She tried to interrupt, but he put a finger on her lips. "*If* she poisoned him, there is no way to prove it any longer. We have only suspicion. And she has not poisoned Tony—he will be fine now. We will take care of her, and everyone will be safe. Even Delphine."

He smiled, and she almost believed that he could make it all come true.

Chapter Thirty-five

WHEN TONY CORNERED THEM THE NEXT MORNING, IT WAS obvious that his health was no longer a matter for concern. He had been searching for them, and was almost bouncing with delight.

"Where have you been? I've been looking all over for you."

Since he had been in Marguerite's bed, Ned did not want to answer that question, and he didn't want her to succumb to a fit of honesty and answer it either. But he needn't have worried. Tony wasn't interested in an answer.

"I told the old man what we found, and he was ecstatic. He knew that was what it was all along. Can you believe it?" Tony was striding around the library enthusiastically, paying no attention to his audience. "He knew what it was. He didn't tell us because he was afraid we wouldn't search for it. And he isn't nearly as senile as we thought. He perked up as soon as I told him we'd found it."

"That is good to know," Marguerite said politely.

"Well, I confess I wanted to shake him when I realized. But he has promised to make up the rest of the funding we need for the steel works, so all is well." Tony paused uncertainly. "I say, Delphine isn't going to cut up rough over this, is she? About not having a treasure to restore the chateau?"

"There's no need for you to worry about Delphine. She will be fine." Ned smiled, a trifle stiffly, and squeezed Marguerite's hand to keep her still.

"Well, if you're sure…" Tony's uncertainty vanished as quickly as it had appeared. "In any case, I need to send a telegram to let Georges know we are set. And then I must go down to the village."

Tony grinned. "It seems I can't just pick up that thing and haul it down to the church. The esteemed patriarch feels that some ceremony is necessary. I must speak to the mayor and the priest so that they can come to receive it from his hands." Tony rolled his eyes, but did not really seem upset. He was probably too delighted to have his financial worries relieved. "We must all be dressed in our finest, preferably draped in decorations, for the formal transfer—and that includes you. I told him you were the one who started us hunting for rosettes, and he will probably want to present you with some sort of reward."

"That is nonsense," Ned protested.

"Too late for objections. Your contribution has already been noted." Tony turned to leave, but paused. "Oh, by the way, this came for you." He handed Ned a telegram before he left.

A telegram? To say Ned was startled would be an understatement. He fingered the envelope nervously. Like many people, he thought of telegrams as harbingers of disaster. Why else would someone need to communicate with him so urgently?

"As you pointed out to me when I was hesitating over my letter, the only way to know what it says is to open it and read it," Marguerite said.

The worry eased as he looked at her. She was smiling, and he did not think she had ever teased him before. If she was now that comfortable with him, how bad could the news in the telegram be?

So he opened it.

"Ned? Ned?" Her voice seemed to be coming from a long way off. "What is it? Is it your family? Is someone ill?"

He recovered himself enough to manage a smile. "No, or rather yes. It is my family, but they are well. In fact, my parents have just been in Paris." He looked at the telegram again and took a deep breath. "And they have decided to pay me a visit."

"A visit?" Marguerite lost her smile. "Here?"

"Yes, here." He looked uncertain. "They probably plan to stay in a hotel."

"*Pftt.*" She waved a dismissive hand. "That is ridiculous. Impossible. There are no hotels here. I doubt that the village boasts so much as rooms above a tavern. They will stay at the chateau. I will tell the servants. When do they arrive?"

He looked back at the telegram, just in case he had completely misread the message. He hadn't. "Tomorrow. They arrive tomorrow."

She grew a bit paler, but nodded. "Tomorrow. I see." She started to leave.

"Marguerite," he called. When she turned back to him, he said, "They will love you, Marguerite. You will see."

"Did you tell them about me, then?"

"That we are going to be married? No, I thought that was something that should be said in person." He did not like her smile—it was too disbelieving, too cynical. But he persisted. "But of course I have told them about you, and everyone else here at the château. It is just that my mother has a habit of jumping to conclusions on very little evidence."

"Unwarranted conclusions?"

"No," he acknowledged wryly. "She is right more often than not."

Marguerite shook her head gently. "Which do you think is more likely, that your parents would come racing here to make the acquaintance of a woman they would welcome as a bride for their son? Or that they would come racing to rescue him from an unacceptable entanglement? No, do not answer that."

His increasing panic had nothing to do with the imminent arrival of his parents. She was withdrawing—he could feel it. He grabbed her by the shoulders to pull her to him. She did not resist, but neither did she respond. He had to keep himself from shaking some sense into her.

"Marguerite, you are going to marry me. You gave your word."

He did not think he had ever seen anything as sad as the smile on her face as she pulled back to leave. "We shall see what your parents say."

This was the end, then. She had not expected it so soon. She had thought there would be more time. But it was probably just as well. She was starting to depend on him too much.

When his parents arrived, he would see how impossible it was. She was a musician who played in public concerts, from a family of musicians who did the same. She had charge of a cousin who was clearly mad, an elderly quasi-aunt and a simple-minded servant. She had to earn a living to support all of them.

He came from a family of wealthy aristocrats and had been safe and secure all his life. He probably didn't even know the cost of a loaf of bread. It was not a gap that separated them—it was a chasm.

Hurrying to her room, she turned a corner too quickly and crashed into Tante Héloise.

"*Tiens!* Calm yourself." The older woman held her by the shoulders. "There is no need to rush. I have just left Delphine and she is quite calm."

"Delphine?" Marguerite put her fingers to her forehead and tried to think. Should she be worrying about Delphine?

"Yes. She is happily trying on gowns with a helpful maid to adjust the fit. It seems she has quite forgotten about the treasure, at least for the moment."

"The treasure. Of course." Marguerite made an effort to smile.

Tante Héloise was not fooled. "Something else is the matter. Something new? What is it?"

"Nothing. Really nothing. It is just that Lord Edward's parents will be arriving tomorrow, and I wanted to see about preparing rooms for them."

"His parents? Already?" Sympathy swept across the older woman's face. "Oh my poor child."

"It's all right. Really it is."

Tante Héloise shook her head and drew Marguerite into her embrace. "I know, I know. You thought to have more time with him. I thought you would, too."

Marguerite simply buried her face against the older woman's shoulder and let herself be rocked gently until she felt able to stand without support.

Tante Héloise cupped Marguerite's face in her hands then and looked at her with both pity and resolution. "You had to know this time would come. It is sooner than you expected, but still…"

"Yes, I always knew."

The older woman looked at her for a long moment before nodding her head. "Good. You will manage. I will see to it that Delphine does not bother you today. Would you like to go lie down for a while?"

"There is no need." Marguerite stiffened her back and held her head up. "I will go talk to the servants and make sure all is prepared. And by then it will be time to change for dinner."

She turned to leave but stopped and turned back. "Don't worry about me. I will be fine."

It wasn't until later in the evening, after an interminable dinner when Ned kept shooting worried glances at her, that Marguerite was able to curl up in her bed, pull the covers over her head, and let the tears flow. She didn't even notice when Ned came into her room until the bed sagged as he lay down beside her.

"What are you doing here?" She didn't know if she was angry or pleased.

"I am joining my beloved, just as I do every night." She could hear the smile in his voice. So foolish, his refusal to see that things had changed.

"But…" She couldn't find the words to convince him.

Then it didn't matter.

His mouth covered hers, silencing her, and then growing more and more insistent, demanding, possessive.

She could not help herself. Why should she resist? Her arms reached up to pull him close and tightened to keep him there.

One night. They could have this one last night.

They made love slowly and tenderly. It seemed as if every brush of their fingers, every breath they exchanged, was magical.

Afterward, she lay beside him, listening to his slow, even breathing. He was asleep. They were precious, these moments with him. "Never will I regret this time I have had with you," she whispered. "I have been so happy."

"And I intend to keep you happy for many years to come."

Startled, she lifted her head to look at him. "I thought you were asleep. Why were you pretending?"

He didn't look in the least bit drowsy. Just amused. "If I had been asleep, I would have missed that poignant confession."

The tears threatened again. She would not let them fall. "I suppose I should be glad that you are not greatly pained by our parting. I have never wished sorrow and regret on you."

"You are such a ninny. The only thing I could regret is losing you. And that is not going to happen."

She pushed away and lay on her back, staring up into the darkness. "My mother always regretted the estrangement from her family. Even though she loved my father, she always missed her mother and her sister. I don't want to cause you that kind of regret."

"And do you think she would have had no regrets if she had parted from your father instead? And how do you suppose your father would have felt if they had parted?"

"But you love your family. I can hear it in your voice when you talk about them. You would mind terribly if they disowned you."

He snorted in exasperation. "Really, Marguerite, not everyone is as foolish as your grandparents seem to have been. You must stop making yourself out to be a bloody martyr all the time."

"I am not doing anything of the sort." She sat bolt upright in outrage.

"Of course you are. You think you are responsible for everything and everyone, and you must always sacrifice yourself. You need to learn a little humility and admit that other people can solve problems, too."

"Why, you, you *arrogant*…"

"You see?" He grinned. "You don't want to let anyone else do anything."

She glowered at him. "I do not make myself a martyr."

"I am very glad to hear that. Now, come get some sleep. We have some interesting days ahead of us." He pulled her down and wrapped himself around her. "Pleasant dreams, my love."

She couldn't stop herself from sinking into the safety of his arms, but she did have to have the last word. "I am not a martyr."

Chapter Thirty-six

THE PENWORTHS ARRIVED FAR EARLIER THAN ANYONE HAD expected. The servants naturally coped with aplomb, ushering them into the warmest of the sitting rooms and providing them with refreshments. The butler, who seemed quite pleased, explained that the vicomte's family and guests were all gathered in his room rejoicing over the discovery of the treasure.

Once they were alone, Lady Penworth looked at her husband. "There actually was a treasure? I must confess that I am surprised."

"Hmm." He was looking around in a distracted way. "You know, this really is an odd place. From the way Ned wrote about it, I was expecting suits of armor draped in cobwebs with skeletal hands reaching out. Not…not this." He waved his hand at the furniture. "It looks more comfortable than my club."

"Yes, I see what you mean. Not that I've been in your club," she sniffed—that was a sore spot—"but all these leather chairs and sofas. The feminine touch is not much in evidence."

"Well, the vicomte has been living here alone for a good many years." He smiled gently.

They seated themselves and Lady Penworth had just taken a sip of really excellent coffee when a young woman swept into the room.

Lady Penworth froze momentarily, then put her cup down carefully and came to her feet. Her husband was already standing and looking at her with a plea for help in his eyes. She could understand his distress.

The young woman was quite beautiful. That was undeniably true. She had large blue eyes, a rosebud mouth, and a tiny chin. Her blonde hair was piled high on her head with a ringlet dangling down over her shoulder.

She was also wearing a gown of pale pink silk printed with a trellis of ribbons and small bouquets of flowers. The bodice was cut square—and very low—across the bosom and the narrow sleeves ended in a frill of lace. The skirt opened over an underskirt of a slightly darker pink and was held out straight on hoops for at least a foot at the sides.

In short, she was wearing a dress that would have been the height of fashion more than a century ago.

What on earth was going on? Did the inhabitants of this chateau habitually dress up in costumes? Were visitors expected to do so as well? Lady Penworth had no intention of doing any such thing.

Then there was her companion—a servant? Lady Penworth wasn't sure. He stood behind her, but not with the passive expression one expected of servants. This fellow, with his round, pasty face, looked worried. And the way his mouth hung slightly open—really, he looked simpleminded.

The girl sank into a graceful curtsy. *She did that very well*, thought Lady Penworth, *and it can't have been easy in that outfit*. Perhaps she was an actress and there was some sort of performance going on. Then the girl spoke, in English but with a pleasant French accent. "Monsieur le Marquis, Madame la Marquise, Lord and Lady Penworth, you are most welcome to Morvan."

Having survived far more awkward encounters over the years, the Penworths smiled graciously and inclined their heads in acknowledgment. "Delighted," said Lord Penworth. Then they waited.

"You cannot know how pleased I am that you have made the journey to meet me," said the girl. The Penworths looked at each other, unable to think of the proper response to that. The girl laughed lightly. "How foolish of me! Since Lord Edward is not here to present his betrothed properly, you must permit me to do so myself. I am Mademoiselle Delphine de Roncaille."

At that she curtsied deeply once more. Lady Penworth was grateful for the depth of that curtsy, since it meant the girl could not see the look of horror she shared with her husband. They had composed themselves somewhat by the time she rose, but before she spoke to them, she noticed that her companion was making distressed noises. She turned on him and waved a hand in dismissal. "Go find Madame."

Returning her attention to the Penworths, she assured them, "You must not distress yourselves. My parents and I are of *la noblesse ancienne,* the true nobility. Never has our bloodline been contaminated by the *bourgeoisie.* Nor do you need to fear that I will look down on Lord Edward because he is a younger son. It does not distress me at all."

"I am certainly glad to hear that," Lord Penworth said with a touch of acid in his voice.

Lady Penworth could not quite manage to speak. She was too angry. This nonsensical creature was going to marry Ned? Her son? Absolutely not! Thank heaven they had come here.

Mlle. de Roncaille apparently noticed a certain lack of enthusiasm, so she spoke reassuringly. "You need not worry yourselves. Since I am French, I understand how things should be arranged. You need not fear that I will make scenes or carry on."

"Carry on?" Lady Penworth's throat was so tight that her voice came out as something between a squeak and a crack.

The girl nodded and gave the Penworths an understanding smile. "I know how it is with gentlemen. I saw it with my own father. I know how these things are done. So you can trust that I will not interfere with any little arrangements Lord Edward chooses to make. Obviously there can be nothing more than an arrangement with Marguerite, but she will be in Paris. He can provide for her a home there. I, of course, will be here, once we have restored the rest of the chateau, or at Versailles."

"Versailles?" It was Lord Penworth's turn to sound befuddled.

"Yes, at the court." Mademoiselle smiled. "And you can rest assured that my lineage will suffice to make your son welcome there."

"Will it indeed." Lady Penworth spoke softly, but her fingers were curving into claws. Oh, she was very glad they had come here. It wasn't too late, but any more delay could have spelt disaster.

There was a flurry of noise—hurried footsteps, rustling clothing, and Ned burst into the room, followed closely by a woman in black.

Ned came to an abrupt halt. Mlle. de Roncaille turned to him with all the hauteur of a grand lady interrupted by her underlings. Lady Penworth noted the worried look on her husband's face and looked at her son with exasperation. He had better have a good explanation. She did not like having her husband distressed.

Ned and the woman in black exchanged a quick look. Then she hurried to Mademoiselle's side—perhaps she was the girl's keeper—while Ned went to his parents.

"I have been welcoming Lord Edward's parents," Mademoiselle informed the other woman. "And I have told them that I will not interfere with any little arrangement you have with him."

Lady Penworth allowed Ned's kiss on her cheek, but she was listening carefully to the women's conversation. What could the girl mean? There was no way Ned—her son—would carry on an affair with a servant. That would be a despicable abuse of privilege.

"That was most courteous and gracious of you," said the servant, if that's what she was, softly, moving so that the girl was drawn away from the Penworths. "And you are wearing a very beautiful gown this morning."

"Yes, I am." Mademoiselle looked down at it complacently.

The servant put a hand lightly on the girl's shoulder. "And

what will you wear to luncheon? I think it must be time for you to change. It is already past noon."

"Is it so late? Then I must indeed hurry. You will have to help me dress."

"Of course." The woman in black threw an apologetic glance over her shoulder as she led the girl out of the room.

Ned, meanwhile, had greeted his parents with a touch of embarrassment. "I apologize for not being here to greet you. We had not thought you could arrive so early."

"Your mother couldn't sleep, so we had an early start," said Lord Penworth dryly. "Very early."

His wife sniffed and gave her son an extra hug before stepping back. "Your young lady greeted us. Quite impressively." She spoke quite as dryly as her husband.

"She's very pretty." Lord Penworth sounded as if he was not sure that was the appropriate comment.

"Pretty?"

It sounded as if Ned did not know who he was talking about, so Lord Penworth said, "Mlle. de Roncaille. The young lady who greeted us. She is a very pretty girl."

Ned grinned. "Yes. That's the first thing people notice. Did you talk to her long enough to realize that she is also as mad as a hatter?"

Lady Penworth collapsed into a chair. She had not realized how tense she was until the fear evaporated. "Thank God."

"What's the matter?" Ned ran to her side.

She glared at her son. "You do realize that she introduced herself to us as your betrothed."

"Ah, yes. That." Ned rubbed the back of his neck. "It's a bit difficult."

"You do not mean you are planning to marry her?" Lady Penworth was horrified and made no effort to disguise the fact.

"Of course not." Ned sounded actually affronted. What had he expected them to think?

His father raised his brows. "Well, she is quite pretty in a fragile, damsel-in-distress, sort of way. And I suppose one might consider her in need of protection."

Ned still sounded annoyed. "Yes, but I can't believe you'd think me such a fool as to marry her. It's Marguerite that I'm planning to marry."

"Marguerite," repeated his mother. His parents exchanged glances. "Do you mean the musician you mentioned in your letters?"

"Yes. Mlle. Benda." Ned's face softened into a smile. "You saw her just now, but I didn't have a chance to introduce her. She's the one who took care of Delphine."

"The young woman in black?" Lady Penworth frowned slightly. "I thought she was a servant, so I didn't really look at her. She seemed to be the girl's keeper."

"I suppose she is, in a way. They're cousins, and Marguerite feels responsible for her. And, of course, since we're getting married, I am too."

"That must be a considerable relief to Miss Benda," said Lady Penworth. She looked at her husband again. "She sounds like a very clever girl."

Ned finally seemed to notice that his parents were less than happy about something, but before he could ask for an explanation, Tony came bursting in. Now there was someone in the room who was completely happy.

"Lord and Lady Penworth, welcome!" Tony greeted them exuberantly, with French embraces and kisses on each cheek. "You could not have come at a better time. Did you know? No, how could you? It was only the other day that we found the Morvan Treasure, thanks to your brilliant son."

"The treasure?" Lord Penworth said. "The butler mentioned it. So there really was one?"

"Indeed, and but for Ned's cleverness, we might never have found it."

"The treasure?" Lady Penworth couldn't help being interested in spite of herself.

"No, Mama, we did not dig up chests of gold and jewels," Ned said with a laugh. "The treasure turned out to be a reliquary containing the bones of St. Mael, and will now be restored to the church in the village, where it belongs."

"Bones." Lady Penworth said the word as if it had an unpleasant flavor.

Tony laughed at the fallen faces. "You look as disappointed as my cousin Delphine. But cheer up. In a few days we will have an elaborate ceremony. The priest and all the village officials will come, there will be speeches, and a procession will carry St. Mael back to his place of honor in the church."

"And you? Are you not disappointed that there is no treasure to invest in your steel factory?" Lord Penworth asked.

"It doesn't matter." Tony could not stop smiling. "My great grandfather is so pleased to have the treasure found that he has promised to provide the funding we need to get started. Our lost investors no longer worry me."

"That reminds me," Penworth said. "Ned had asked if I knew anything about a fellow named Louvois. I didn't, but I asked some people in Paris, and it seems that he may have been behind the hesitation of some people at the Crédit Mobilier to back you. Have you had problems with him before?"

Tony looked startled. "I've never even heard of him."

Ned was aghast. "No. He went after you because you are related to Marguerite. He probably thought he could punish her through you."

"But why?" Tony looked even more confused.

"He is that bastard who showed up here not long ago—he was trying to force Marguerite to be his mistress," Ned explained. "When he failed, he must have been trying to get revenge by targeting you, Tony."

"Force her…?" Lady Penworth was finding this more and more distasteful.

"Yes, Mama. It seems he had enough influence to prevent her from working in Paris, but that's all taken care of now."

"Yes," she said softly. "I suppose it is."

Lord Penworth was frowning. "An unpleasant fellow. I discovered that he had also caused some uncertainty about the funds Matthias Benda had on deposit. But he shouldn't cause any more trouble. Alphonse de Rothschild doesn't like it when people try to insert personal vendettas into the banking system."

"I'm sure Miss Benda knows she has nothing more to worry about," Lady Penworth said. Her words were perfectly amicable, but Ned looked as if he was unsure of her meaning.

Good.

Chapter Thirty-seven

THAT AFTERNOON, MARGUERITE FOUND HERSELF ALONE WITH Lady Penworth. They were in the small parlor where Ned had once fed her tea and cakes. It was still a pleasant room with a warming fire, but Lady Penworth did not look as if she was planning on a cozy chat over the teacups.

Ned's mother was a formidable woman, still beautiful though she must have been near sixty and did not pretend otherwise. There were lines on her face, but there was no stooping in her posture. Her dark hair was shot with silver but becomingly arranged. Her gown, of deep red silk faille trimmed with black velvet, was the acme of the dressmaker's art. The bustle was more pronounced than anything Marguerite owned, and she felt quite shabby in her black wool.

That momentary reaction made her stiffen her own posture. Why should she be embarrassed by her unfashionable gown? She was not some languid daughter of wealth who had nothing to do all day but change her clothes. She owned a few gowns that she wore for performances, and the rest of her dresses served for all other activities. They had been chosen for practicality, not style.

But at the moment, she would have traded them all for a gown a tenth as stylish as Lady Penworth's.

The maid brought in a tea tray and placed it in front of Marguerite. It reminded her that here she was acting as hostess. Lady Penworth accepted a cup from her—milk first, one sugar—

and one of the small cakes called madeleines. Then she waited.

Lady Penworth took a small bite, barely a nibble. "Delicious," she said.

"Yes," Marguerite agreed. "The vicomte has an excellent chef."

Lady Penworth looked down at her tea as she stirred it and then looked up at Marguerite. "I notice that you refer to the vicomte by his title, and not by his relationship to you."

Marguerite lifted her shoulders and offered a French *moue*. "That is a matter of courtesy. It is a distant relationship. He is my what, great-great-uncle? Or should there be another great? In any case, his family disowned my mother, so I do not feel any particular kinship."

"Yet here you are, living in his chateau."

"Here I am," Marguerite agreed. "And I am very grateful for his invitation, which came at a difficult time for me, after my father died."

"Very fortunate. And now you are to marry my son."

"Is that what he told you?" Marguerite permitted herself a small smile.

Up went Lady Penworth's brows. "Was he mistaken? Has he not asked you to marry him?"

"He has. But I told him I would hesitate to marry him if his family disapproved." Marguerite sipped her own tea, proud of the fact that her hand did not tremble.

The silence was growing uncomfortable by the time Lady Penworth spoke again. "Tell me, Miss Benda, is there some reason why his family should *not* approve of you?"

The corner of Marguerite's mouth lifted in what might be considered a half-smile. "You have met my cousin Delphine, have you not?"

Lady Penworth nodded.

"She is my responsibility, and she seems to be sinking further into madness." Marguerite abruptly stopped. She had not put that realization into words before, and the truth of it came as a bit of a shock.

"Many people have relatives who…need to be cared for." Lady Penworth spoke carefully. "There are hospitals…"

Marguerite cut her off with an abrupt gesture. "No. I promised my mother, as she promised Delphine's mother, that she would not be put in an asylum. But that is not the main problem, is it?"

"Is it not?"

"Let us not pretend, Lady Penworth. I am a professional musician, from a family of professional musicians. You and your family are aristocrats. We both know that while aristocrats often patronize artists and musicians, admire them, and even befriend them, they do not marry them."

Lady Penworth put down her cup and sat back in her chair. "Well, that is plain speaking."

Marguerite lifted a shoulder. "I have not lived in aristocratic households, as you have, but I have encountered aristocrats over the years. They generally consider themselves a higher order of being, as if the fact that they know the names of their ancestors for half a dozen generations confers special privileges on them. Those privileges entitle them to whatever they want, whenever they want it. Are you telling me that your family is different?"

"A somewhat jaundiced view, one might say."

Another shrug. "Or perhaps simply realistic."

"Yet the world is full of people who would be more than happy to join the ranks of those privileged aristocrats. After all, if you marry my son, you would no longer be obliged to perform on the stage." Lady Penworth's smile, though cold, was a trifle smug.

It was Marguerite's turn to sit back in surprise. "Obliged? You do not seem to understand, my lady. I am a musician. I play and I compose. That is what I do. I could no more stop doing it than I could stop breathing. Ned understands this, even if you do not."

"Well, of course many ladies play…"

"*Pfft.*" Marguerite made a face. She was growing seriously

angry. How could a woman of so little understanding be the mother of a man like Ned? "They play for guests who chat or sleep. Oscar Villoteau, the impresario, is arranging a concert tour for me that Liszt himself will sponsor. And I will play my own sonata, that I have composed and that Liszt has praised. Do you think I do this because I am *obliged*?"

She stood up and stared down at Lady Penworth. "Think about it, my lady. If Ned marries me, you will not be getting a decorative little daughter-in-law who can be brought out to entertain the company." Suddenly Marguerite was furious. "I am a Benda. My family have been musicians, known and honored for well over a hundred years. My father was the famed Matthias Benda, the most brilliant violinist in all of Europe. You think I am not good enough for your son? What has your family done that makes you think you are good enough for me?"

With that she flung out of the room, head high.

Left alone in the room, Lady Penworth sat immobile for a moment, then picked up one of the madeleines, dipped it in her tea, and took a bite. As she chewed, she thought. She considered the uncomfortable possibility that she had misunderstood the situation.

No. It was not a possibility. It was a certainty. She had made insulting assumptions about Miss Benda, and she had seriously underestimated Ned. She grimaced. Apologies were uncomfortable, but it appeared they would be necessary.

Then she smiled. A musician. She had attended innumerable concerts over the years, and had learned quite a bit about music from the listener's point of view. And while she had on occasion shaken hands with the performers and murmured a few words of thanks, she had never actually known any musicians. Now she would have one right in the family.

This would be interesting.

A whole new world was opening up for her.

Ned took his father up to the tower where the archives were stored. He spoke enthusiastically about the incredible resources he had found here, the letters he planned to edit, the light that would be shined on the attitudes of the lesser aristocracy, all the while noting with amusement that his father was paying no attention at all.

"And then," he said, "I thought I might take the remaining papers, fashion them into wings, and fly out over the ocean."

His father nodded. "Very interesting."

Ned sighed. "Suppose you just say what it is that's on your mind."

Lord Penworth looked slightly embarrassed. "I don't want to interfere in your life…"

Ned grinned. "Of course you do. At least, Mother does."

"Well, she worries about our children. As do I, of course." He seemed to be avoiding his son's eye. "And we couldn't help noticing that while you mentioned this young woman in your letters, you did not actually say very much about her."

"Young lady," Ned said. His grin vanished. "Miss Benda is a lady."

"Of course." Lord Penworth looked at his son then. "She is a lady who appears on the public stage."

"You make it sound as if she is some music hall performer." Ned glared at his father. "She is a brilliant musician. Her father was Matthias Benda, who was the finest violinist of the century, and her mother was the daughter of French aristocrats. Her birth is at least equal to mine, if not better. I'll not have you sneering at her."

"Is that what I was doing? I thought I was simply endeavoring to get my facts straight."

Ned paced over to the window and stared out while he collected himself. When he turned back to face his father, he spoke, he thought, quite calmly. "I intend to marry Miss Benda, and I need you and Mother to approve and welcome her into the family."

"Are you asking my permission?"

"No. Your approval. Marguerite says she will not marry me without it."

"Ah." Lord Penworth smiled slightly. "She is worried about her acceptance in society."

"Don't be ridiculous," Ned snapped. "That does not matter in the least to either of us. But her mother was disowned by her parents when she married Benda, and Marguerite says she does not want that to happen to me."

"We could never disown you." Penworth looked horrified. "We could never disown any of our children!"

"I know that." Ned did smile now. "But Marguerite's experience of her mother's family has left her…distrustful. And there is a long distance between welcoming acceptance and disavowal." Noting the uncertainty on his father's face, he added softly, "She is not a fool, you know."

"No, I understand that. Indeed, I begin to think she is very clever."

Penworth's dry tone was not encouraging, but Ned refused to consider it definitely *dis*couraging.

"You must try to understand," Ned said. "No one has ever needed me, not really, but she needs me. She does not realize it, but she does. Just as I need her. She can take care of herself, just as she has always done, but I can protect her, make her life easier in a dozen different ways."

A light of understanding grew in his father's eyes.

"And I need the fact that she needs me," Ned continued. "She has no family to take care of her, only people who depend on her, so she needs me. I know that you and Mother and all my family love me, but you do not need me. Marguerite does."

Lord Penworth stood still, saying nothing for a long moment. Finally he nodded. "I think I understand, but speaking of family, I don't quite understand her relationship with her cousin."

"Ah, yes." This was probably going to be a bit difficult to explain, but it couldn't be avoided. "I have a plan for that," Ned said.

Penworth was waiting when his wife returned to their room. *Waiting* was perhaps not quite the correct term. He was wandering around, picking things up—a statuette here, a small vase there—not really looking at them, and putting them back down again, rarely in their original place.

"There you are," she said. She sat down in one of the chairs flanking the fireplace and held out her hands to the warmth of the flames. "I think we may have misunderstood the situation."

"Misunderstood? After talking to Ned, I can assure you that he is quite determined to marry Miss Benda. And he seems to have put quite a bit of thought into how to deal with the various problems." Penworth smiled wryly. "Indeed, he is far more practical about the whole thing than I thought he could be."

"Practical? Ned?" Lady Penworth thought about it for a moment. "Well, I don't suppose he has ever had to be before. But I was thinking about Miss Benda. She is not quite what I expected."

"No?"

She waved a hand. "Yes, I know you said he wasn't a fool and wouldn't fall in love with an avaricious little harpy. But I couldn't help worrying. And a performer, practically an actress."

"Well, as to that…"

"I know, I know. I exaggerate. And when I saw that pretty little blonde lunatic, I was sure he had just decided to ride to the rescue. I am not precisely enamored of Miss Benda, but at least she seems to be sane. And she certainly isn't spineless." Lady Penworth did not precisely shudder, but she felt some discomfort as she recalled their interview.

"Yes, about Miss de Roncaille." When his wife looked momentarily blank, Penworth said, "The lunatic."

She nodded. "I had forgotten her name. What about her?"

He took a deep breath. "Well, it appears that Miss Benda considers herself responsible for her cousin."

"Commendable, I'm sure. And I am sure no one would wish to see the girl consigned to a public madhouse. But surely a place for her can be found in some private hospital. Don't the Quakers have some sort of establishment that is quite highly thought of?"

Penworth shook his head. "No. It seems that Miss Benda promised her mother that she would not let her cousin be locked up in an asylum."

Lady Penworth was taken aback. "Promises are all very well and good, but surely it is obvious that something has to be done about the girl. I mean, she is clearly under the impression that she is living during the *ancien régime*. She cannot be allowed to simply wander about. And I hope Ned doesn't expect to have her live with us."

"I told you he was being very practical," Penworth said, with a slight smile. "No, he does not intend to foist her off on us like one of those wounded animals he used to acquire. He thinks to buy a place in the country, perhaps somewhere between Oxford and London, with enough land to have a cottage for the cousin, where she can live with people to take care of her."

"Keepers, you mean."

"Well, yes. But where he and Miss Benda can keep an eye on her."

Lady Penworth looked skeptical. "Keep an eye on her so that she isn't abused, or keep an eye on her so that she doesn't harm anyone?"

"Both, I suspect." He cleared his throat.

"There's more?"

"In addition to the girl, there is also an elderly relative, Mme. d'Hivers, and a young man, somewhat simple, who will have to live with them."

Lady Penworth's eyes widened. "A simpleton? An elderly relative, yes, that's ordinary enough, but where on earth did the simpleton come from?"

"He's an orphan. It seems her father rescued him from some

boys who were tormenting him and he somehow ended up part of the family."

"And Miss Benda considers herself responsible for all of them?"

Penworth nodded.

Lady Penworth stared at the fire for a moment, and then began to laugh. "I must say our children never seem to marry into boring families!"

That evening, Marguerite was not in bed when Ned came to her room. She was sitting by the fire, wrapped in a shawl, and gestured for him to sit in the chair opposite her.

He did so and waited. She kept her face averted while she seemed to be trying to decide how to say something.

"I have been thinking," she said.

There was a long pause. She did not seem to have finished thinking, so Ned sat there and watched her. She looked dreadfully serious. Serious enough to make him worry about the direction of those thoughts.

"I lied to you, and I lied to your mother as well," she finally blurted out.

"Did you?"

"I did not mean to do so. At the time, I thought it was the truth. I think perhaps I was lying to myself as well."

"Really?" This sounded more promising. He was finding it difficult not to smile.

"Yes. I told her what I told you—that I would not marry you unless your family approved." She looked at him them. "I have changed my mind. I am too selfish, not as honorable as I should be. I want you too much and I will not give you up."

"Thank heaven!" He fell back in the chair. "It's about time you realized that. I was beginning to think I would have to keep you in bed until you were too dizzy to think and then drag you in front of a priest before you could recover your wits."

She could not repress her smile, but still shook her head. "You are a fool, you know. I will be a very bad wife. I get lost in my music and forget everything else. Meals will not be on time, and I will neglect to order the coal."

He stood and pulled her up into his arms. "I have been known to forget meals too when I am working, and the housekeeper will order the coal."

"Ah, I keep forgetting." She laughed softly. "You are an aristocrat and don't have to worry about such things."

"And you are an artist, and don't worry about such things."

Suddenly serious again, she said, "I do love you, you know. I cannot seem to help myself."

"That is all that matters." He kissed her and a future full of promise lay before them.

Chapter Thirty-eight

TO THE ASTONISHMENT OF LORD AND LADY PENWORTH, THE vicomte de Morvan made a remarkable recovery. He was bright-eyed and alert, welcoming them with courteous ceremony when they were presented to him, and while he was not precisely vigorous, neither was he the feeble, bedridden invalid they had been expecting.

Ned, after noting the doctor's calm acceptance of the change, was less astonished. He commented on this to Tony, who also failed to be amazed.

"Did he think we wouldn't bother to look for the blasted thing if he'd told us what it was?" Tony shook his head in disgust.

"Well, to be fair," Marguerite said, "we might not have looked with quite as much enthusiasm. Delphine wasn't the only one envisioning a chest full of gold and jewels."

They turned to look at the girl, who seemed to have recovered from the shock of disappointment, at least sufficiently to be dressed in normal fashion. She was fluttering prettily around the vicomte, who was sitting up in a throne-like chair by the fireside. He wore a dressing gown of crimson velvet and his legs were covered with a thick blanket, protecting him from any chill.

Although he smiled benignly at his relatives and other visitors, and thanked Ned most graciously for his perspicacity in unraveling the secret, his attention was focused on the ceremony that would restore the Treasure to the village. The steward, a man

Ned had never even seen before, acted as second in command, noting down the vicomte's orders and sending minions off to do his bidding.

It took almost a week for the preparations to be in order. This was in part because the vicomte wanted the presentation to take place in the hall of the chateau, the place where the priest had died. While his young relatives had made some effort toward cleaning up while they searched for a treasure, they had made only the slightest of inroads into the dust of decades. Every servant in the household was put to work dusting and scrubbing and polishing.

The Penworths would have departed but the vicomte insisted that, far from intruding, they were necessary for the celebration. After all, it was their son who had penetrated the secret that had kept the Treasure hidden all these years. In addition, he said with a smile in Marguerite's direction, he suspected that their families might be united in the not too distant future.

While the cleaning proceeded, Delphine set about creating floral decorations—a task at which she excelled, Tony attempted to compose a speech that would meet with his great-grand-father's approval, and Marguerite supervised the moving of the harpsichord to the hall, where she was to provide musical accompaniment for the ceremony and procession.

Although Marguerite approached her part in the coming extravaganza with tense concentration, Ned's first reaction had been amusement. "I'm surprised the vicomte doesn't want an entire orchestra," he said.

She did not even seem to hear him, so intent was she on getting the three footmen who had been carrying the instrument to place it precisely where she wanted it. But she had heard. After she had dismissed the footmen, she turned to him. "He would have liked that, but there are no musicians in the village and there was not time to import an orchestra from Paris." With that, she took a deep breath, lifted the lid of the harpsichord, and propped it open.

Although he had heard her playing for the vicomte, Ned had never seen the harpsichord before, and he was sorely tempted to laugh. Not that the instrument was not beautiful: the sides were painted a deep pink with garlands of roses and gilded swirls, all very artistic. It was the painted interior of the lid, visible only when the harpsichord was open, that prompted his reaction.

A naked goddess reclined on a couch amid lush draperies, with servants laying offerings of flowers before her and cherubs hovering above her.

Trying to keep a straight face, he asked, "Won't the priest be a bit shocked by the instrument?"

She looked confused for a moment, then realized what he was looking at and laughed. "Do you know, I'm so accustomed to her that I no longer notice. But you need not fear that she will cause a scandal. No one will see her, because I will be playing behind a curtain. Now you must go away. I need to practice." She made a shooing motion with her hands before sitting down at the keyboard and ignoring him completely.

Ned started to say good-bye but realized it was pointless. She had started playing and did not even notice the noise of the servants busily working in the hall. It seemed as if her entire being was concentrated in her fingers. With a smile, he left her to it. He was going to have to get used to this.

The day of the presentation dawned bright and clear. For once, the sky was blue, not gray. The wind was, if not vanished, at least subdued—a breeze, not a gale. Though the November sun rose late and hung low on the horizon, it was still strong enough to provide some warmth for the villagers who arrived at the chateau gates.

It looked as if the entire village had turned out—the male half of the village, at any rate. An acolyte, holding high a ceremonial cross, led the procession. He was followed by a priest in splendidly embroidered vestments, accompanied by two more acolytes with censers. Four more acolytes followed, carrying something that looked rather like a stretcher. Then came the schoolboys, neatly two by two, in their blue smocks. And after them came the villagers, somberly dressed in dark coats and top hats.

Ned was suddenly grateful that Marguerite had warned him to dress formally in a black dress coat and pantaloons, with a silk waistcoat and top hat. Anything less would have been an insult to the occasion. His parents, standing beside him, were naturally dressed in the proper formality. His mother wore a costume—it had too many parts to be called just a dress—in two shades of violet, bright enough to be festive, sedate enough to prevent her from becoming the center of attention.

Tony, representing the family, greeted the procession at the door and led them into the hall where the vicomte sat enthroned on a gilded chair upholstered in tapestry. No one could mistake him for a young man. He was pale and shriveled, almost insubstantial. Yet his eyes were bright and he held himself erect and looked on the procession with a benign air. Beside him, Delphine hovered like a butterfly in her bright silks. The music from the hidden harpsichord floated over them all like an otherworldly benediction.

Tony gave his speech of presentation, the priest gave his speech of acceptance, and the mayor spoke of the gratitude of the village. Then the vicomte raised his hand. His voice was thin, but did not quaver. "Many years ago, l'abbé Seznec entrusted the Treasure of Morvan to the care of my family. Now, at last, we fulfill our responsibility and restore the Treasure to its rightful place." He gestured to the table at his side. Tony moved the Treasure to the front, and the vicomte lifted the silk cloth.

The reliquary had been carefully cleaned so that the gold shone and the gems glowed. Marguerite's brooch now gleamed in its proper place. Whether the placement had been deliberate or not, the sunlight coming through the glass cupola bathed the

Treasure in glory. A collective gasp ran through the gathering, and many of the villagers fell to their knees.

The priest held out his hands and chanted a prayer in Latin, of which Ned understood not a word but he bowed his head along with everyone else. Then two acolytes waved their censers about, and the smoke of the incense surrounded the reliquary before drifting up to the dome. The stretcher brought in by the remaining acolytes proved to be a palanquin. The reliquary was placed on it; they hoisted it to their shoulders and led the procession out while the schoolboys followed, chanting a *Te Deum.*

Ned found himself unable to move. He wasn't sure what he had expected. Emotional outbursts, perhaps. Sobs and cries of joy. What he had not expected was this dignified reverence. There was joy, but joy restrained by awe. He had not been able to help himself—he had bowed his head when the reliquary was carried past him and stared after the procession till it was out of sight. When he looked around, he was struck by the expression of peace and joy on the vicomte's face. Beside him, Delphine smiled angelically and put a protective hand on the old man's shoulder.

Those remaining in the hall stood in silence until they heard the outer doors close, shutting off the sound of the chanting. The vicomte relaxed then, leaning against the back of his chair and smiling up at Delphine, patting her hand.

At that moment, his attention was drawn back to his parents. Lady Penworth reached out a hand to her husband, who passed his handkerchief to her.

"Are you all right?" Ned asked. His mother did not go in for public displays of emotion, and it was unnerving to see her dabbing at her eyes.

"I don't know what's the matter with me," Lady Penworth whispered. "I was prepared to be polite. I know this is all superstitious nonsense. But somehow…all these people…and the music…it was really very moving."

Chapter Thirty-nine

Dinner that evening was the most peaceful meal Marguerite had ever eaten at the chateau—and Delphine was not present. All the tension of the past weeks and months had dissipated, and not only because the Treasure had been found and restored to its rightful place.

Assured of funding for his factory, Tony was a relaxed and charming host. It probably helped that his digestive woes were at an end now that he was no longer being poisoned—thank heaven. She could not believe that they had escaped tragedy so easily. But there he was, enthusiastically tucking into his boned quail stuffed with *foie gras*. She could not remember seeing him so cheerful. Of course, she recalled, when she had first arrived she had been so wrapped up in her own worries that she hadn't paid a great deal of attention to him.

She was relaxed as well. And, she admitted to herself, she was pleased with her appearance. Her black velvet gown, trimmed with satin, was becoming even if it was nowhere near as fashionable as Lady Penworth's blue silk splendor. Since she had no jewels, she had tied a satin ribbon around her neck.

Ned's parents were also being charming and…friendly. Not that strained graciousness of people who would like to drown you in the nearest ditch but are too courteous to say so. No. They had been warming to her over the past week. This evening, the smiles they gave her were truly welcoming, and Lord Penworth complimented her on her appearance.

Had it been her own defensiveness that saw dislike and distrust when she first met them? She did not think so. But whatever the reason, she was grateful, especially since she had told Ned that she didn't care what his parents said. She was going to marry him.

They also seemed to look at their son differently. When they'd arrived, their affection for him had been obvious, but it had been tinged with exasperation—rather the way parents look at a beloved child who has fallen into a mud puddle and ruined his good clothes *again!* Now, however, father and son were discussing some point about English politics and Lord Penworth was listening to Ned's comments with respect.

As for Lady Penworth, she was talking to Marguerite about music—quite knowledgeably for someone who was not herself a musician. She wanted to know about the piece Marguerite had played during the presentation. "It sounded rather like Bach, but it was not, I think, anything I had ever heard before," she said.

"It was a concerto by someone named Telemann."

"Telemann." Lady Penworth frowned in thought. "I don't believe I have ever heard of him."

"Nor had I. The harpsichord is not my instrument, so I am not familiar with the repertoire, but it soothed the vicomte to hear me play it. I had to go through the music stored here to find pieces to play, and this was one of them. It seemed to belong to the age before all the violence took over."

"Before the violence took over," Lady Penworth repeated. "Yes, that is a good way to put it. Do you suppose this recent foolish war with Prussia will mean the end of it?"

Marguerite shrugged. The only thing she knew of wars and politics was that the farther from those in power one was, the safer one was. However, she had gathered from Ned that his parents were near the centers of power in England. Perhaps it was safer in England than on the Continent. This was something she would have to grow accustomed to.

Ned had accepted her family with all its problems and oddities—not just Delphine and her delusions but also Tante Héloise and poor, simple Horace. Even if, as he assured her, he could easily afford to provide for them, how many men would be willing to do so?

In her turn, she would have to grow accustomed to his family. It wasn't that they were odd, but they had a different way of looking at the world. They did not have to treat the powerful with caution, because they were themselves the powerful.

Lady Penworth certainly didn't seem to find questions of war and peace intimidating. She discussed them as casually as Marguerite's father and his friends debated the merits—or lack thereof—of Berlioz and Wagner.

However, at the moment Lady Penworth seemed prepared to put political debate aside. She raised her glass in a small, private toast and said, "Let us hope that there will now be peace, not just for France, but for all of us."

Yes, peace. There was peace at the moment. Better yet, there was no fear. Marguerite had lived with fear for so long that it had taken her a while to recognize its absence. She caught Ned's eye across the table and for a brief moment they both sat motionless, smiling, happy.

She was very grateful that Delphine had declared herself too weary from all the ceremony to dine with the others, and ordered a small collation brought to her room. But even thoughts of Delphine could not distress her too much. Ned's plan to provide her with a house of her own and guardians in the guise of servants sounded as if it would not only solve that problem but solve it painlessly for all of them.

She rose from the table, still trying to come to terms with the realization that she did not have to be afraid any longer. She was going to have everything she had ever wanted—Ned, music, opportunity to perform, time to compose—and those who depended on her would be safe.

Before she reached the doorway, Tante Héloise stopped her.

"It is all right then?" the older woman asked, tilting her head in Lady Penworth's direction. "His parents, they are agreeable?"

"Yes." Marguerite felt like spinning around with joy, but held herself to a smile. "Yes, all is well with his parents."

Tante Héloise raised her brows, surprised, but nodded. "If it is well—then I am happy for you. It is time for good things to come to you."

The vicomte had been too weary to dine with them, but they were to join him in his rooms for coffee. Marguerite walked down the corridor with her hand on Ned's arm, savoring the warmth of his nearness, the hidden strength of him. In front of them, Tony was burbling away about the new steel process they would be using, waving his hands about in a thoroughly French fashion.

Leaning down to Marguerite, Ned murmured, "You would never realize it to look at him now, but Tony was the complete English schoolboy when we were growing up. Now he seems more French every day."

Marguerite started to laugh, but the smile froze on her face when she stepped through the vicomte's door. Delphine was seated beside the old man and he was patting her hand.

Behind her she heard low voices.

"The young woman appears to have recovered from her fatigue," Lady Penworth said.

Tante Héloise was less charitable. *"Diantre!* I should never have left her alone. Horace cannot control her."

Obviously. Marguerite could see Horace hunched over in a corner of the room, looking miserable.

The vicomte and Delphine, on the other hand, were looking delighted with each other.

"There you all are!" The vicomte beamed at them. "I trust you dined well. This pretty child has been keeping me company." He patted Delphine's hand again, and she ducked her head shyly.

Marguerite hissed in a breath. As if Delphine had ever been shy! But before she could say anything, Ned pressed her hand

and gave her a warning look. He was right. This was no time to make a fuss, especially when she did not know if there was anything she should be making a fuss about. There were times when Delphine behaved in a charming, perfectly sane, manner.

This seemed to be one of those times. Delphine was dressed appropriately in her favorite dinner dress of mauve gros grain trimmed with flounces of satin and lace, and she sat quite still with a small smile on her face. Marguerite was not sure she trusted that smile, but there was nothing she could do. Or was there?

The vicomte was near the fire, sitting up in a high-backed armchair with a blanket covering his legs. Delphine was sitting at his left and there was a small table to his right on which rested a cup of coffee. Great God in Heaven! Delphine had been giving him his coffee? What if there had been seeds they did not find? What if Delphine had some other poison hidden away?

The chair next to him should have been for Lady Penworth, the highest-ranking lady in the room. Too bad. Marguerite didn't care if her future in-laws considered her rude and mannerless. She had to get at that coffee cup.

Hurrying across the room in front of Lady Penworth, Marguerite seated herself beside the vicomte. Ned followed but looked at her quizzically. She met his eye, then glanced at the coffee cup and looked back at him.

Thank heaven he was not a fool. He understood immediately and took the chair next to her.

Once they were all seated, servants came around, bringing coffee and small glasses of liqueur. Marguerite removed the vicomte's cup, saying "This must be cold by now," and replacing it with a fresh cup. At least she hadn't needed to knock it out of his hand. He looked startled, but said nothing.

Delphine noticed the maneuver, but looked amused rather than frustrated. There had probably been nothing wrong with the coffee. Probably. Marguerite would give a great deal to be certain.

The vicomte waited until they were all served before he spoke again. "I believe I owe you an apology for being less than forthright about the Treasure."

Marguerite found it amazing that his voice was so much stronger. A week ago, the vicomte had been as fragile as a desiccated leaf. Today it was difficult to remember that he was ninety years old.

"It had been entrusted to our family, and the burden of having lost it weighed on me more and more as the years passed. I should have trusted you, but I feared that you might not view it in the same way. So much of the past has been overturned. Men view with disdain what we once viewed with reverence." He shook his head.

Tony looked a bit uncomfortable, a feeling Marguerite shared. She knew that Tony was inclined to share the anticlerical views of the revolutionaries. Her own family had been more indifferent to religious observances than anything else. Ned, who was fascinated by the past and sought to understand vanished ways of thinking, was the one who truly appreciated the significance of the Treasure.

"But now I need no longer feel ashamed to return to the home of my family," the vicomte continued. "As I have been telling my young niece here"—he smiled at Delphine—"I can now restore the chateau to its glory."

"Oh yes," Delphine said softly. Her face was positively glowing as she turned to the others. "Did I not tell you, Marguerite? It will be the perfect setting for me. The chateau is the home I have always dreamed of."

Marguerite started to open her mouth, but she could not think what to say.

"And you, my child, are as lovely as the setting." The vicomte beamed at Delphine. "You will be a worthy chatelaine for the Chateau Morvan."

Marguerite finally found her voice. "But, Delphine, I thought it was agreed that you would live with me."

Sudden fury flooded Delphine's face, making her almost ugly. Marguerite flinched before it.

"Not now," whispered Ned, putting a hand on her arm. "There is no need to talk about it now."

His face was white—he knew what she was afraid of—but what he said was sensible, she knew. Any protest she could make would provoke a scene and accomplish nothing. It would make things worse. Already she could see Ned's parents looking at each other, wondering what was going on. She was going to have to tell them. How were they going to react to the news that Delphine was not just mad but murderous as well?

The old vicomte seemed oblivious to the tension. "There is no need for you to worry, Marguerite. The little Delphine is more than welcome to make her home here." He continued to talk about his plans for the renovation of the chateau.

Delphine smiled smugly.

Marguerite tried not to panic.

Chapter Forty

"Not tonight," Ned said, grabbing hold of Marguerite's arm when she was about to follow her cousin down the hall to their bedrooms. "You can't accomplish anything at the moment."

Mme. d'Hivers joined them. "Do not worry. I will take care of her."

"How? You cannot…" Marguerite shook her head violently.

"Stop that!" The older woman spoke sharply. "Calm yourself. I will see that she creates no difficulties and goes quickly to sleep this evening. We will talk about it in the morning." After a quick nod in Ned's direction, she hurried after Delphine.

"But Delphine can't be allowed to think that she will actually live here with the vicomte." Marguerite sounded on the verge of hysteria. "I have to stop this nonsense."

"Shh." He pulled her around a corner and held her tightly, pressing her to his chest. He had no idea how to deal with this latest development, but that didn't matter at the moment. He could figure that out later. Right now his main concern was to take care of Marguerite.

"Hush, my love, hush. If you confront Delphine at the moment, she will just get hysterical, and you will achieve nothing." He could feel her trembling in his arms and rubbed her back gently until she calmed.

When she was no longer shaking, she pulled back, but she did not look pleased. "You are doing that again. You rub my back to calm me down as if I were a baby. Or a pet kitten." She pressed her lips together and glared at him.

He wanted to smile but managed to restrain himself. "Don't be insulted. You had a shock. Of course you were upset."

She sighed and nodded in resignation. "It was just… Earlier I had been thinking that all my problems had been solved." Her mouth twisted in an effort to smile. "Foolish of me, wasn't it?"

"Not at all." He turned her to shepherd her to her room. "But that doesn't mean you need to berate yourself. There are all sorts of wise little adages that tell you things will look better in the morning."

She did not resist as he nudged her along, but she did give him a sardonic look. "You are humoring me."

"Am I?" He smiled. "Is it working?" He opened her door and followed her in. "You seem to be calmer."

A cheerful fire blazed on the hearth, but she ignored it and went to stare out the window. He waited in the warmth.

"Can you see anything?" he asked.

She shook her head. "Only my own reflection. But I know that the sea is out there."

"Do you find that calming?"

She lifted a shoulder. "It's cold and indifferent. Yes, I suppose that does make it calming."

He shook his head. "You're being melodramatic again." She lifted her head to a defiant tilt, but he ignored it and continued. "You are also getting cold. I can see the drapes moving with the draft. Come down by the fire and warm up."

When she came close, he pulled her down to sit in his lap. She did not resist, and rested her head on his shoulder while he held her. For a tall woman, she felt remarkably small in his arms. Thin, still too thin. He wanted to feed her delicacies that would tempt her appetite. What would she like? Something savory? Morsels of pheasant breast? Or sweets? Cream cakes? Chocolates? What were her favorite foods?

He smiled into her hair. So much he had to learn about her.

Her sigh brought him back to the present.

"Your parents don't know yet, do they," she said.

"Know what?"

"That she is a poisoner. That she was trying to kill Tony. That she may have killed her uncle." She was not looking at him. Her face was still hidden against his chest.

"You make her sound like La Voisin."

That made her lift her head and look at him with a frown. "Who is La Voisin?"

"A sixteenth-century fortune teller with a sideline in poisons. For a while, poisoning was quite a popular activity at the court of Louis the Fourteenth. Do you suppose that's why your cousin thinks she belongs at Versailles?" He grinned.

Marguerite did not seem amused. "Do you think it will improve matters if you treat it as a joke?"

"It can't hurt. If it will make you feel better, I could stand on my head or put on a fake nose." He leaned his head back to see if his nonsense was working.

She shook her head but couldn't entirely hide her smile. "Perhaps not. But I must consider what to do."

"Yes." He regarded her seriously now. "We won't be able to hide it. She is a danger, and people have to be told. They have to be warned. Tony. My parents."

"And what should I do about the vicomte? He could be in danger."

"You thought she might have poisoned his coffee." He smiled at her look of chagrin. "No, don't feel embarrassed. It was my first thought too. But I think he's safe for the time being."

"Because the seeds have been discarded?" Marguerite shook her head. "She might have something else. I don't know."

"Yes, she might, though I doubt it. Where would she get any poison? Has she even gone to the village here? If she had bought poison, Seznec would have said something. But she isn't going to want any harm to come to the vicomte until he has restored the chateau, or at least handed it over to her."

"Yes, you are probably right." Marguerite wrinkled her nose. "She may not be rational, but she has a certain cleverness. She is shrewd enough to see what is to her advantage and she acts in ways that appeal to people, at least when they first meet her."

Then she tilted her head, considering. "But we still have a problem. We have to warn the others. We know that. But once they know, are they going to let us just take her away? When Tony finds out he has been poisoned, won't he want her punished? And are your parents going to be content to have a woman who is not just mad but dangerous living near their son?"

He smiled happily at her.

She took exception to that. "*Now* why are you smiling? Do you find this amusing?"

"No." He couldn't seem to stop smiling. "But you finally said *we*. You said *we* have a problem."

"I'm sorry." Her eyes were averted again. "I should not burden you…"

"Stop that!" He grabbed hold of her shoulders and managed to keep himself from shaking her, though that was what he wanted to do. "I love you, Marguerite, and you love me. That means we share our burdens just as we share our joys. That's what it means to love each other."

She looked at him for a long moment then reached up to trace her fingers gently along his cheek. "I love you so," she whispered.

He would never tire of hearing her say that. "Come," he said, "let's go to bed. There will be time enough to deal with shared problems in the morning. Now it's time for us to share some of the joy of love."

Chapter Forty-one

CANDLE IN HAND AS SHE WENT WEARILY DOWN THE CORRIDOR, Mme. d'Hivers stopped abruptly at the sight of Lord Edward. Shoes in hand, he was approaching the door of his room. He stopped abruptly as well.

"Madame." He nodded courteously.

She glared at him. "I will not ask where you are coming from. I will endeavor to forget this encounter."

"As you will." He inclined his head again. But before she could pass on her way, he spoke again. "Madame, please. I wished to ask about Mlle. de Roncaille."

She considered. Well, if he was truly going to marry Marguerite, she might as well tell him. "She grew a trifle excited last night. I finally persuaded her to drink a tisane."

"A tisane?" He cocked his head.

She shrugged. "A tisane with a bit of laudanum in it. She sleeps soundly now, but just in case, I locked her door."

"You have the key?"

"Of course." She took it from her pocket to show him. Did he think she was a fool?

He smiled then. "Good."

She started to leave, but he caught her sleeve to stop her once more.

"Madame," he said, "you and I will keep Marguerite safe. Agreed?"

Was that truly his goal? If so… "Agreed." She watched until he had entered his room. Aristocrat or not, he might perhaps be a good thing for her Marguerite.

Marguerite woke to the chill gray light of morning. The chill was caused by the absence of Ned. She slept so soundly in his arms that when it was time for him to go to his own bed, he could slip away without waking her.

Appearances must be maintained, even if everyone knew, or at least suspected, that he was spending every night with her.

Ah, but the chill left by the loss of his warmth was almost painful.

She wanted to laugh at herself. Little more than a month ago, she had not even known that Lord Edward Tremaine existed. Now she was bemoaning a few hours' separation. But she didn't want to laugh.

Nor did she want to get up and face the day.

She wanted to curl up under the covers and feel sorry for herself. Which was idiotic. Ned's arrival—simply his existence— had transformed her life so utterly that she had no business feeling sorry for herself, even for a moment.

She made herself get up and get dressed in one of her simple black gowns—a skirt and bodice of soft wool, with only the gathers at the back of the skirt to suggest a bustle. To keep her costume from looking too stark, she tucked a white fichu around her neck before fastening the jet buttons of the bodice.

She paused, stricken, with her hands on the last button, realizing that she was looking forward to an end to her mourning. It was only six months since Papa had died. Was she forgetting him already?

No. What she sometimes forgot was not Papa, but the fact that he was dead. There were moments when she turned to ask what he thought about some passage she had just played, about the phrasing. At those times she could almost hear his answer.

But then so much had happened, there had been such turmoil, that Papa seemed to be part of another life completely.

She took a deep breath and straightened her spine. Meditations on life and death must wait for another time. There were things she had to do here and now, so she had best get on with them.

It was time for breakfast, but she could not break bread with Delphine at the moment. The girl would either have forgotten all about the events of yesterday or she would be bubbling over with delight. Marguerite did not think she could sit calmly through either performance.

What she needed to do was make sure that Delphine didn't have any other substances—Marguerite gave an abrupt laugh. Was she trying to fool herself? Did she think not saying the word even to herself would change things? *Poisons.* What she needed to do was make sure Delphine didn't have any other *poisons* in her possession.

Since Delphine would almost certainly be at breakfast, this would be a good time to search her room thoroughly. When she and Ned had searched, they had stopped as soon as they found the *agrostemme* seeds. It had not occurred to them that Delphine might have any other poisons. She probably didn't— where could she get them? But it was necessary to be sure.

Before heading down the corridor, she pocketed her room key, just in case Delphine had decided to lock her room. Marguerite was fairly certain that the same key opened all the bedrooms.

As it turned out, that had been a sensible precaution. Delphine's room was indeed locked, and it took a bit of jiggling to get it open. Feeling a bit smug about her foresight, Marguerite opened the door.

The smugness promptly evaporated.

Delphine was inside the room, with a drawer in her hands and all her stockings dumped out on the bed. She had turned to the door and was looking haughtily affronted.

She was also dressed in one of the ancient dresses, one of the milkmaid ones, with the skirt pinned up to show the underskirt. Dear God, did this mean Delphine was living in another century again?

"What are you doing here?" she demanded.

Marguerite ignored that and walked into the room. "What are you doing, Delphine?"

"That is none of your affair."

"Are you looking for something?" Marguerite asked.

"That is none of your affair," Delphine repeated. "Do not presume to question me."

"If you are looking for the bottle of little seeds, the *agrostemme* seeds, they aren't there any more. We found the bottle and threw it into the sea." Marguerite stepped closer, keeping a cautious eye on her cousin.

Delphine backed away, clutching the drawer in front of her. "You have no business taking my things." Her voice began rising.

Marguerite stopped. Perhaps she should not have mentioned the *agrostemme*. She did not want to provoke Delphine, so she tried to speak gently. "Are you looking for something else? Perhaps I can help you."

"You took my seeds! Who are you to touch my belongings? You had no right!" Delphine's voice had risen to a shriek.

"Calm yourself, Delphine." This was worse than usual. Much worse. There was a hectic look about Delphine that she had never seen before. This time, Marguerite did not know how to approach her cousin, but she had to say something. She kept her voice low and calm. "Perhaps if you sit down…a tisane, perhaps?"

Delphine did not seem to even hear the words. Her eyes were blazing with fury.

"How dare you enter my room? You are nothing! You should not even approach me without my permission."

"Delphine, please." Marguerite put out a hand toward her cousin.

"No!" Delphine sprang back from her cousin's hand, holding

the drawer in front of her like a shield. Terror replaced the fury in Delphine's eyes. "I know you. You wish me harm. You want to send me back to that school. I will not go back there!"

Suddenly she darted toward Marguerite and swung the drawer at her.

The attack was completely unexpected. Never had Delphine attacked her this way. Marguerite barely managed to put up an arm to deflect the blow, and a corner of the drawer hit her elbow. Crying out in pain, she clutched the injured arm to her and tears filled her eyes. She fell to her knees. She could not believe how much it hurt. She could not straighten it.

No, not her arm. Her arm could not be injured. She gasped and closed her eyes against the pain as she tried to straighten her arm.

She did not even notice when Delphine swung again. The second blow caught her on the temple. Everything went black.

Ned hurried to the breakfast room. There had been no sound from Marguerite's room. She might still be sleeping, and if so, he did not want to disturb her. But perhaps she had not waited for him and had gone down to breakfast alone.

He stopped in the doorway. No. She wasn't there. The only people present were his parents. He would just as soon not have had to face them right now, but they had seen him.

Since there was no escape, he made an effort to look cheerful and said good morning.

His mother gave him one of her looks, the one that said, *I know perfectly well what you are about, and don't think you're going to get away with it.*

Since there were no servants in attendance at the moment, she felt free to speak. "I trust you are prepared to explain that little drama we witnessed last night."

"Drama?" he asked vaguely.

Lady Penworth held up a hand. "Do not play the fool with me, young man. You know perfectly well what I am talking about. Why was Miss Benda in such a rush to get next to her uncle..."

"Her great-uncle," Ned interrupted to say. "Or really, I suppose it's her great-great-uncle. Or should there be another great in there?"

His mother looked at him and he subsided. Nonsense never worked on her.

"What was so important about his coffee?" she asked. "Miss Benda was so determined to get hold of it that anyone would have thought it was poisoned." She raised her brows questioningly.

Ned knew how a mouse felt when the cat had him trapped. He opened his mouth and then closed it.

"I thought so!" Lady Penworth pinched her lips closed. Then came a resigned sigh. "Her cousin isn't just mad, is she? She's actually dangerous."

"We're not entirely sure." He wasn't ready to explain. Not yet. Ned turned to his father, who shook his head.

"No use looking to me for help," he said. "I'm as worried as your mother is."

"You aren't sure," Lady Penworth said to her son, "but you are certainly suspicious enough. I think the two of you are the ones who are mad. If that girl is actually dangerous, you cannot possibly allow her to live anyplace where she could roam free. She must be kept confined."

Ned shook his head. "Mother, you know what those places are like. You cannot possibly suggest that Marguerite condemn her cousin to such horror."

She waved a hand in dismissal. "Not all those places are the same. I am certainly not saying that she should be consigned to a charity ward. I am sure we can find a hospital where she can receive decent treatment."

When Ned opened his mouth to protest, his mother held up a hand. "I think we should go talk to Miss Benda right away.

There's is no point in allowing this farce to continue any longer."

Just then Mme. d'Hivers hurried in and looked around. "Is Marguerite not here?"

Ned stumbled slightly in his haste to get out of his chair. "She may still be asleep."

"No." Madame shook her head. "I wanted to talk to her, and I thought to catch her before she came down. But there was no one there."

Ned had an uneasy feeling about this, but before he could say anything, his mother broke in. "We should check again. You may simply have missed her," she said.

Madame looked slightly offended, but even more worried. "I hope so."

"You did say that you had locked Delphine in, didn't you?" Ned spoke sharply.

"Yes, but…" She shook her head. "We should look again."

She and Lady Penworth led the way, but it was Ned who rapped sharply on the door. "Marguerite? Are you there?"

When there was no response, his mother made an impatient noise and pushed past him.

The room was empty.

They were looking at each other uncertainly when they heard the shrieks.

"What is that?" Looking horrified, Lady Penworth put her hand to her throat.

Ned did not wait. He raced down the corridor toward the noise. There was a key sitting in the lock of the room the screams came from, and he was jiggling it to get the door open when the shrieks stopped.

That did it.

He stepped back and lifted his leg to kick the lock open. His success was immediate, and he went tumbling into Delphine's room, trailed by his parents and a number of servants who had been attracted by the noise.

He pulled himself to his feet and saw Marguerite, collapsed

and motionless, blood running down the side of her face. For a moment he was frozen, unable to even breathe. Then he realized that Delphine was there, pulling Marguerite toward the open window and the balcony over the sea.

"No!" The sound tore from his throat. He dove across the room to grab hold of Marguerite, a task that proved to be not difficult at all. As soon as she saw him, Delphine let go and began backing away. Ned barely managed to catch Marguerite before she crashed to the floor.

He was cradling her in his arms when the shrieking began again.

His parents were still outside the door, trying to get in. Half a dozen servants—both male and female—were crushed against each other, blocking the entrance and making loud exclamations. But it was Delphine who was shrieking as she pointed at them.

"They have come for me, the *canaille, les sans-culottes*, the mob! No! I will not go!" She kept backing away toward the window. "Never will I let them take me." She stepped through it and stood upon the balcony. "I will not be imprisoned again!"

"No, no, mademoiselle, you must be careful," Lord Penworth called out, finally breaking through the crowd.

"My dear girl, calm yourself," said his wife.

But they were too far from the window. Ned only half noticed them as he held a handkerchief to Marguerite's head, trying to stop the bleeding.

Delphine pulled herself up onto the wall, and posed defiantly. "I will not let them drag me to the guillotine. I am of *la noblesse ancienne*. I will not be humiliated by these pigs. I will not be jeered at by the mob. I have my own escape."

"Delphine!" Mme. d'Hivers broke through the wall of servants and spoke commandingly. "You must stop this nonsense at once." She reached out, but she was too far away.

Delphine lifted her head, flung out her arms, and stepped back into space.

Chapter Forty-two

NED WAS FAIRLY SURE HE WAS GOING TO GO OUT OF HIS MIND waiting for someone to tell him how Marguerite was. The hours since they had broken into Delphine's room filled a cauldron of nightmare memories.

Tony's casual "I'm sure she'll be fine" did not help.

Ned turned on him with a snarl. "You didn't see her. There was blood all over her. And that lunatic cousin of yours was trying to kill her."

"You can't know that," Tony protested.

Ned seized him by the shirtfront. "She was dragging her to the window. She was going to throw her out. Doesn't that sound murderous to you?"

"All right! All right!" Tony held up his hands in surrender. "I was just trying to reassure you."

Ned released him with a contemptuous shove and resumed his pacing. He had been permitted to carry Marguerite back to her own room, but then his mother had taken control. She shooed him out with orders to fetch the doctor and go find himself a place to wait.

The waiting place he chose was the room across the corridor from Marguerite's. It was empty, and wide enough for pacing. Every time he passed the open door he glared out at the closed door of Marguerite's room. A few servants had gone in and out, carrying pitchers and basins and towels and suchlike, but no one had come out to tell him what was happening.

Horace had joined him. He did not pace. He just sat and stared at Marguerite's door. His lips moved slightly, but no sound came out. Ned thought he might be praying.

"Damnation! I'm not waiting any longer!" He strode across the corridor and flung open the door.

Dr. Fernac looked up from fastening his cuffs with a smile. "Ah, the impatience of youth."

Ned wasn't interested in Fernac. His eyes focused instantly on Marguerite. His mother was tucking her into some sort of frilly jacket thing, but Marguerite saw him and smiled. "It's all right," she said. "She didn't really hurt me."

In an instant, he was on his knees at the bedside, holding her hand to his cheek. "Of course she hurt you. You were unconscious and there was blood all over."

She laughed a little at that. "Well, she did hurt me a bit, but no lasting damage. The doctor says that nothing is broken in my elbow. Just a bruise."

"Your elbow? But your head…" His hand hovered over the small bandage on her temple. A bruise was spreading around it.

Fernac chuckled. "An unusual young woman. She awakens to find herself covered in blood, and all she worries about is her elbow."

"It hurt," she protested, but with a smile. "And I cannot play the piano if I cannot bend my arm. But Dr. Fernac has promised that there is no real injury there."

Ned looked over at the doctor for confirmation.

"True enough," Fernac said. "The first blow caught her on the elbow. And such a blow causes pain, no doubt. It was the second, the corner of the drawer, that caused the cut and the bleeding. But it did not even need a stitch, there are no signs of any lasting effects, and her arm will be fine in a day or two."

On the far side of the bed, his mother and Mme. d'Hivers stood side by side, arms folded in identical fashion. They exchanged looks, and both nodded.

His mother was the one who spoke. "She is going to rest in bed at least for today." She looked pointedly at her son. "She needs peace and quiet, and she should not be upset. You do understand, don't you?"

"Yes, of course." Why did his mother think he would do anything to upset Marguerite? And why was she giving him that exasperated look?

"I don't understand it. Delphine has never had an outburst like this. She has never been violent—at least not to me. Not like this." Marguerite sounded worried, and he suddenly realized. She did not know what had happened.

"There's no need for you to worry," he assured her, and gave his mother a look intended to convey *Yes I understand. I'm not an idiot.*

"Tante Héloise is usually able to handle Delphine, but she may need some help this time," Marguerite said carefully. "Will you be able to manage?"

Madame shook her head. "Do not worry yourself, child."

But Marguerite was still looking at him. He was still holding her hand, so he kissed it and then he leaned over and kissed her on the forehead, taking care to avoid her injury. "Yes, of course. And I will take care of Horace as well."

Lady Penworth nodded her approval. "And later on, you may bring a book and sit here with Marguerite if you promise not to disturb her and to let her rest."

Suddenly Ned felt much better. Not only did it appear that Marguerite was not seriously injured, but his mother was no longer calling her "Miss Benda."

The rest of the day was spent on practicalities and explanations. Ned found himself grateful for his parents' presence. They were so reassuringly *competent.*

By afternoon, when Marguerite was worrying more about

her cousin than about her elbow, Ned was allowed to tell her what had happened. Her first reaction was to hide her face in her hands. Ned was less worried about the possibility of tears than he was about the fact that she wasn't moving.

He put a hand on her shoulder. "Marguerite?"

She shook her head and lowered her hands. There were no tears. "I feel so ashamed. My first reaction after the shock was relief. I was…I was *glad*. Glad that it was all over."

His arms went around her to shelter her. "It's all right. It's all right, my darling. I think we all felt the same way." He kept murmuring to her as he cradled her against him.

The tears came then, and he held her until they finally subsided.

At last she lifted her head. "She was terrified, you know, when she first came." Her voice was clogged with tears. "All the time, she kept being afraid that people were going to take her back to the school, but after a while she trusted me. I was the one who took care of her."

"But now," he said, "it had reached the point where no one could take care of her anymore. There was nothing good in the future for her."

"It was such a waste." More tears came until finally she fell asleep. He laid her down gently on the pillows.

Mme. d'Hivers, once it was clear that Marguerite was not in danger, seemed to collapse. The moment she left Marguerite's room she began to berate herself for having dismissed Delphine's delusions as tiresome when she should have recognized the seriousness of the way they were taking over the girl's mind. Finally, Dr. Fernac dosed her with laudanum and sent her to bed as well.

That left the door open for Lady Penworth. She gave full vent to her maternal instincts, cosseting Marguerite in ways Ned couldn't ever recall her cosseting her own children. To his recollection, when he had fallen off a horse or tumbled out of a tree, he had been efficiently cleaned up and bandaged, but the look on his mother's face had implied that his aches and pains were his own fault.

Now, however, she was all but wrapping Marguerite in cotton wool. And from the way Marguerite was sinking into it, he suspected that nobody had been taking that kind of care of her in a long time. Maybe ever.

Well, there would be plenty of cherishing in her future. He would see to that.

Tony had been only moderately distressed to learn that Delphine had killed herself. He was considerably more distressed to learn that she had been trying to kill him. "I knew her whole branch of the family was obsessed with their bloodline, but this is outrageous." He stormed about the room, waving his arms in good Gallic fashion. "She must have been out of her mind."

"I believe that has been pretty clearly established," Ned said dryly.

Tony pulled up abruptly. "Yes, I suppose it has." A shamefaced grin appeared. "And I never did pay much attention to her. Was that why Marguerite was always so...so...nervy?"

"Probably. But don't feel too guilty. She and Mme. d'Hivers were trying to keep it more or less secret, and even they didn't realize how bad it had gotten."

"Well, that's that then." Tony recovered his self-confidence. "Probably just as well she killed herself. If it ever got out that she was trying to poison people, it would make a terrible scandal, and people would start worrying that there might be madness in the family. Investors don't like that sort of thing."

One could always trust Tony to keep his priorities straight—his own priorities, that is. Ned shook his head and said, "I thought your great grandfather was providing all the funding you need."

"Yes, but you never know what the future may bring."

Before Tony could begin his lecture on the future of industry, Lord Penworth came in. "I've spoken with the mayor and with the priest and told them about this dreadful accident. There are a dozen or so fishermen out looking for the body." He looked sternly at Ned and Tony. "You will be very careful to remember that this was an accident, won't you?"

"We can do that easily enough," Ned said, "but what about the servants who saw her jump?"

Lord Penworth sighed and pinched the bridge of his nose. He looked on the verge of a severe headache. "There can be no guarantees, of course, but I have spoken with them at length. They value their jobs here. It seems decent employment is not easy to come by in this area. At any rate, they do not want to cause problems for the old vicomte and have agreed to keep silent."

Tony looked doubtful. "And how much did that cost?"

Lord Penworth shrugged. "A few hundred francs."

"Really, Papa." Ned couldn't resist. "Bribery. After all the times you have told me how important it is to be open and aboveboard."

"I believe I have also told you to use your common sense. Which reminds me." He turned to Tony. "We are all agreed that your great-grandfather should not be told of the girl's madness, are we not? As far as he is concerned, it will be a tragic accident."

Tony shrugged. "If you think so."

Lord Penworth frowned. "What I think does not matter. What Dr. Fernac thinks is that the vicomte can survive learning about an accident. He might not survive madness and suicide."

Tony lifted his hands in surrender. "You are perfectly right. There is no point in distressing him unnecessarily. I wish him many more years here in his chateau."

Lord Penworth pursed his lips as he contemplated the younger man. "You do realize that you are going to have to spend a fair amount of time here."

"Me? In this antiquated pile? Whatever for?"

"Because," Lord Penworth explained patiently, "your great-grandfather is a very old man. He can continue here, cared for by servants and Dr. Fernac, but there should be a member of his family watching out for him at least occasionally. And that would be you."

"But…"Tony turned to Ned. "Marguerite could do it, couldn't she?"

Ned shook his head, feeling no regret at all. "Sorry, my friend, but she will be busy taking care of me. Besides, this is your inheritance. You'll need to take care of it."

'What do I want with a musty old heap of stones like this? An unwanted relic. A monument to history best forgotten. It's been standing here for centuries, utterly useless." Tony glared at the walls around him, and his expression slowly turned to contemplation. "Standing here for centuries," he repeated. "Even the Revolution didn't damage it."

A slight smile lifted the corners of Penworth's mouth. "You can contemplate the future of the building later. Just now you will have to come with me to break the news of Mlle. de Roncaille's demise to the vicomte. As for you, Ned, you should probably join your mother and Marguerite. I believe your wedding is being planned, and you may want to call for some restraint."

Ned looked at his father with horror and hurried from the room.

Chapter Forty-three

MARGUERITE HAD ALWAYS ASSUMED THAT WHEN SHE married—*if* she married—it would be a simple affair. She and the groom and two witnesses at the mayor's office, and afterward, dinner at a good restaurant, perhaps with some friends and champagne. She might have a new dress. A new hat, at least.

That was not Lady Penworth's idea of a wedding.

"Finally," she said with satisfaction, "we shall have a wedding at Penworth Castle."

When Ned said something about a simple ceremony, she dismissed him with a sniff. "It is high time for a wedding to take place from the castle. Our neighbors will never forgive us if once again they are deprived of the opportunity to celebrate with us."

She turned to Marguerite. "It would be different if your parents were still living. In that case, you would naturally be married from their home. But you would not, I think, wish to be married from the chateau here?" She shot her an inquiring glance.

Marguerite shuddered. She had recovered from the blows, and she was beginning to come to terms with Delphine's fate, but she still had nightmares. She wanted desperately to leave the Chateau de Morvan behind her. "No," she said. "Not here."

"Very well." Lady Penworth smiled with satisfaction. "The wedding can be held two days after Christmas."

"But that's a month away," Ned protested.

His mother looked at him with a tinge of exasperation. "You know that the vicar has High Church sympathies. He will not permit a wedding during Advent. It must be after Christmas. Even so, that gives us almost no time to prepare." She turned to Marguerite. "But it must be as soon as possible after Christmas because you will need time to prepare for your concert tour. When does it begin?"

Marguerite was startled. She had assumed that the concert tour was something not to be discussed with Ned's parents. They might not actually oppose it, but she thought they would prefer to ignore it. "Yes, that will give me time. The first concert is not until the end of May, in Vienna."

"Good. That will please Susannah and Max. Although I should ask—will it be desirable for the Prince and Princess of Sigmaringen to attend? Or will that create problems?"

Marguerite's mouth dropped open. A prince and princess? She managed to find her voice enough to ask, "Why...?"

"I shall have to ask my husband," Lady Penworth said, "and I must send some telegrams." She bustled off, leaving Marguerite staring after her in confusion.

"You will get used to it," Ned said.

"I'm not sure about that. Who are Susannah and Max?"

"Susannah is one of my sisters. She's married to Count Maximillian von Staufer, who's a friend of the Prince of Sigmaringen. And the prince is married to Olivia, whose brother Harry is married to my sister Elinor. They're the Earl and Countess of Doncaster."

He grinned at Marguerite, who was looking pale. "Don't worry. It'll be easy to keep them straight when you meet them."

She sent him a look of exasperation that imitated his mother's look. "Are all your sisters countesses?"

He thought about it. "You know, they are. I never realized it. Isn't that odd?"

"Very," she said dryly. "I will try to remember to curtsey to them all. But I do not understand your mother. I thought she disliked that I am a musician."

"Oh, that was when she thought you were a greedy little adventuress, out to take advantage of her naive son. Me." He grinned. "Now she's changed her mind. You are now the brilliant artist of whom the family is extremely proud. She will ooze sympathy for all her acquaintance whose sons married insipid little creatures."

"You talk such nonsense." Marguerite had relaxed somewhat and looked around. She smiled. "But we are, for the moment, quite alone."

"So we are." Ned locked the door to assure that their moment of privacy continued.

A few days later, they were both swept away, Marguerite to Paris with Lady Penworth and Ned to England with his father.

Marguerite had spent most of her life in Paris. Had anyone asked, she would have said that of course she knew the city well. But now she was in a Paris she had never experienced before. They stayed in a suite at the Grand Hotel, where they were joined by one of Ned's countess sisters.

This one, a cheerful woman with honey-colored hair, insisted on being called Emily. Her husband, the comte de la Boulaye, preferred to be called Lucien *au sein de la famille,* as he called it, in the bosom of the family. He was not a strikingly handsome man, but he had a lively, expressive face and a ready smile.

Although he had accompanied his wife to Paris, he joined the women only for dinner, being busily occupied during the day with Marguerite knew not what. Then on the fourth day of their visit, he drew her aside to speak privately.

"I have written to Ned already, but you might wish to write to your cousin Morvan as well," he began. Then, when she looked confused, he said, "Ned did not tell you? *Eh bien,* I explain. Ned told me of the difficulties you had with this swine Louvois. I investigate a bit, and there will be no more trouble from him, I think."

The smug smile with which he said this made Marguerite a bit nervous. "No more trouble?"

Lucien smiled even more smugly. "He is a fool, this Louvois. The sort who pays more attention to his waistcoat than to his investments, and who will ignore his banker's advice and insist on investing vast sums because he overhears a conversation between two men in a restaurant. Tomorrow he will wake up and find himself bankrupt. And everyone will know of it."

Marguerite was torn between delight and worry. "You didn't do anything that will cause you trouble, did you?"

"Me? Never. I simply sat down with a friend and described to him a scheme that promised vast riches to its investors. I fear that Louvois, who was at the next table, hurried off before I explained to my friend that it was all a swindle and would soon collapse." He stopped smiling and looked at her nervously. "You do not mind?"

She smiled slowly. "Mind? Oh no, I do not mind in the slightest." She knew she should be horrified, but she was not, and she refused to feel guilty about that.

The rest of their time in Paris was devoted to clothing. Gowns from Charles Worth, mantles from Emile Pingat, hats from Caroline Reboux. Marguerite had always tried to be properly turned out, but it had never occurred to her that people could spend so much time discussing colors and fabrics and trimmings.

She had also acquired a maid, Janine, who not only helped her dress and arranged her hair twice a day—once in the morning and again in the evening, but who also clucked over Marguerite's existing wardrobe and proceeded to alter and retrim most of the dresses. Marguerite had to admit that all this activity made her look far better than she ever had before, but it also took a great deal more time.

She hoped that she and Janine could work out an amicable

modus vivendi as time went on so that she did not spend her entire life changing her clothes. Meanwhile, whenever she could, she escaped to the music room with the piano the hotel had put at her disposal.

There were both advantages and disadvantages to marrying into the aristocracy.

Chapter Forty-four

WHEN THEY FINALLY LEFT PARIS FOR ENGLAND AND PEN-worth Castle, they were accompanied by a massive number of trunks and boxes filled with clothing, and more to follow. Lady Penworth insisted that they had bought only the minimum needed. Janine was delighted to have scope for her talents.

Marguerite thought—and hoped—that she now had enough clothing to last her for years. Ned had, after all, said that he preferred a quiet life and avoided the social whirl.

It was a different kind of whirl that she tumbled into when the reached the castle. Ned was there—thank Heaven. But so was the rest of his family. There were sisters and brothers and their husbands and their wives and their children. There were in-laws and cousins and friends and relations. And they all wanted to welcome her.

Marguerite had never been in a family like this. When she had been growing up, it had been her and her parents. There had been friends and acquaintances—mostly other musicians—but no relatives. That was why she had been so glad when Delphine arrived. She finally had, if not a sister, at least a cousin.

Delphine. She pushed aside the memory. Perhaps some day she could remember those early days with her cousin, the good times, but not yet. The pain was still too raw.

Now she stood at the door to the drawing room where half a dozen adults and even more children were all talking and laughing at the same time. It was difficult to come to terms with all the changes.

Ned came up behind her and put his arms around her waist. "Do you mind?" he asked softly. "I expect they are all a bit overwhelming."

"Mind?" She leaned her head back against him and considered. "I certainly don't mind. It is just that it is so different from anything I have known before. I think…I think I like it. I think I will like being part of your family."

The days sped by quickly with people coming and going and preparations for Christmas as well as the wedding. They gathered greens and holly, trimmed the tree, and a book of carols was discovered so Marguerite could play while the others sang.

Early on Christmas morning, Ned and Marguerite stole away to exchange Christmas gifts. While in Paris, she had found for him a medieval miniature, a painting on vellum of St. George slaying the dragon to rescue the watching maiden. He had for her a manuscript of a Chopin etude. They thanked each other without words.

At last the day of the wedding arrived. It was rather like giving a concert. Instead of only Tante Héloise, there were two of Ned's sisters to help Janine get her dressed. Instead of black silk, she wore cream-colored satin and velvet. Instead of the short walk onto the stage, there was a long walk down the aisle of the church, with Tony beside her. There was the familiar feeling of panic when she felt the eyes of the audience on her.

No, far more panic than she had ever felt on the concert stage. She was certain someone would stand up and forbid the marriage. No matter what Ned's parents said, surely there were some here who would object. Someone who would forbid a marriage between a musician and an aristocrat.

But at the altar was Ned, looking worried until his eyes met hers. Then he smiled, and everything was all right. She floated the rest of the way down the aisle. The other people in the church vanished from her mind. The vicar asked questions—"Will you,

Marguerite…" and "Will you, Edward…"

They joined hands and made their vows. Nothing else mattered.

And then they were married. Ned looked as amazed as she felt. They began to laugh with joy and couldn't stop as they hurried down the aisle and out of the church.

The rest of the day was a blur of people smiling and laughing and wishing them well, of music and food and more good wishes. It was not until they were in the carriage on the way to some secret destination that she felt as if she could catch her breath.

The farewell shouts faded into the distance. The carriage doors and windows fit so well that she could barely hear the sound of the horses' hooves as they drove away. Suddenly she felt shy. She peered sideways at Ned, who was smiling a bit uncertainly.

"Wife?" he said—half greeting, half question—and reached out a hand to her.

Her hand went to his on the instant. "Husband? Is it really true?"

"It had better be." He pulled her to him and buried his face in her hair, turning into chaos the curls Janine had so carefully arranged. "I was so afraid you would take fright, that my family would drive you mad, and you would run away."

She in turn rubbed her cheek against the smooth silk of his ascot. "I have missed you. Even when you were there, I felt as if you were always just out of reach."

"I thought I would go mad with longing for you." His arms tightened around her and his mouth found hers.

Some time later, she tucked her head against his shoulder and smiled happily. "Where are we going? Can you tell me now?"

"Well, I have found a house for us. I told my family that we would go directly there. But it's near Oxford, and we wouldn't arrive until late tonight. I thought that perhaps you would prefer to spend the night at an inn not too far from here and continue on tomorrow?" He raised his brows in question.

"I hope the inn is not too far at all." Her hand slid up his chest.

"Just a few more miles," he said thickly.

It was late morning before they finally set out on their journey, but by train the trip was not long at all. Ned saw to it that his bride was well supplied with periodicals and cushions and a plaid rug, since even a first class carriage might prove drafty. Not that he wouldn't have been more than willing to keep her warm himself.

Although they behaved with exemplary propriety, sharing a boxed lunch of cold chicken, crisp rolls, and a thermos of tea, other travelers glanced in, smiled, and decided to sit in another compartment.

On the carriage ride from the station, when the winter sun had almost set, Ned began to worry. "I've only leased the house, you know, so if you don't like it, we can look for something else."

"Why wouldn't I like it?" She smiled at him as if she couldn't imagine disliking anything he suggested.

"Well, it's not terribly big or impressive. It's nothing like the castle or Morvan."

"And may I give thanks for that! You do remember that all my life I have lived in rooms in cities—not in country mansions. Although," she tilted her head, "I would prefer that it not be a hovel."

He smiled. "It isn't a hovel, but it isn't a mansion either. Just a simple manor house."

"With room for a piano and for a library?"

"With room for both." The carriage rounded a bend in the road and he looked up. "There. You can see it now."

The setting sun struck the honey-colored stone and gleaming windows of a square Georgian house, two stories high plus dormered attics, plain except for a small porch over the front door. On one side, the lawn sloped down to a stream.

Marguerite's eyes opened wide. "Ned, it's lovely."

Her enthusiasm did not wane as he led her into the house where Tante Héloise and Horace were waiting to greet them. She had nothing but praise for the drawing room and morning room and breakfast room and dining room, though she laughed and said they would have to invite guests to fill up all the space.

With a smiling shrug he said, "There are six bedrooms." She stopped in shock, so he added, "In case we have guests."

At the rear of the house, he led her to a pair of broad doors. "This is what I wanted to show you." He opened the doors on a large room with windows on three sides and gaslights for evening illumination. Low shelves holding books and sheet music circled the room under the windows, with a chaise and a pair of comfortable chairs in one corner and a ceramic stove in another. But pride of place went to a platform at one end of the room on which sat a piano, gleaming in its moiré mahogany case.

She stood in silent awe, then slowly walked over to the piano. She caressed it gently with her fingertips. "My Pleyel. It is my very own Pleyel. You brought it from Paris." She turned to face Ned. "You have brought me my parents' gift." Her eyes filled with tears. Running to him, she threw her arms around him. "You are the most wonderful man in the world."

His laugh was a mixture of relief and joy at her reaction. "You're sure you wouldn't rather have jewels? One of my brothers said that I should have bought you diamonds instead."

"*Pfft*. Diamonds." She dismissed the notion with a wave. "Paste looks better on stage, anyway. But this… I thought I had lost everything of my family. Everything that tied me to my parents." Returning to the piano, she pressed down a few soft chords. "It's been tuned. You even had it tuned."

"Oxford, you know. You can find all kinds of people here."

Left unmentioned was the effort required to unearth the name of such a craftsman, but Marguerite's smile indicated that she knew.

Twining her arms around his neck, she said softly, "You are the kindest, most thoughtful, most generous man on the face of the earth."

"I know." He smiled into her smile. "That's no doubt why you love me."

"No doubt."

They knew that the years to come would be filled with music.

Author's Note

THE CHATEAU DE MORVAN, THE VILLAGE, AND THE FAMILY are all imaginary. The historical background, however, is real.

During the 1790s, there was considerable opposition to the French Revolution, particularly in the west of France, in the Vendée and in Brittany, where the Chouans appeared. This resistance included both peasants and aristocrats in an alliance of religious and royalist opposition to the Revolution. Many of the revolutionaries were strongly anticlerical, so a jeweled reliquary like the Treasure would have survived only if hidden.

Honoré de Balzac's novel *Les Chouans* is a romance set in this period of conflicting rights and divided loyalties, and that is where I first met them.

As for more current events (current as far as my characters are concerned), the Franco-Prussian War, foolishly declared in 1870 by Emperor Napoleon III, was won with humiliating speed by Prussia. The Siege of Paris lasted from July 1870 to January 1871, at which point France surrendered. The Parisians did not, however, and the radical Commune of Paris continued to resist until May, when the official French army marched in and brought it to an end.

It was an unpleasant time for the residents of Paris. In his *Journals*, Edmond de Goncourt, who lived in Paris throughout the siege and the Commune, tells of seeing an old woman sitting on the curb and crying. When he asked if he could help her, she shook her head and said, "It is only that I am so sad." The hunger was real as well, and the zoo animals from the Jardin des Plantes, including the elephants Castor and Pollux, were indeed slaughtered and sold in butcher shops.

And the musical part of the story? Many members of the Benda family, originally from Bohemia, have been important in music from the early 1700s to the present day. They include instrumentalists and singers, performers and composers and conductors, and among them are two women composers, Juliane and Louise Reichardt, the daughter and granddaughter of violinist Franz Benda. I didn't think anyone would mind if I added two more musicians to the family tree.

The Pleyel piano company no longer builds pianos, but beginning in the early nineteenth century its instruments were favored by musicians from Chopin to Stravinsky.

Franz Liszt appears in the story because his music is wonderful, but also because his generosity to younger musicians is legendary, so I feel sure he would have helped Marguerite.

About the Author

WHEN SHE RETIRED AFTER TOO MANY YEARS IN JOURNALISM, Lillian Marek felt a longing for happy endings and stories where the good guys win and the bad guys get their just deserts. Having exhausted her library's supply of non-gory mystery stories, she started reading romance novels, especially historical romance. This was so much fun that she thought she'd like to try her hand at writing one. So at the age of 70 she took her computer keyboard in hand, slipped back into the 19th century, and began. She was right—writing romance novels is as much fun as reading them.

www.ingramcontent.com/pod-product-compliance
Lightning Source LLC
Chambersburg PA
CBHW071305170626
46809CB00001B/340

* 9 7 8 0 9 9 9 0 1 8 0 1 9 *